TERMINAL 3

MÖBIUS

BOOKS

TERMINAL 3

Illimani Ferreira

First printing: September 2020, Mobius Books LLC

ISBN: 978-1-7333225-5-3

ebook ISBN: 978-1-7333225-4-6

To Jim and Billie

PROLOGUE

CIDA BROWSED THROUGH THE movie options on the small LED screen facing her airplane seat. It was like going through the apps of her smartphone but with less flickering and more tapping. Her son was next to her, occupying the other middle-seat among the four in the central row of the Economy Class aisle of an American Airlines' Boeing 747. He had showed her how to navigate through the airplane's vast movie library just before the flight attendant had dropped the tray of tasteless food that passed for dinner in front of her. He was now transfixed by Chris Pratt running away from an explosion. She looked beyond his seat, which was occupied by a middle-aged lady who wore too much perfume under and over her garish, mauve blouse perfectly matching her mauve skirt and mauve stilettos. The woman's bored eyes suddenly lit up as they met Cida's eyes. Cida nodded curtly and turned her attention back to the screen in front of her seat, resuming the endless browsing through the airplane's movie library before she could say anything.

Since the moment they were boarding in Guarulhos Airport, the mauve woman stuck to her like a tick, first asking if the boy was her son – the kind of blunt and straightforward question that could only be asked in a non-inquisitive way when coated by the casualness that Brazilians allowed between themselves, especially when in line. The whole social fabric of Brazil would shred to tatters of sequined nylon if it wasn't for the bonds and network that were birthed through harmless conversations between two or more Brazilians in lines. As soon as Cida confirmed that, yes, the boy was indeed hers, the woman started a rant about how her son and she were alike, which Cida knew too well they were. They both had the same dark straight hair topping their long light-brown faces that framed their almond-shaped eyes. Those were very average physical features in their home country that always made them dissolve in a crowd in Brazil. Hopefully they wouldn't stand out in the US either like they were to the eyes of the mauve woman. She was not the first stranger bored in a line who pointed out to Cida how similar she was to her son in a complimentary way. His jaw was stronger though, and his nose was smaller. Like his father's.

And then the mauve woman switched gears, from commentaries on their appearance to questioning Cida about their business in LA. That's where Cida tensed. The small-talk was as Brazilian as her, but she knew that in a few hours, the questions she would have to answer would either lead her and her son to liberation or doom them to a life of limitations. Questions like the ones that woman had just started asking: "Why LA?"

"Disneyland and Universal Studios," answered Cida mechanically. She was ready for that one.

"Why not Orlando, closer to Brazil and much cheaper?"

"There are no beaches in Orlando," answered Cida in a blink. That was going well.

"Oh darling, you can just take a bus or rent a car and drive to Tampa from Orlando," pointed out the mauve lady in a condescending tone. "Did you know that?"

"There's no Hollywood sign in Orlando," Cida said sharply, improvising this time.

The mauve woman then started talking about how the Hollywood sign was overrated, and LA was overrated and how she would love to move to Orlando where the Brazilian community was larger and she could live there while speaking Portuguese, but her husband had a solid job as a set carpenter for the film industry in LA, and before she could talk more about herself or ask more questions the line moved as the boarding started.

Cida sighed in relief and thought it was the last she would see of the woman. She actually enjoyed the chance to have that exchange, as it allowed her to practice the answers she had trained for the customs officers upon arriving in Los Angeles the next morning. However, Cida discovered with dismay that the nosy, mauve lady was in the aisle seat next to her. And she seemed jubilant with the prospect of more talking and rambling. Cida put her son between them, but that turned out to be a mistake since the mauve woman started asking him questions, to which Cida had to speak over him before he had a chance to answer. The questions were harmless and shallow just like the woman asking them. But he was just a six year old boy. He could spill the beans. And she couldn't trust that woman. She looked like the dozens of women Cida used to clean for. The ones that revered Miami as the Muslims worship Mecca, traveling there two or three times every year for their shopping sprees and Red Lobster/Olive Garden dining experiences that they took as refined. And yet they never paid Cida fairly, switching in a blink from bitching about this or that aspect of her cleaning to some act of familiar generosity, such as giving away some old dress that didn't fit them anymore. Cida accepted both their abuse and used clothing in silence. This time, she had been facing her abusers' look-alike with the muttered answers to her inquisitions. She thought about just saying that she was a domestic worker in Brazil, and maybe that would make the mauve woman stop pestering her and her son. But that could backfire and result in even more questions, or worse, a job offer. Cida decided for a different strategy: she turned to the person seated next to her at the opposite aisle, hoping that, by ignoring the mauve woman she would shut down her questioning and maybe make her fade away from her life like her former employers did.

The first thing she noticed about the man seated next to her was that the grease-stained wife beater he was wearing revealed a profusion of blond hair in the chest that contrasted with his shaven armpits. Yes, she could see and – to her consternation – smell his armpits because he had his hands tucked behind his bald head, elbowspreading into her personal space. His blue eyes met hers as soon as Cida turned to him only to dive into her breasts for a fraction of seconds and then bounce back, what seemed to trigger a toothy, goatee-framed smile. The first thing the man said after Cida greeted him with a slight nod was that he liked Brazilian women very much, that he found them hot, that he liked boondah, all rushed into one eager sentence. The second thing he said was that he was a limo driver in Anaheim who was spending a week in Brazil because, again, he liked boondah. The third thing he said was a question: he asked Cida what her name was. Her answer was "I don't speak English", even if she did. She spent so many hours online, taking classes on Duolingo, and then watching Hollywood movies with the subtitles in English instead of Portuguese. Her English was far from perfect, but she sure understood everything he said: the text, the subtext and the sext. Cida knew too well his type. She was running away from a man that couldn't let her boondah alone. Who would profess his love while holding her in a choke with an arm, alcohol stink wafting from his breath. Not that she was ever afraid of his grasp. He did grab and control, but he knew, even in his alcoholic stupor, where the line was. He did not have the balls to cross the line, she thought. But then he did.

Cida was ironing his clothes when he stormed out of nowhere and punched her. Her reaction was swift: she pushed the hot iron against his bare chest – he was always shirtless when he was in a violent mood. She did not love that man, she realized that she never did. Or any man. But she had a son with that man and, for that reason only, she allowed him to linger around. The last straw wasn't the punch. It was what he said after it, while wincing in pain from his burnt chest. He said that he was going to take her son away from her. She decided that it was time to not ever let any man have power over her. Cida saved every penny she could. She endured every abuse the father of her son inflicted on her for the months it took to amass the small fortune required for her next step. She even pretended that she loved him, even though she had never loved him at any point of their intertwined unhappy lives. And then she got passports stamped with American tourist visas for her and her son, as well as a permit faking her husband's signature that stated she had his leave to take their child out of the country. With those documents she boarded a bus that left her hometown of Goiânia and dropped them in São Paulo twelve hours later. And in São Paulo she boarded a plane.

The boondah man and the mauve woman cornering Cida and her son tried to engage a few times after the airplane took off, but Cida was curt, almost rude, using every opportunity to seem distracted. Her last strategy, after dinner, was to erratically browse through the movie options. She was not interested in any of them at this time, even if she did love movies. An awful long movie in her life had ended and a new one was about to start after she got through customs the next day, in a new city, in a new country.

The mauve lady started dozing and the boondah man had been watching a movie. Cida concluded that it'd be finally safe to stop browsing through the on-board movie options. She rubbed her index finger, which was numb, and realized with a certain horror that the movie the boondah man and her son were watching happened to be the same Chris Pratt action movie. She would raise him right. She would raise him to be better than his father, or her father and his grandfather and every man she ever knew. She would raise him to be the decent man she has never met in her whole life, so that the love she had for that boy would persist, unscathed, when the time came for the boy to become a man.

***

A terrified Cida eyed the customs agent flipping through the pages of her passport and her son's with his thick fingers. She feared that those ham-sized hands would just rip the page where the tourist visa was stamped and drag the two of them onto the next airplane headed to Brazil. The fingers suddenly stopped at the passport's pages that featured her name and picture. As she raised her eyes, she realized that the man was looking deeply into her face. Like the boondah man from the airplane, he was bald and had a goatee, which made Cida wonder for a moment if that was a trend among American men. The goatee did not frame a smile, though. And the blue eyes focused on her did not have the boondah man's warmth of arousal. They were cold.

"Maria Aparecida Silva Chagas." That was her full name and that was the first thing he said. Cida nodded as an answer.

"What brings you to the US?" he asked.

"Disneyland and Universal," she answered, and stressed it by pushing her son ahead who was now wearing the cheap hat with Mickey Mouse's face she bought from a street vendor in the filthy sidewalks of Anhanguera Avenue.

"Why didn't you go to Florida instead?"

"There's no Hollywood sign in Florida."

"Are you planning to do the climb to the Hollywood sign?"

She chuckled but he didn't. It wasn't a joke.

"Yes," she answered, insecure.

"It is illegal to climb to the Hollywood sign. Are you planning to do anything else that is illegal during your stay?"

Cida sweated and didn't know what to answer as his gaze lowered. At first Cida thought that his gaze would park by her breasts as usual. But it kept going and only stopped by her belly. Cida shivered.

"Ma'am, please turn right and go to the third room. You are gonna need to be screened."

Cida complied and, as she went through the customs booths, she followed to her right instead of the left where all the cleared passengers were going. Cida and her son were not cleared.

They walked through a corridor until Cida and her son reached the third door, as the customs agent had instructed. Before that door there was a small line of women. They were all in her age range. The door was open and Cida peeked inside quickly just to see what seemed to be an X-Ray machine. No. No more lines. She would have none of that. Cida squeezed her son's little hand and kept walking. Another door, but closed. Another one. And another one. The corridor in front of her ended in a wall. She tried the handle of the last door, which had a sign that read "Lost and Found". It was open and she slipped into the room, closing the door behind her.

The room was dim but not dark. Dim was good. She would wait there as long as needed until they forgot about her and then get out of this airport. One or two or ten hours. The room had two rows of shelves filled with all kinds of objects that grouped objects of the same kind together. Sometimes two completely different kinds of objects were shelved together, although Cida could guess that whoever was in charge of storing the objects in this room had some sort of organizational intent in mind as, for example, flip phones and dentures shared the same shelf. Cida looked down and met her son's expectant gaze. She was scared but she couldn't help herself—she had to smile. Cida went down to her knees and put her hands on her son's shoulder and whispered: "We are gonna play hide-and-seek."

He smiled, excited. Her son liked to play. They hid behind a large box on the last row of shelves. For one or two or ten hours, Cida was not sure since she drifted off to sleep with her son in her arms, whispering in his ear every time he started to get restless *meu anjinho* – my little angel. Cida liked angels. She often prayed to them. She named her son after one of them. That may be why she was determined to start over her life in the City of Angels.

When Cida woke up, her son was nowhere close to her. She heard a chuckle. Her son's chuckle. He was exploring the content of one of the boxes on the shelf next to her. "Do it quietly, meu anjinho," appealed Cida in a whisper. He fished out what seemed to be a toy gun. Even in the dim room, the reflective metallic surface of the object could be seen. Too shiny to be a real gun. Too weirdly shaped too, even if it had a trigger. Her son pointed the gun at the wall and pulled the trigger. And then, the room was no longer dim. It shone in purple and green and purple again, as wavy lights on the surface of the wall started expanding in a circle that soon became darker in the center: a hole.

Cida's first reaction was to run toward her son and yank him away from the lights. As she did so, he slammed against the opposite wall and looked at her with wide, scared eyes. Cida's second reaction, after realizing that the hole in the wall was pulling her toward it as if it had its own gravitational force, was to try to run away from the hole like prey scurrying away from the angry maw of a predator. Her efforts were to no avail, as her feet simply slid on the dusty linoleum floor despite her frantic efforts to escape. Her son stood up and tried to approach her.

"Stay away!" she commanded. And he did, just observing with fear as his mother was lifted in the air and then dragged into the hole, which closed after it swallowed her.

***

Cida was in another room. This one was not dim; it was dark. She banged the walls and yelled her son's name to no answer. The walls first felt like a slick, cold surface until, in the tentative exploration of her fingertips, she felt some sort of velvety fabric underneath them. She pulled that fabric and it revealed a window through which Cida saw the Hollywood sign, lit in the mountains at night. The sign was at a distance, and her view of it was sometimes blocked by a passing car or a bus that darted in high speed. Cida was assaulted by a feeling of vertigo when she realized that those passing vehicles were hovering several meters above the ground. They were flying.

"The jewelry is in the second drawer, take what you want but please don't hurt me," said a voice behind Cida that sounded weirdly… dampened?

Cida turned and realized that she was facing not a person, but a water tank in which some sort of octopus was swimming. An octopus that could talk.

The octopus was not the only thing Cida saw now that the blinds were open. She also noticed a door and rushed toward it, more confused than scared. She went down a row of stairs when suddenly a green wall appeared in front of her. Cida tried to stop but, in her rush, she clumsily tripped over the steps and dove straight into the wall. A literal dive as Cida realized that what she thought was a solid wall was actually a mass with the texture of jell-o. And now she was surrounded by it. Cida waved her arms like a swimmer inside the green gelatinous substance as she heard an echoing voice reverberate around her: "Stop! Stop it! I don't like to be touched!"

Cida felt the jell-o moving around her until it spilled her at the base of the stairs. As she turned back she noticed that the green wall of jell-o was actually a blob topped by two smaller spheres: eyeballs, and they were locked on her.

"You perv!" yelled the outraged jell-o. Cida didn't engage. Instead, she ran to the front door of the building. Once outside, she halted in her tracks. She was too overwhelmed by what she was seeing. She wanted to run, but to where? Above her head were the flying vehicles she saw before. Along the edges of the street, buildings – some made in familiar shapes and of known materials, others not. But what definitely paralyzed Cida in stupor was on the street with her. A crowd of men and women, but also jell-o creatures like the one she encountered, and feathered quadrupeds that were talking happily to what seemed to be a bouncing, pink helical spring that a more detailed look revealed to be a coiled serpent. A quite chatty one with a strident voice. Creatures in all colors, forms and sizes were parading in front and behind her on the street. And then, she shook away her stupefaction when she realized that, despite being in a crowd, she was alone. Cida looked around, but among all those unfamiliar alien faces, there wasn't the one she was looking for. She had lost her *anjinho*.

PART ONE

SPACE

"One day, perhaps, there will be a sign of intelligent life on another world. Then, through an effect of solidarity (...) the whole terrestrial space will become a single place. Being from earth will signify something. In the meantime, though, (...) The community of human destinies is experienced in the anonymity of non-place, and in solitude." —Marc Augé

DAY 1

GABE STARED WITH WIDE, GLAZED eyes at his own reflection in the underground Maglev train's window. There was nothing particularly special in his features that morning. He was still his usual wimpy, light-browned self, his wavy black hair on the verge of needing a trim. He couldn't take his nervous eyes from his reflection because it was, at the moment, his only company in the train's car. Gabe was alone, and, as is the case for many of those whose upbringing took place within the early 22nd Century's Greater Los Angeles foster care system, loneliness had been a constant for at least half of his eighteen years.

Gabe found solace in the fact that his loneliness on the train was meant to be brief, as his trip from the shittiest, cheapest corner of Pomona to his final destination would only last a few minutes. He knew this because until yesterday he was a janitor for Los Angeles Metropolitan Transportation Office, commanding a squad of robots to clean the insides of shiny metal Maglev train cars like the one he was riding right now. He worked at night and, except for the company of the non-sentient robots, he worked alone. The job was easy, the paycheck was decent, but the nights were long and he could only go so far pretending that the robots were his friends when reality he was all alone with his work tools. That's one of the reasons he quit his job. The other one was that he was notified that the first position he applied for, as soon as he reached the legal age to leave the foster care system, finally had an opening. Through a letter, he was invited to training day. It was with a certain relief that Gabe felt the Maglev train's slowing until his reflection in the window was replaced by the station lights. Gabe sighed as soon as he noticed the station was as deserted as the train car.

"Welcome to Kornelia Kardashian-Bezos Spaceport's Terminal 1!" informed the cheerful voice of an invisible announcer, "This is the final station of the Pomona-Terminal 1 express line. All passengers are requested to exit the train."

Gabe complied and stepped out of the empty train and walked across the white tiles of the equally empty station toward the escalator. Until a day ago he was a janitor, and yet he had never seen a station so clean. Now that he thought about it, he never saw a train as clean as the one he just rode. The Pomona— Terminal 1 express line was never one of his assignments. Gabe kept pondering on this as the escalator transported him upward, but before he could arrive at any conclusion he emerged in the vast main lobby of Los Angeles Spaceport's Terminal 1, and the magnificent array of pleasing colors and lights that flooded his retinas turned all his janitorial musings small and irrelevant.

Gabe was used to aliens. He was the only human on his whole block in Pomona, as all the other apartments were occupied by a hive of refugees from Mu Normae 7 whose telepathic communication with each other would sometimes mess up the wifi in his place and also make Gabe's head buzz lightly – which he didn't mind, since that reminded him that he was not alone. His landlord was from Gamma Malvina 6 and apparently had slashed the former tenant of the apartment he lived in with one of his rear claws – and got away with murder because apparently it was ruled a case of self-defense. Gabe saw that claw just once, when he asked his landlord for a delay in paying the rent. After such a sight, Gabe never skipped paying his rent on the due date, even if that meant not having cash for his other basic needs.

Besides the humming from the Mu Normae 7 hive, his whole neighborhood had sounds and smells from the street vendors that clogged the sidewalks, as most aliens didn't rely on the online delivery purchase systems used by most humans to shop for groceries. Not Gabe, though, or the majority of humans in his Pomonan neighborhood, as he quickly learned that most of what the street vendors had to sell was cheaper than buying online if you could tell the edible from the poisonous, the authentic from the counterfeit, and the real from the manufactured photonic illusion which would turn out to be just a rock three hours after purchase instead of a decent imitation of those cool sunglasses Gabe had been coveting for months. This was Pomona, which was part of Los Angeles Megalopolis, which was part of Earth, the Human Homeworld, which was, for no more than a few decades, part of the Democratic Confederation of Planets, which was accessible beyond the halls of the Spaceport to those aliens whose applications for tourism, business or immigration visas weren't rejected. Earth was safer than other places, Gabe heard, even if he had been mugged five times just in the last year, although only once by aliens.

Gabe was used to aliens, that's a fact. What took Gabe's breath away as soon as he emerged from the Maglev train station into the Spaceport's lobby was not the canopy of aliens that walked around him, but the nature of those individuals and how different they were from his neighbors in Pomona. None had the oozing tentacles or the cracked exoskeletons he was used to seeing. Instead, they paraded perfectly tended tendrils carrying small metallic purses, or slender, violet, long bodies snaking their way through aisles made of pristine glass, white marble and light-gray vinyl, or many other shapes and colors of mostly embodied sentient existences that hinted at elegance, sophistication and wealth. Even the smells and sounds in Terminal 1 were appealing. Whereas in Pomona the air was saturated by a mix of acrid or rotten stenches with a hint of something that actually smelled appetizing accompanied by a non-stop battery of screeches, gurgles and screams, in Terminal 1 all that Gabe could smell was a faint whiff of lavender from the ground mixed with the almondy, sugary treats from a lounge café that were probably some sort of universal pastry, suitable for any kind of digestive system, since not only mouths but also beaks, trunks and suction cups were feasting on those snacks through the most polite series of nibbles. Amid them, a translucent octopus played a hypnotic ethereal song with their delicate tentacles on a silvery, triangular harp. That music seemed to merge harmonically with the mild chitchatting hum of the up and coming passengers as well as the announcer's velvety voice saying something about a last call to board a rocket headed to Triffid 2. Not that Gabe was paying attention. Mesmerized and fascinated by all the pleasing stimuli, it took him several minutes to realize that he was on unknown grounds, that he was quite lost.

After shaking his head to get rid of all those sensorial baits and get his mind back on track, Gabe noticed two human security guards passing before him on top of their hovering scooters. One was a man, the other a woman, with respectively Herculean and Amazonian allures that could have given them, at any time, a place in the world of modeling. They were clad in white uniforms, composed of a buttoned up shirt which had on the right sleeve a golden badge labeled "T_1". It surprised Gabe that they wore shorts instead of pants, which revealed the absolute lack of hair that their sturdy legs displayed between their shorts and the almost knee high boots.

"I guess I'm gonna need to shave," pondered Gabe to himself as he approached a donut-shaped counter of white vinyl that displayed on its front, in golden letters, the word "Information". Within the donut was a single clerk clad in white and gold, although their body lacked the bulk and their attire the ornaments that would single them out as another security guard. They displayed their pearly white teeth in a huge smile, which topped an unyielding gaze that relentlessly scanned Gabe's approach to their vinyl enclosure.

"Hello sir, you seem to be lost," said the clerk, cheerfully, "How can I be of assistance this morning?"

"Hi, I'm looking for the security guard quarters. It is my first day."

The clerk's smile slowly, and somewhat painfully, receded. "That's probably at Terminal 3. Next!"

Gabe looked back but there was no one behind him. "Can I ask you where Terminal 3 is?"

"Certainly not here. Please...dislodge yourself from the premises of Terminal 1."

"I... Sure, where's Terminal 3 then?"

"Sir, if you are not moving, I will be forced to call security."

"I just asked—"

The Clerk pressed a red button and, almost immediately, two security guards built like linebackers darted toward the counter on their hovering scooters.

"What's the emergency?" asked one of them.

"We've got another lost *thrurd*," informed the clerk, eyes almost rolling out of their orbit.

"This is Terminal 1, not Terminal 3," explained one of the security guards in a condescending tone, "Can't you read?"

"Wouldn't be the first illiterate person they've hired at Terminal 3. Their standards are *that* low," said the other security guard.

"I really just need directions to Terminal 3," insisted Gabe.

Each security guard put a hand on one of Gabe's shoulder blades, steering the smaller man away from the clerk booth.

"Come on, *thrurd*. We'll show you to your place."

Gabe struggled to stick to the faster pace of the two security guards, as they pushed him from the top of their hovering scooters toward a gate in a secluded corner of Terminal 1's main lobby, which displayed a sign:

Connecting Flights at Terminal 3
NO RETURN AFTER THIS POINT

After crossing the gate, they emerged in a long, damp concrete corridor through which Gabe had to hurry as the unyielding hands of the security guards kept pushing his back until he reached another gate, this one closed and guarded by two other towering Terminal 1 guards.

"Lost *thrurd*?" asked one of them while obviously knowing the answer, already removing the heavy bolts that kept the gate closed.

"What is a *thrurd*?" Gabe asked.

Instead of an answer Gabe got a boot in his buttock. The kick propelled Gabe forward just as the gate opened, and he landed with his face on the ground.

Just like within Terminal 1, Gabe was assaulted by a battery of sensations as soon as the pain caused by the impact of his face on the ground relented. However, what had been a gentle breeze of mixed, pleasant sensorial stimuli in Terminal 1 was now in Terminal 3 an unraveling whirlwind that had for *pièce de résistance* an unidentifiable stench paired with the feeling of stickiness to his skin. Gabe soon realized that the stench came precisely from the sticky, green substance glued to his clothes and surrounded him. The whirlwind expanded to a tornado as soon as Gabe stood up while trying to clean himself from the stinky goo. His ears detected a metallic bang from behind and, after turning around, he realized that the gate he had been kicked through was now closed, and a message crudely sprayed with red ink on its surface read:

DOESN'T LEAD TO TERMINAL 1! STAY AWAY!

That's when Gabe began to realize the sounds in this new environment. They were loud and mixed: voices in hundreds of inflections, cackles, mutterings, screams and grunts. When Gabe turned around again, now no longer facing the ground or the door, he saw the source of that cacophony. Aliens, but not like those from Pomona nor the ones he had just seen in Terminal 1. The aliens from Pomona were trying to make a living. Even if things could be messy, it was a predictable mess for a native like Gabe.

TERMINAL 3

Whatever problems Pomona had they were neighborhood problems, the ones he almost always knew how to go through or circumvent as he followed the path of the daily routine he was used to as a resident. Aliens or humans, they were all denizens of Pomona. The aliens from Terminal 1, on the other hand, were of different kinds, but also converged into a single status: passengers. Some walked calmly to their boarding gate, and the ones that were not moving were doing so only temporarily, as they waited in a lounging chair or at a café table. The aliens from Terminal 3, the ones that Gabe now faced with wide, terrified eyes, were... something else.

Gabe couldn't say they were not moving. Everything there seemed to be moving, even fixed features such as the dangling boards that barely concealed the semi-exposed electrical wires, some of them showering the passerby with sparks, or the eroded concrete pillars that seemed to be crumbling at an extremely slow pace. But of course most of the movement came from the denizens of that decayed space. These aliens were not passengers as, clearly, they wouldn't limit themselves to just passing by. They were barreling, rushing, trampling as a stressed, angry crowd composed of individuals in a myriad of shapes, colors and sizes. Terminal 3 wasn't a place of residence like Pomona, or passage, like Terminal 1, but a place of shuffle, of struggling denizens that wanted to stay afloat by means of constant movement without which they'd all perish.

The only reason Gabe was not yet another element of that mass of frenetic, nervous lifeforms was that he was positioned at the very edge of the vast lobby, as the Terminal 3 mob was also composed of fellow humans. A few of them were travelers – often the sketchiest kind. But most were clad in a uniform that was similar to Terminal 1's security guards, with a few differences. They were black instead of white, and included long trousers instead of tiny shorts, which was not surprising since the bodies those uniforms were outfitting had little of the Olympian allure from the security guards of Terminal 1. Some were overweight, others were scrawny, others were just in between, like Gabe's own body, although they were all taller than him –

which was not a surprise, Gabe sometimes thought that he was the shortest man in the world at 5'6''.

A bronze badge labeled "T_3" was fixed to the security guards' right arms, although Gabe wasn't paying particular attention to this kind of sartorial specificity. Instead, he was especially transfixed by the fact that the security guards' motion amid the mass of creatures was akin to ants trying to stop a tsunami. Some were barking instructions at confused yet reluctant aliens. One of them was running after a humanoid alien with a slender, orange, elastic body that was quickly gaining terrain over the chasing guard by the ease with which he dodged the numerous obstacles in his way. A whole group was trying to stop an immense, clearly irate elephantine creature, by charging their tasers at them. The alien suddenly snatched one of the security guards with their trunk and, despite the deafening buzz in the Terminal's main lobby, the sound of a bone cracking was loud enough to be heard by Gabe.

Gabe looked away from that mess and his eyes met a crab-like alien pushing a delicate cart that carried a cushy basket containing a dozen purple, pulsating eggs. The overwhelming sensorial whirlwind around Gabe suddenly calmed down, and he couldn't help himself but to sigh in relief. A mother and her offspring. There was nothing grotesque or brutal there, on the contrary, that was a soothing sight he desperately needed. The crab-like alien suddenly halted as one of the eggs cracked. A smaller version of the creature emerged from it, their tiny claws struggling to push the eggshell bits away from their slimy body. Their mother deftly cleaned the baby from the eggshell cracked bits with one large claw, while the other lifted the baby to her face. Gabe almost cried, overwhelmed by the cuteness, as he assumed that the mother was going to give her newborn baby a kiss. However, instead, the creature tossed the baby inside her mouth. Cracking exoskeleton sounds ensued.

Gabe liked to think of himself as resilient. He was a Pomona man after all, and before that he was a Pomona boy since he was nine years old, the age when he became an orphan and moved to a foster care home there from Santa Monica. A boy that, during his time in foster care, once spent three days in Hergsh's paracloaca after he refused to share his lunch with her (Hergsh was an Alpha Scuti flabby alien over two tons of weight, with a below average intellectual capacity). And still, everything that he saw and heard and smelled and felt against his skin was a bit too much. He needed a break already. He needed to sit down. To Gabe's surprise a whole row of benches were unoccupied by the wall next to him. He lowered himself on the bench just to feel it yielding and crumbling under his weight. And again, he was back on the ground.

"You lost?" asked a masculine voice above Gabe.

Gabe raised his head. He first saw a pair of black boots parked right before him, which were topped by the Terminal 3 black uniform. The uniform wrapped a large, burly body that could, at first sight, belong to a security guard from Terminal 1. A second take however showed that the brawn contained in that body seemed to be less akin to the expensive cosmetic and physical enhancements the security guards at Terminal 1 must have gone through in order to obtain their defined muscles. Nothing about the man in front of Gabe was defined. His muscular expansiveness was not cultivated—he simply came into the world in that bearish way. That's when Gabe finally met the man's eyes. He had a five o'clock dirty blond beard that matched his fuzzy hair and a half smile that was less cocky than goofy. For some reason, Gabe immediately trusted that man.

"I... am a little lost," admitted Gabe.

"Sorry for the bench, we are having some issues with metal scavengers, they got the metal supports under the plastic," the man extended a ham-sized hand to Gabe, "Here, let me help you up. Where are you going?"

Gabe grabbed the man's hand who started to yank him up to his feet.

"To the security guards' headquarters. Today is my first day."

The burly guard immediately let Gabe go, who fell over the broken bench. Gabe looked at the man's face, and noticed that the goofy smile was gone and was now replaced by a bitter sneer.

"Get out of here while you can," advised the guard darkly as he turned his back to Gabe and walked away.

For a moment, all that Gabe could think was that the ground felt just right. He could spend a moment there, and then just go home, have a shower, scrub all that funk off his skin, have a long night of sleep and then beg for his former job back. Cleaning Maglev trains was boring, mostly uneventful and terribly lonely, but he didn't need to deal with an alien eating their offspring. Or any other kind of alien. Or humans. Or sentient creatures and their proneness to bizarre behaviors. Gabe eyed, for a moment, the crab-like Medea pushing her stroller calmly amid them as her jaw kept munching the baby she just swallowed. And then he remembered that he didn't apply for this job only because he hated his long, lonely nights as a janitor. He was there for a reason. He was there because that's how he would finally find out the truth that was denied to him throughout his life. He had a plan, and it was time to follow that plan.

Gabe stood up and scanned through the hectic flow of aliens and humans before him. He quickly spotted the security guard that he had just met, as he stood taller than most. He was walking slowly through the crowd, pushing any unfortunate passerby that stood in his way. Something that a big man in a position of authority could afford to do and get away with. What the burly guard couldn't do was run through the cracks in the crowd, dodging, bending, finding his way in the interstices. And that's what Gabe, a smaller than average man could excel at. He reached the tall security guard just in time to see him opening and entering a door upholding a sign that read simply "Personnel only". Gabe had a feeling that his destination had to be behind that door.

Gabe walked through the door and found himself in a corridor framed by the same kind of brutalist concrete walls of Terminal 3's main lobby. He listened to a voice at the end of the corridor. Gabe concluded that he had to be at Terminal 3's security guard headquarters as, in his stroll toward the source of the voice which he now noticed was a hoarse and commanding alto, he passed by the entrance of a musky-smelling locker room and another doorway that lead to what seemed to be a Spartan cafeteria. As he reached the end of the corridor, he emerged into a medium sized conference room, where he realized that the voice was coming from a sturdy, middle-aged woman. Based on the black uniform she was wearing, Gabe assumed she was another security guard, although a beret topping her short, salt-and-pepper hair and a bronze star pinned to the left side of her chest indicated her status: she was the one running the joint. And that leader was speaking to a dozen of what seemed to be rookies who were still wearing their day-clothes while surrounded by another dozen security guards.

Nobody but the big security guard that harassed Gabe noticed as he scurried quickly to a seat, doing his best not to be flagged as the guy who was late on his first day. The fact that the leader of the security guards was in a heated exchange with a curious yet obnoxious rookie helped Gabe to be less conspicuous: "... and no, there are no benefits for emotional support pet ownership, " Clarified the irritated leader. "Honestly, I always wonder why people apply for this job—"

The rookie to whom she had been speaking when Gabe arrived stood up excitedly as a few moans could be heard in reaction to his enthusiasm: "I thought you were never going to ask! I want to travel to the stars one day, Brenda! It's too expensive for me now, but if I can nail this job—"

"First, I wasn't asking, Brock—"

"Blake," corrected the over-enthusiastic recruit that identified himself as Blake.

"Second, sit down," continued the leader who seemed to be named Brenda, "Third, you should refer to me as ma'am, not by my first name. Fourth, your unwanted answer to my purely rhetorical question is wrong! The reason any of you applied for this horrible, terrible job is not for career perks or professional advancement. You did so for no other reason than the fact that you are worthless losers that couldn't find anything better. Maybe you torched the fast food joint when you tried to flip a burger. Or you tried burglary but landed in jail after the cops had to use lube to remove your fat ass from a chimney... Whatever the failure in life that brought you here… that's fine! I don't give a fuck! Just follow my orders and don't screw up. Do you think you can do that?"

Blake raised his hand but Brenda ignored him.

"Good," she continued, "I assume none of you guys have much education, so there's some facts to get through."

A holographic projection of the Milky Way appeared between Brenda and the rookies.

"This is our galaxy—"

"Hi, my name is Mason and I'd like to ask what a galaxy is," said a chunky rookie with a drawl.

"You clearly have the intellectual skills required for this job. Just don't ask any other questions. It's annoying. Also, I don't care about your name. Anyway, our solar system is here…"

A yellow dot appeared within a small galactic arm squeezed between two larger arms.

"…right between the Sagittarius and Perseus arms, which are known as the 'fabulous side of the galaxy'. We joined them in the galactic confederation twenty years ago, but in return we agreed to build, right here, where we are, a hub for space flights coming from the Norma and Scutum-Centaurus arms, also known as the 'fucked up side of the galaxy'. Are you following me, so far?"

Blake and Mason raised their hands.

"Excellent!" continued Brenda, "So, the aliens from the fabulous side of the galaxy get to use the fancy-schmancy Terminal 1, while here, at Terminal 3, we get all the scum from the fucked up side—"

Blake started frenetically waving his raised arm and Brenda yielded: "Spit it out."

"What about Terminal 2?"

"We don't talk about Terminal 2," said Brenda ominously, "Now, back at what matters. Our jobs as Terminal 3 security guards isn't to make things safe. We can't make chaos safe. Our job is to be dispatchers. We dispatch all that scum up and down and, if necessary, beyond. Now, let's start your day by—"

TERMINAL 3

Brenda stopped talking and rolled her eyes when she heard the sound of someone clearing their throat by the conference room's entrance. A petite woman standing at the doorway seemed to be the source of the interruption. She wore a sweater made of some sort of gooey alien fiber that had four extra-sleeves, which she tied as improvised, decorative ribbons that fell over her shoulders. The big, warm smile on her face suggested that she was, just like her fashion sense, the kind who tried too hard to find any way possible to make a broken thing work, as long as it didn't involve actually fixing it.

"Now you'll get to listen to some legally mandatory bull crap," said Brenda in guise of introduction to the newcomer at the door, who ignored the jab and took the floor.

"Thank you, Brenda. First congratulations on your admission to an exciting career! My name is Wendy Lin, and I'm Terminal 3's resident exoethnologist. It means that I'm here to counsel you on any case involving 'friction' with the passengers in transit. I assure you that most situations can be solved with a bit of empathy—"

"Just so you know, this is empathy," said Brenda while showing her taser.

"—and willingness to understand."

"This is all the understanding you need," said Brenda, as she showed her nightstick.

Wendy sighed and shook her head, even if the smile never left her face: "As you can see, Brenda has a very different idea about the wonders of the diversity of passengers in transit. She is not very fond of my... perspective. However, the door of my office at R Wing is always open for any security guard—"

"And I'll fire anyone I see wandering there. You done, Wendy?"

"No, I still—"

"Good," said Brenda as two security guards escorted Wendy out of the conference room, "Now, let's move on to business. It's okay that you guys all suck, but you still need to prove to me that you can suck it up, so today is your probation day! Screw up and

25

you are out! To be sure that things are gonna run smoothly I'll pair you with a senior security guard for the day."

Brenda consulted a holotablet: "Blake Hamilton, you'll get Sunanda Patel. Liliana Castro, you get Anne Beauchamp..."

Every time Brenda said the name of a rookie, they stood up and sought their either sullen or bored senior security guard that would serve as their mentor, whom, by their turn, nodded or pointed the way out to the exit of the conference room.

"And last but not least, Gabriel Chagas..." said Brenda as she made a quick pause and took a short glance at the last rookie in the room, "...you get Christopher Davis."

"I won't take that guy!" protested the burly security guard that had harassed Gabe, "He's a shrimp and won't last one hour."

"Computer decided based on your psychological stats, Chip," said Brenda as she turned her holotablet to Chip's line of sight, "You have an over inflated level of confidence, while Gabriel there has a very low level, wait... is it the opposite?"

"Nevermind, let's go, shrimp!" said the big security guard as he stomped out of the conference room.

Gabe quickly trotted after him as he noticed that Brenda followed him with scrutinizing eyes. He thought about thanking her for this opportunity or even wish her a good day, but she clearly was the kind that would see that sort of politeness as obsequious flattery, so Gabe decided to give her a curt nod. Her reaction to his nod was squinted eyes that clearly hinted that he had gotten way too familiar with his new boss.

Once out of the conference room Gabe noticed that the rookies and the mentoring seniors were assembled at the locker room. As soon as Gabe joined them, the security guard named Sunanda and paired with Blake snickered at him before throwing a provocative glance at his mentor: "You are gonna lose, Chip."

"Shut up, Sue." growled Chip.

"Lose what?" asked Gabe.

"Lose your clothes," said Chip, to Gabe's confusion until he realized that he was not answering his question, but barking a command. The fact that the other rookies were stripping off their daily clothes and dressing up in the security guard uniform was a hint.

"Yes, sir!" said Gabe, as he immediately complied with his order.

"Don't call me 'sir'. Name's Chip."

"Cool, I'm Ga—"

"You are a shrimp who won't last the day."

"I get the feeling that you don't like me."

"This job is not for you, shrimp."

"You don't know me."

As soon as Gabe was undressed, Chip tossed him a uniform that smelled of sweat and was slightly moist. Gabe soon realized the source of the moisture.

"This one has blood on it."

"Told you this job isn't for you."

Gabe hesitantly started putting on the uniform without another peep until he was fully dressed: "Which one is my locker?"

"You don't need a locker since you are not gonna last the day. You can put your crap in there."

Chip pointed at a cardboard box that read in a crude calligraphy:

~~Lost and Found~~ Free Stuff

***

In his first three hours of mentoring, Gabe discovered that not all the space within Terminal 3 was as crowded and hectic as the main lobby. The Terminal had a total of twenty wings, and most had the specific purpose of conveying passengers towards the arrival and departure gates that lead to the space rocket boarding docks. Others had a different kind of function, accommodating, for example, a food court (L wing), retail stores (N wing) or all the administrative facilities other than the security guard headquarters (R wing). Gabe learned all of this by staring at a panel featuring Terminal 3's map while Chip went to the restroom. So far, the senior security guard ignored all his questions and the mentoring seemed to be limited to strolling in circles inside S Wing, which, according to the Terminal 3's map, was categorized as "Under Renovations". There was no sign of any construction workers, Chip and Gabe apparently were the only people in the middle of the bare concrete walls, deserted counters and still escalators.

Gabe grew progressively bored from this pointless hike and tired of all the silence and walking for hours without a break. He didn't want to complain or be demanding, and since his mentor refused to answer any of his questions so far, he decided to try a different engagement strategy by making a general statement: "I thought we'd get one of those hovering scooters."

"That's for T1. T3 is too crowded and underfunded for that."

Gabe couldn't help but smile as Chip frowned, realizing that he broke his own rule of trying to bore the rookie to death. The fact is that Chip was bored too and could use the conversation.

"Those guys at T1 are such assholes," pondered Gabe, again, avoiding questions.

"I know, right?!" reacted a suddenly enthusiastic Chip, "Their benefits are awesome, apparently they even have a jacuzzi in their headquarters. They select T3's from time to time, hope I can make the cut next year! I belong there!"

"I'm sure you do," stated Gabe in an accusatory way that Chip took as flattery. And unlike Brenda he wasn't averse to flattery.

"So that's the reason you work here?" asked Gabe.

"There you go with your annoying questions again."

"Look, like it or not you are stuck with me for the rest of the day—"

"As I said, I don't think you are gonna last that long. Do I need to repeat that?"

"I'm here to stay. I can repeat that as many times as you need."

"What are you doing here, anyway? You look way too nice and smart for us. Like a preschool teacher."

"Thanks."

"That's not a compliment, shrimp. Just want to know your damage. Let me guess, you were a preschool teacher who got fired when they found out you are a pedo or something!"

"What the hell, no!"

"You wouldn't be the first pedo working here, there was—"

"I'm not a pedophile!"

"That sounds like something a pedophile would say."

Gabe suddenly halted as Chip kept walking while making a couple of other uneducated guesses about Gabe's background until he realized that his mentee was not by his side. Chip turned around and noticed Gabe standing a few feet behind him.

"Hey, no slacking, we still have 23 loops inside this Wing before we take a break for lunch."

"What's going on over there?" asked Gabe, as he stared at the crook underneath the concrete base of an escalator.

Even if he had been walking around S Wing for hours, it wasn't a surprise that he would only now notice that they were not entirely alone in that part of Terminal 3 as their company was barely visible. A family of three. Aliens unlike any he had seen before, with mantis heads topping fragile looking, extremely slender bodies that were as gray as the surrounding concrete. The secluded corner of the Wing under the escalators seemed to be their nest, the ground around them covered in a yellow paste that was the source of a light stench.

"Nothing to see here. Let me show you another Wing," suggested Chip with a sudden sense of urgency.

"Shouldn't we do something about them?" insisted Gabe.

"Let them be, man."

"Looks like they are struggling," said Gabe, as he took a tentative step toward the squatting creatures.

"You heard Brenda," said Chip in an increasingly alarmed tone as he noticed Gabe's movement, "We are here to dispatch people, but those guys aren't going anywhere. Forget them."

"I'll talk to them," announced Gabe with determination.

But before he could reach them, Blake suddenly showed up and shoved Gabe aside as he darted toward the aliens, while his mentor Sue ran way behind, yelling at Blake to not move.

However, Blake ignored her, and barreled into the alien family's perimeter with his baton in hand: "Hey bums, this isn't a hotel! You can't—"

Blake stopped midsentence as the three aliens turned their gaze to him. Their bubbly eyes, usually as gray as their exoskeleton, suddenly lit up green. As they did, a trickle of blood dripped from one of Blake's nostrils and, one second later, the rookie security guard crumbled to the ground.

Gabe was close enough to Blake to be able to reach out to his feet and drag him out of the perimeter of the aliens, whose eyes went back to their normal grey as they resumed their ostensive disinterest for the security guards. Gabe took Blake's pulse as Sue and Chip surrounded him.

"He's alive," stated a relieved Gabe. The other rookie seemed to have simply passed out.

"I won!" celebrated Chip, "You can give me my cash now, Sue!"

"Day isn't over yet!" barked a sullen Sue as she turned on the intercom device attached to her lapel, "Headquarters, we have a ripe rookie at S Wing in need of medical attention."

"What are you guys talking about?" asked Gabe, less confused and more shocked by the two senior security guards' callous stance.

"Every time there's a mentoring day, Sue and I make a bet to see whose rookie is gonna badly injure themself first," explained Chip with clear delight over his triumph, "And today I win!"

"You were just lucky yours is a puppy while mine was a wannabe vigilante," argued Sue.

"Actually, the shrimp here was about to get close to the roaches when you guys arrived."

"To help them!" clarified a now appalled Gabe.

Gabe's outrage with his seniors' callousness was making him feel lightheaded again, just like when he was tossed into Terminal 3 by the staff of Terminal 1. And Chip noticed this with sudden concern. "Are you okay, buddy? You look pale."

"Don't patronize me," said Gabe, "I know that you don't care, you just want to win that bet."

"Well, maybe I pushed you too hard this morning," said Chip with a show of empathy that took Gabe aback, "Why don't you go sit down for a moment while Sue and I handle this issue?"

Gabe nodded and walked to a bench nearby while Chip and Sue eyed him. And as he sat down, the bench crumbled under his backside, making Gabe land heavily and painfully onto the ground. Chip and Sue high-fived each other while laughing their asses off as Gabe, at first dumfounded, and then angry, cursed himself for falling for that cheap prank.

***

Gabe and Chip were now patrolling R Wing. Just like S Wing, R was a long, rectangular aisle made out of concrete. However, this one had a row of small offices and headquarters for support services in the Terminal, such as the firefighter squad, the maintenance crew and the custodial unit. Most of those offices also displayed signs such as "Out for Lunch", "Will be back in 5 minutes" and "Fuck Off", all of them permanently attached to the office doors. This time, Gabe was the silent, sullen one while Chip was doing all the talking. Gabe was still angry about the incident at S Wing, but most of his outrage was that, for some reason, the laconic façade that Chip displayed when their day together started was gone, giving way to a continuous self-centered monologue. At first Gabe wondered what prompted Chip to suddenly open up to him, but the babbling was just incessant, consisting of Chip's narcissistic inclination and his vain sexual urges. All Gabe could do was squirm silently and wish that Chip would shut up. And then he had enough: "Hey, Chip—"

"Wait, I'm not done. So, after the Beta-Centauri dude stuck his tendril into my—"

"Seriously, what are we doing here?"

"It's rude to interrupt, did you now that?"

"You are…supposed to mentor me."

"Fine, you get three stupid questions. What do you want to know?"

"Why did you bring me here?"

"R Wing is safe. Only S Wing has less transit than here, but it's clear that taking you there was a bad idea because of the squatting roaches. Here, on the other hand, there are just offices, most of them closed. If you stay alive and unharmed until the end of the day I will win my bet with Sue."

"Do you only care about winning your stupid bet?"

"Well, to be fair, the restroom in this wing has some rad action if you need to go for a quick BJ. Front stall to give some and back stall to get some. Now, pay attention because this is very important. If you'd rather have anal, you should instead—"

"Right, I got it. You care only about your bet *and* sex."

"And not creating any trouble for myself. You are gonna give up at the end of the day anyway, so it's better to keep you in one piece till the shift ends."

"For the last time, I won't give up. Why do you keep saying that?"

"Because you tried to help those roaches that were gonna fry up your brain if you had taken just one more step toward them. If you want to help people, you are in the wrong line of business here."

"Hey, isn't this the place where that woman who showed up for the briefing works?" said Gabe as he noticed one of the few offices that seemed to be open – mostly because it didn't have a door. A sign at the entrance read:

Assistance to Passengers and Staff

"That'd be four questions, but I will give you that because I'm feeling nice today. Yes, that's where that nutjob Wendy Lin works. They used to have a door, but it was made of metal."

"We should tell her about that family in S Wing."

"Dude, I told you, forget about the roaches."

"Yes, but—"

"Do you have the hots for Wendy?"

"What?"

"I can get why you have the hots for her, but she's too nuts. Not worth it."

"I want her professional advice on—"

"So you don't have the hots for her then."

"No, I mean... I—"

"Don't you like girls?"

"I'm straight!"

"Straight? This is the 22nd century!"

"You are... confusing me."

"If you want to find the hot girls and dudes you got to go to the Terminal's fire station. Those guys are always on fire, sometimes literally. Come on, I'll show you the way, it's right over there."

"I'm gonna talk to Wendy."

"So you have the hots for her."

"Are you coming or not?"

"Nah, if Brenda sees me there I'm fired. Plus you need some space for your 'talking' thing," said Chip, as he winked to Gabe.

"There won't be 'talking' with a wink. It will be just talking. Winkless talking."

"Sure, and while you do that I'm gonna go to the restroom to 'relieve' myself," said Chip, as he winked again.

***

Gabe was a polite, small man. He discreetly approached Wendy's office and, since there wasn't a door, he just stood at the office's entrance in silence, hoping to be noticed. That didn't happen immediately. The office was not more than a windowless cubicle furnished with only two desks and four chairs. A doorway inside the room lead to what seemed to be a mostly unoccupied infirmary (if Gabe looked closely, he would have noticed that the robotic nurses had placed a currently unconscious Blake in one of those beds). Wendy was seated at one of those desks, the other being occupied by an androgynous, green-skinned, four feet-tall humanoid alien, a native of Nu Lyrae. The Nu Lyraese were the first alien species to settle down on Earth as refugees, after the catastrophic collapse of their homeworld's sun. Although there weren't many of them in Pomona, Gabe heard about them, as their arrival on Earth was taught at school as the historical landmark of when Earth changed its status from a Galactic Indigenous Reserve to an Open Self-Governed World with a seat at the Galactic Confederation Senate. Most Nu Lyraese settled down in the suburbs far South of LA such as San Diego and Tijuana, and spoke with the local accent while incorporating some elements of the local culture to their own. The Nu Lyraese alien wore a scrub and seemed to be a medical doctor. He and Wendy were carrying on a conversation that Gabe didn't dare to interrupt.

"You should try power yoga for your stress, José," said Wendy, "It's like... you know when you have to hold your pee the whole day and, at night, you finally can let it go?"

"I can't know, urination isn't one of my physiological endowments, but I must say that this human custom is a big and puzzling waste of energy."

"What I mean is that you need to let yourself go. You're so repressed sometimes!"

"If I were human I'd drink nothing but my urine. There are many precious vitamins and enzymes in there."

"That'd... kill you. Eventually."

"So will your constant inhalation of environmental air as oxygen slowly corrodes your DNA. And yet, I don't see you stopping your unhealthy breathing, despite my effusive warnings."

Wendy shook her head in amused disbelief and, by doing so, she noticed a very uncomfortable Gabe at the doorway. And so did José: "Hello sir, your face seems to be abnormally flushed. You may either be embarrassed or having a stroke. Do you need medical attention?"

"I...I'm actually here for her," said Gabe, as he shyly pointed at Wendy.

"For me?" said Wendy, in disbelief, "Is it another one of Brenda's nasty charades? Because if it is, tell her that—"

"I'm here because you said this morning that security guards could get your help," clarified Gabe, "Today is my first day."

"Wait, do you actually want my help?" asked Wendy, her skepticism turning into sheer joy.

"Yes, unless this is a bad time."

"There is no bad time for your exoethnological advisory needs!" said Wendy louder than she intended, "The door of my office is always open!"

"You don't have a door."

"But I do have a chair. Please, have a seat!"

Gabe stared at the empty chair facing Wendy's desk with a frown that wasn't unnoticed by her: "Don't worry, this one is made of plastic."

Gabe sat down as Wendy gave him a big, slightly scary smile.

"As you know my name is Wendy and my colleague over there is José, our resident doctor."

Gabe was used to aliens adopting Earth names. That usually happened when humans didn't have the necessary muscles to pronounce their actual names. He was also streetwise enough to know that, even if there weren't many Nu Lyrae aliens in Pomona, if he tried to shake his hand he'd be called a *pendejo,* whatever that word means, as the act of extending your hand was considered obscene in their culture. Instead, Gabe turned back and gave a curt nod to José.

"I am Gabriel, but you can call me, Gabe."

"How can I assist you, Gabe?" asked Wendy.

"So, there is this alien family squatting in S Wing. My mentor Chip calls them the 'roaches'—"

"He shouldn't be employing such a derogatory terminology. Instead, we must refer to them by the politically correct term, 'insectoids'," said Wendy.

"Sure... so you know those guys?"

"I'm aware of their situation. As far as I know they are immigrants from the fourth planet of Epsilon Apodis, but there's very little academic material about that planet or their species. There is some sort of food shortage in their homeworld that is forcing families to flee. We don't know exactly what is going on since their planet is too small, too poor and too tucked into the fucked up side of the galaxy to gain attention from researchers and media outlets."

"Can you help them?"

"I'm sorry, Gabe, but my hands are tied. Legally I'm not allowed to perform a direct outreach intervention. Whoever needs my assistance needs to come to me either directly or indirectly and... they never came for my help. And if they did I'm not sure what I could do. Earth doesn't recognize them as a species legally entitled to the status of refugees, so they are just stranded here in Terminal 3. The only reason I think Brenda hasn't deported them yet is because of their psionic powers."

"Then tell me what to do!"

"Have you tried talking to them?"

"They fried the brain of the last security guard who got near them!"

"Maybe he used the wrong approach?"

"What do you mean?"

"Well, Brenda and most of the other security guards may think of Terminal 3 as some sort of cesspool. But the truth is that Terminal 3 isn't a place with problems, it's actually a place with individuals who are facing problems. The insectoids aren't the only ones struggling around here," said Wendy, as she stood up, waving to Gabe to follow her.

Gabe and Wendy exited the office and were soon joined by José, who would never skip a chance to witness humans behaving in what were, for him, puzzling, unpredictable ways. The corridors of R Wing had, like before, a smattering of aliens, most of them seeking assistance from offices that were closed.

"Find an alien and try to be helpful," suggested Wendy.

"That's... it?"

"You need to start somewhere. If you want to help that insectoid family you need to learn how to interact with aliens in general."

"I'm from Pomona, I interact with aliens all the time."

"Oh please, don't come at me with the 'I have an alien friend' card. That's an entitled human privilege fallacy that won't—"

"I don't think I have... friends."

"Ah."

They fell into an awkward silence that lasted a few seconds.

"But... still... you have the wish to help, that's what matters!" announced Wendy, breaking the brief silence through a far-fetched cheerfulness.

"I guess."

"Then go for it. Pick an alien and try to help them."

"Hello sir, can I assist you in any way?" said Gabe to José.

"You can go fuck yourself, *pendejo,*" answered José.

"Ah, in José's culture offering assistance is basically requesting sexual favors. And I wasn't talking about him. I meant a passenger that clearly needs some sort of help. Like..." Wendy scanned the passing aliens and locked on a crab-like one that was pushing a stroller filled with pulsating eggs.

"Not her!" promptly said a horrified Gabe as soon as he recognized the alien, "I saw her before, she ate her own baby!"

"Nonsense. The natives from Stephenson 2 aren't known for feasting on their offspring," pointed out José.

"And even if they were, it'd be a cultural matter, not to be judged or frowned upon," added Wendy.

"Now you are just being weird, Wendy," said José.

"I'm not helping her!" protested Gabe, "I saw it when she swallowed the baby and chewed! It even crunched—"

Suddenly the crab-like creature stopped in her tracks. She rocked her head slowly at first, and then faster, in an almost convulsive fashion. And then her head busted open. A smaller version of the creature emerged from the cracked-open head, crawling through the busted shell of their mother's head.

"What...the...hell..." whispered Gabe, transfixed by the sight.

"When the mother swallowed her offspring, she was merely constricting it within her skull cavities in order to submit the child to an unnatural and forceful development of the muscle tonus," explained José, "A standard procedure for Stepherson 2 newborns and certain human adults, although the latter call it Crossfit®."

The crab-like mother carefully picked up her baby from the crack within her head and put it into the cart amid their to-be brothers and sisters.

"Hey... can I... help you?" asked Gabe in tentative shyness.

"Would you have an Advil by any chance?" asked the crab.

"Ah, José over there is a doctor."

"Over where? I can't see shit. In case you haven't noticed my head is cracked."

"He's talking about me, Ma'am," said José, as he grabbed one of the creature's red claws and gently steered her toward his office, "Please follow me."

Gabe turned his attention to Wendy who smiled supportively to him while showing her thumbs up.

***

By the time Gabe was done with his crash-course in empathy toward aliens it was lunch time. Wendy invited him to share her packed lunch, and Gabe was inclined to accept her gentle offer as he enjoyed her company and felt that she was the only living creature in Terminal 3 that was not treading on him either intentionally or accidentally. But when she excitedly announced that her meal was some sort of noodles from 35-Vulpeculae 1, which were also the gelatinous wool of the six-sleeved sweater she was wearing, Gabe realized that Wendy's sartorial choices didn't seem particularly appetizing. He politely declined her invitation under the pretext that he was on the clock and had to find his mentor.

Gabe searched for Chip all over R Wing, including the restroom. Although he couldn't find Chip in any of the stalls, he got a chance to see all the action taking place in there. It lifted a little bit his self-esteem that he was complimented on his physical appearance by a couple of the users of the restroom. He also had to decline the invitation for lunch from a large, furry, bear-like alien, who was very proud of the benefits of the intake of proteins and vitamins contained in the glandular secretion that he wanted Gabe to consume. Gabe realized how hungry he was when the sight of the orange, milky substance oozing over the alien's fur made his stomach growl. He then remembered that he saw a cafeteria in the security guard headquarters in the main lobby.

The security guard cafeteria was a noisy, busy, smoky room. It featured the same windowless, brutalist, concrete walls that were the signature of the whole terminal, but in this case they were stained by layers of grease deposited by the fumes coming from the kitchen. However, when Gabe stepped into the cafeteria it wasn't the noise or the appearance of the room that stood out, but the heavy smell of overcooked cabbage that had been left to rot for who knows how long. Gabe wasn't bothered by the smell. He had eaten worse things and he didn't consider himself picky with food, even if he had just realized a few minutes ago that he had qualms with food that could also be used as a sweater. He found Chip at the end of the line of security guards waiting for their meals.

"Chip! I looked for you in the restroom!" said Gabe while posting himself behind his mentor in the line.

"Back stall or front stall?"

"I... Anyway... I talked to Wendy—"

"Ah, forgot to tell you. Never, ever, accept her invitation for lunch. It's a trap and you'll get sick. Believe me, that woman can digest anything."

"She did invite me to stay for lunch. I said no."

"Good, with nutjobs like her you just go for a quickie and walk away."

"Wait... no! We just talked!"

"Less talking and more action, buddy! You'll never get some with that attitude!"

"Listen to me, dammit! She gave me an idea!"

"And her intercom number, I hope."

"No! She—" Gabe was interrupted by the sight of a parade of metallic trays containing a gray paste scattered with a few condensed knots. The trays were being handed by the cafeteria robots to the security guards at the front of the line. "I thought it was gonna be something with cabbage," muttered a perplexed Gabe.

"It is cabbage," confirmed Chip, as a robot handed him out one of the trays.

"How can you even know that?" asked Gabe, also picking up a tray, "It doesn't even look like cabbage."

"It's Monday. We always have cabbage on Monday," said Chip matter-of-factly as he followed Gabe to a free table.

Gabe touched the gray paste with his spoon and was surprised to see that it was harder than it looked, as if it was made of a solid substance that had been carefully sculpted to look like a flat splatter of goo on his tray. Gabe tried some of the cabbage-smelling cream-that-was-not-actually-creamy and his tongue was suddenly assaulted by a barrage of flavors that were surprisingly harmonic, all of them aligned to the sweet and sour range that oscillated between a citric, fruity sourness and the delicate tanginess of frozen yogurt mixed with a preserve of wild berries. But the most surprising aspect of the cafeteria food was that, once swallowed, it left the unique, unmistakable aftertaste of hot, steaming crap in the mouth. And all that was crowned by the lingering smell of cabbage.

"I've eaten worse," shrugged Gabe as he helped himself to a second mouthful of the food.

"So, you were talking about Wendy," reminded Chip.

"I told you I did not have sex with Wendy."

"I know, but you said that you talked to her and you couldn't shut up about that."

Gabe frowned. He had given up on sharing the outcome of his meeting with Wendy, as Chip had acted like a shallow douchebag that seemed to have the attention span of a hamster when he tried to do so in the line. And now, he was the one bringing up the topic. Gabe thought that maybe Chip was one of those types that swing between two different personalities. A quick look around in the cafeteria, at the human resources that were the bulk of Terminal 3's security personal, made Gabe realize that, whatever Chip's deal was, it wouldn't make him the craziest person in the room. And the fact was that Gabe had Chip's attention for once, and he decided to keep it short so he wouldn't risk losing it again: "We need to talk to the insectoids."

"To whom?"

"The... squatting cockroaches in S Wing."

Chip dropped his spoon, giving Gabe a severe stare. "Do you want to get your brains fried too?"

"Blake tried to kick them out of their spot. I want to actually talk to them."

Sue suddenly slammed her tray of food on the table and sat next to Chip: "Talk to whom?"

Gabe was taken aback by Sue's sudden, unceremonious appearance, but Chip's indifference to her presence gave him the confidence he needed to try to win a second ally for his cause: "The insectoid family."

"Who are they?" asked Sue as she chewed a mouthful of the gray cafeteria food.

"He's talking about the damn roaches." clarified a sullen Chip.

"Yes! You absolutely should!" affirmed Sue with confidence and a sudden jerk of her spoon that made some bits of the gray food fly all over the table.

"See, Chip? It's a good idea!"

"It's not," said Chip while throwing a spiteful glare at a grinning Sue, "She just doesn't want to lose our bet."

"Just transferred 50 credits to your account," informed Sue. She dropped her spoon and started typing on her holowatch. "You won, Chip."

"That's not how we play it," growled Chip as he clenched his fists and gritted his teeth, giving him the aggressive look of a big cat: one that had been cornered by a huntress.

"I've never seen you mad about winning money before," poked Sue.

"Gabe is not going anywhere close to the roaches. That's dangerous and stupid."

"Aww, it's so cute to see you caring," poked Sue, again.

Chip suddenly stood up and yelled: "I don't care! Fuck you two, I'm gonna eat somewhere else!" And then he stomped toward the cafeteria's exit still holding his tray.

"Aren't you going after him?" asked Sue.

"Nah, he's just a horny, selfish prick who only cares about himself," shrugged Gabe, as he helped himself to another scoop of the cafeteria's grub du jour.

"Look, Chip and I have seen lots of you rookies getting injured, some even killed."

"Are you saying that you care?"

"Nah, I'm cool with that. This is a slaughterhouse, we all know what we signed up for."

"The two of you are assholes, so what?"

"I am an asshole. Chip isn't. Every time something happens to one of us, he goes downhill, even if he does his best to pretend everything is fine. I make those stupid bets with him because he needs the encouragement."

"So you care, too... about him at least."

"What can I say... I like how that big booty of his fills those pants."

"You guys spend lots of time talking about asses."

"It's a boring job full of ugly things. When there's something beautiful parading around we kind of cling to it. Which makes me wonder why he's being so nice to you. Ass-wise, you are way below his league."

"He's... not being nice to me."

"He scares away every rookie he mentors before lunchtime. Not you, though," said a pensive Sue, as she studied Gabe. "Maybe he's saving you for dessert?"

"Or maybe he thinks that I can be a good security guard."

"Or that, but probably he just wants to tap your ass."

"My ass isn't 'tappable'."

"Okay then, I guess he cares about you and shit."

"You know, Sue. I think you care too. Maybe you're just like him, a good person pretending to be tough."

"Nah, I'm really an asshole," said Sue, as she produced Gabe's wallet, the one he had left inside the box in the locker room with his other personal belongings, "See?"

"Can... I have it back?"

"Transfer fifty credits to my account and we can discuss that possibility."

***

After a round of negotiations with Sue, Gabe retrieved his wallet and, as a bonus, she gave him the hint that there was an intercom on his uniform that allowed him to contact any security guard. He tried to contact Chip through the device, and either his was broken or Chip ignored him. After that, Gabe decided to go straight to S Wing and try to communicate with the insectoid family. He already made up his mind about doing so and it would be easy without Chip in his way.

Gabe was not prepared for what he saw at the premises where the insectoids had found shelter. Chip was crouching, facing them from a safe distance, while holding the metallic tray with cafeteria food with one hand. The two adult insectoids stayed in their nested positions under the escalators, but the smaller one walked to the limits of the goo-covered ground that also served as a warning to those passing by on where their territory started. He was facing Chip, just a few feet ahead of him.

"Hey little guy, sorry for being late today." said Chip, with a tenderness that Gabe could never imagine he was capable of just before he set the tray on the ground and slid it toward the insectoid child, who grabbed it eagerly.

"Hey," said Gabe from behind Chip, who, startled, tipped to the side from his crouching stance.

"What the hell are you doing here?!" said Chip, trying to keep his composure despite his fallen position.

"Just getting to see you not being an ass, for a change."

"I...I pissed on that food! Yeah! And...I took a dump on it too! I...I like to see those roaches eating shit!"

"Come on…We all need a hand sometimes," said Gabe, who was not buying any of that as he extended a hand to Chip,

Chip flinched, but knew better than to pretend that he was not caught in a moment of weakness. He grabbed Gabe's hand who hauled the bigger man up to his feet.

"If you tell anyone about that you are dead," threatened an embarrassed Chip.

"So… you've been talking to them, huh?"

"Kinda…They don't answer, but they are cool…kinda…" said Chip, as he rubbed his face, none of the former cockiness remaining. He was just tired and wasn't afraid of showing it anymore. He then picked two stickers from his pocket, "Wanna have a drink with me?"

Chip didn't wait for Gabe's answer. He walked around the insectoid family's nest and reached the escalators under which they were based. Gabe followed him sheepishly. Chip removed an out-of-order sign that blocked the access to what remained of the escalators: the metallic parts were removed but there was still a fair deal of plastic and fullerene parts that allowed him to have a seat. He then offered one of the stickers to Gabe.

"It's a bit early for drinks, don't you think so?"

"This is Terminal 3, nobody gives a shit," said Chip, as he pealed one of the stickers and glued it to his neck.

Gabe wasn't in the mood for a drink, but it was clear that Chip could use a drink buddy. He picked the remaining sticker from Chip's hand and glued it to his neck as he sat next to him.

"This is a good bourbon," said Gabe, to which Chip nodded.

They remained in silence for a moment, the quietness fueling Chip's sudden morose. Gabe decided to interrupt the awkwardness: "You know, it's not true that nobody gives a shit in Terminal 3. You seem to."

"Okay, fine, maybe I do! What are you gonna do? Gimme a medal?"

"I could give you…a hug?" suggested Gabe with alcohol-fueled courage.

Chip did not answer and Gabe had the impression that he was blushing, which didn't make sense since shameless people don't blush. He thought that maybe he was waiting for the hug, although he was afraid that, since Chip didn't give him his clear consent, hugging him could be a violation of sorts. Gabe was not really experienced at hugging and regretted having offered it. Since they were seated next to each other in the escalator's vault, he thought about a side-hug, but that could be interpreted as an aloof gesture, as it was essentially just a half-ass hug. Gabe stood up and walked to what remained of the escalator step ahead of Chip. He decided to be bold and try a full hug, by opening his arms broadly and bending his body down towards Chip really slowly, so his mentor could have enough time to acknowledge that there was a hug coming for him and object if he was not down for the gesture. Yup, that would work. The therapist he saw during his teen years at the foster care home, who said that there was a chance he could be on the spectrum but couldn't be sure since she wasn't getting paid enough by the government to deliver an official diagnosis, would be proud of him for trying to be all social for a change and—

"The fuck are you doing?" asked Chip after witnessing Gabe standing still in front of him with his arms wide open for over one minute.

"I...I...was..." mumbled Gabe, as his eyes frantically looked for an explanation. That's when he noticed a trail of the goo from the insectoid's nest oozing towards a sinkhole, "I was... protecting you... from that!"

He pointed at the goo and Chip just shrugged at the sight.

"First, if someone needs protection here, it's you, shrimp. Second, that's just alien shit."

Gabe climbed down the escalators and squatted in front of the slow flow of goo, examining it closely.

"It doesn't look like shit," Gabe took a whiff, "Nor does it smell like shit...it actually smells like...cabbage!"

"So do my farts. Get out of there."

Gabe dipped his finger in the goo. "That's not shit, it's food."

"Now you are just being gross," remarked Chip.

Gabe licked the tip of his finger.

"Now you are just being super-gross," pointed out a slightly nauseated Chip.

"It's cafeteria food."

"Now you are just being ultra-gro—wait, cafeteria food, you said?"

Gabe answered with a nod and Chip immediately stood, outraged. He stomped down the escalators and toward the alien family's camp. Feeding them was the only thing that made him not totally miserable about his job, and at the end of the day they weren't even eating the food. He didn't care if they were going to fry his brains, they were going to hear some before they had a chance. But when Chip and Gabe walked around the escalators and faced the aliens, they were surprised by the sight of the insectoid child feasting on what was now only half of the metal tray that Chip had given him just a few moments ago. The cafeteria food was dripping from the tray's edges and splashing onto the ground.

"That... that explains so much," muttered a perplexed Chip.

In that moment both Chip and Gabe's intercom devices conveyed a message from Brenda: "All guards! Report to headquarters immediately! This is a code D54!"

"What is a code D54?" asked Gabe.

"Deportation of Dangerous Elements," answered a distraught Chip.

***

When Gabe and Chip arrived at the security guard quarters, it was already packed with their colleagues. A dozen wooden crates were aligned against the wall, and a few security guards were opening them with crowbars. Brenda was pacing in circles in the only vacant space in the middle of the crowd. As Gabe and Chip approached, they realized why: Wendy was at Brenda's heels, relentlessly showering her with unwanted advice: "...it is my legal prerogative to remind you that humane standards should be observed in the deportation of any undocumented—"

Brenda suddenly stopped and faced Wendy, who almost bounced against the bigger woman: "And it's my legal prerogative to kick any element causing disruption out of this room. And you've been extremely disruptive with all that annoying, unstopping yapping!"

Brenda sniffed the air and turned her attention to Chip and Gabe.

"Have you two been drinking?" she asked bluntly.

"I...Actually...Ma'am," babbled a panicked Gabe "I... I can ensure you that—"

"Yup," answered Chip with a shrug.

Brenda lifted her hand to Chip's neck and peeled the liquor sticker from it. After studying the object for a few seconds, Brenda shrugged and glued it to her own neck. She then walked toward one of the now open crates. "I have some good news everybody," announced Brenda, "We've just got a delivery from our friends at Theta Muscae." Brenda then lifted a yoga-ball sized helmet from the box: "Anti-psionic helmets. We'll finally get rid of those cockroaches!"

"The appropriate terminology is 'insectoids'," pointed out a sullen Wendy.

"Disruption!" yelled Brenda, "Take her out!"

Sue eagerly snatched Wendy in a headlock and dragged her off the premises while Brenda picked up the helmets from the boxes and distributed them to all the security guards in the room.

"Hey, Chip," whispered Gabe to his mentor, "You... are not gonna do this, right?"

Chip was handed two of the huge helmets from Brenda. He faced Gabe sternly and put one of them on his head, which gave him the grave appearance of a giant licorice lollipop: "Time to see if you can take this job seriously, shrimp," Chip said, as he handed the other helmet to Gabe.

***

Wendy was laying in front of the door of the security guard headquarters. If she couldn't persuade them, she could at least be a human shield. The door opened, and a procession of lollipops exited under Brenda's leadership. Instead of halting in front of Wendy, they all just took a broad step over her outstretched body.

"Where are your humane values?" yelled Wendy, from her ineffective laying position on the ground to the droves of security guards passing over her, "Alien lives matter! Alien lives matter! Alien— ouch!"

One of the guards kicked her before stepping over her. She was pretty sure it was Sue, although she couldn't positively identify them with their helmets on. As the throng of security guards passed through, she noticed that one of them stayed behind, and was looking at her from behind the hermetic black helmet on his head. Wendy stood up and had a good idea of who he could be: "Gabe?"

"Sorry, Wendy I…I have a job to do," said Gabe in a muffled voice from inside the helmet. He then rushed to catch up with the line of security guards headed to S Wing, leaving a disappointed, speechless Wendy behind.

The security guards formed a circle around the insectoid family as soon as they stormed into S Wing. The insectoids remained unfazed, ignoring the intruders' presence, although their gray eyes had a hint of a red spark. Brenda was about to announce her purpose when a security guard stepped forward: "Ma'am, can I do the honors?"

"Who the hell are you?"

"This is my mentee, Blake," said Sue, "He was the one who was attacked by the roaches today."

"I didn't think someone could survive their psionic attacks."

"Apparently there wasn't much of a brain in there for them to damage, and he begged to come back from the infirmary to assist in the deportation."

"Whatever, rookie. Go for it," said Brenda with a shrug.

Blake swaggered toward the insectoids, whose eyes immediately started glowing red. "Your tricks don't work anymore, losers!" gloated Blake, "Now, get those roach asses of yours out of there! You are gonna get deported to whatever shithole planet you came from and—"

Blake couldn't finish his sentence, as he was struck by 6 laser blasts, each one coming from one of insectoid's three pairs of eyes. The lasers perforated his helmet, and he fell to the ground, dead. For a moment, nobody moved, and all the security guards could do was stare in perplexity at Blake's corpse.

"So, they can shoot lasers from their eyes," pointed out a dead-pan Brenda. "Why didn't anybody tell me they have fucking lasers?"

Brutal silence.

"Whatever. Charge on them! If I see anyone retreating, you are gonna wish the roaches had busted your brain too!"

Despite her threat, half of the security guards were fleeing S Wing. Those were mostly rookies on their first day or seniors who had forgotten that there was no place for fleeing on Brenda Roy's team – no matter how bad the paycheck or the conditions of work were. Ironically, the success of their ongoing enterprise relied on the cowards, as Brenda had her most trusted guards ready to use the ones fleeing as the cover they needed to approach the insectoids. Chip and other burly guards were positioned in the back, standing in the pathway of the fleeing guards, kicking or hurling them all the way back toward the middle field, where Brenda and a few others expertly grabbed the ones that were tossed back into the melee, pushing them ahead like a conveyor belt toward Sue in the frontline. She used the unfortunate ones that were hurled at her from the middle field as a shield to the battery of laser blasts coming from the insectoids, gaining ground little by little. And then, there was Gabe.

Gabe was in shock and moving neither forward, nor backward. He saw Sue tossing away a guard's body that was too worn out by the lasers just to grab another with her right hand for her shielding needs, the left hand clutching her taser, ready to employ as soon as she found herself in range. Gabe couldn't blame the insectoids, they were just trying to defend themselves. They were powerful, but they were only three. This had to stop. Gabe didn't think, he just acted. He approached the insectoids, that were too focused on Sue and her human meat shields to notice his meek movement in the sideline. He picked the helmet off a fallen guard and gently put it on top of the insectoid child's head. His parents immediately turned their head toward him. Although their faces were expressionless, he could see the red in their eyes flickering to gray for a moment. And their hesitation was their ruin, as Sue and Brenda imitated Gabe's move and covered the two adult insectoid heads with helmets. It wasn't clear if the helmets on the insectoids' heads deterred them or they had voluntarily stopped, the point is that they were no longer a threat. Despite that, Sue still tasered them to unconsciousness.

The security guards celebrated their achievement with loud cheers. Gabe, who couldn't stop staring at the passed-out insectoids, could feel a few intense slaps on his back. Some of his other peers were securing the helmets on the insectoids' heads with tape. As soon as the insectoids woke up, they were escorted toward the gate where the rocket that would take them back to the fucked up side of the galaxy was waiting. The guards were so enthralled by the success of their deportation procedure that no one even noticed they had left a mesmerized Gabe behind. He only woke up from his shocked stupor when he noticed Wendy and José approaching the premises. Wendy gave him a disappointed, lingering stare while José, with the help of a half-dozen robotic nurses, focused on the dozen dead or badly injured security guards on the ground.

"Yup, not a lot to do here. Most of them are dead," shrugged José.

"What about that one?" said a scornful Wendy as she pointed a finger to Gabe, "He looks like he is dead inside."

"He seems pretty alive to me. Should I examine him more closely to be sure?"

"No need, doctor," said Gabe, as he removed his helmet, "I quit."

"I thought you had a 'job to do'," said Wendy, still with a spiteful tone in her voice, but puzzled by Gabe's decision.

"That's not a job for me, clearly."

Wendy was touched by Gabe's sense of guilt. He still had potential and she was the one who had a job to do now: "Okay, calm down and take a deep breath. Sometimes every job sucks, and—" Wendy suddenly slipped on the cafeteria food on the ground and fell on her back, the goo splattering all over her body. However, she did not lose her composure and continued with her motivational lecture from the ground: "—sometimes shit happens and you... get covered in all this... shit... and then—"

"That's not shit, the insectoids eat metal," informed Gabe.

"Iron, actually," added José.

To Wendy's surprise: "Wait a minute, José, are they the ones who stole our office's door?"

"If by stole you mean ate it, sure. Their planet ran out of iron, they came to Earth because they were starving."

"Why didn't you tell me that?!"

"You didn't ask, and my medical intervention wasn't necessary, since they were getting the nutrients they needed."

"Okay, last question," said Wendy, as she dug a hand into the goo surrounding her, "If this isn't shit, what the hell is this?"

"Cafeteria food," answered Gabe.

"No, I mean, this," said Wendy, as she cleaned a chunky object in her hand from the cafeteria food that covered it. The object was the size of her fist.

"That's the metallic outcome of their digestion of iron," explained José, "Or their actual shit, as you humans would rather say."

"Holy crap..." said a flabbergasted Gabe, as he realized what the object in Wendy's hand was, "Isn't that shit g—"

"Yes, it is!" said an excited Wendy, "Gabe, I think I found a solution, but I'm going to need your help. Can you give your best shot to delay their boarding?"

***

Brenda, Chip, Sue and two other security guards were escorting the insectoid family through D Wing. The wings of Terminal 3 that held boarding gates were less crowded than the arrival wings, but there were still a good number of aliens that were connecting from and to the fucked up side of the galaxy.

They kept their distance from Brenda, her team and the insectoids, as they stopped at gate 183, from where the next rocket to the fucked up side of the galaxy was set to take off. Some of the transiting aliens knew how dangerous the insectoids could be and most knew how dangerous Brenda was.

As the security guards were about to shove the insectoids through the boarding gate, Gabe rushed between them: "Wait! You can't deport them!"

Brenda gave him an irritated frown.

"Ma'am, please listen!" appealed Gabe, "The insectoids came to Earth as refugees."

"Refugees need to fill forms 485 and 2995-B, and present their demand to the Department of Homeworld Security, 6 months before they land. These roaches just waltzed in. They are going up."

"They couldn't wait six months! They eat iron and their homeworld ran out of it."

"Wait, are you saying all that ordeal of benches and other utilities falling apart for weeks was caused by those roaches eating metal?"

Gabe grimaced. Why would he think that he was making a point for them to stay by saying that?

"Don't remove the roaches' helmets after they are boarded," instructed Brenda to the escorting security guards, "It will prevent them from eating the rocket from inside."

"Wait!" insisted Gabe, as he kept blocking their way, "This... None of this is right!"

"Gabe, enough!" appealed Chip, as he noticed Brenda starting to fume.

However, Gabe persisted: "We are humans, dammit! A century ago, there were still people literally starving on half of our planet, and now that is over because we managed to talk to each other and work things through! We are better than this!"

"That rookie has been talking to Wendy, hasn't he?" Brenda asked Chip, who confirmed with an almost embarrassed nod.

"I've been talking to passengers, Ma'am! I've been treating them as my equals!"

Brenda sighed. She could just ask her guards to move the rookie out of her way. Out of her Terminal actually, as he was already fired even if he didn't know it yet. But she noticed that there was an audience around her. Passengers, both aliens and humans, watching attentively, some of them recording the standoff with their holophones. Brenda feared almost nothing, but bad publicity and the hassle that would ensue was one of the few things that frightened her.

"Very well, rookie," said Brenda, amid her gritted teeth, "Show me how to do my job, then! Do your 'talking' magic!"

Brenda released one of the adult insectoids she was escorting and took a few steps back, followed by the security guards who dragged the other two with them. Now, only Gabe and the insectoid remained in the middle. "Hi...My name is Gabe...I...I—"

"Without the helmet," commanded Brenda, from the edge of the circle. Gabe removed promptly his helmet.

"Good," said Brenda, "Now remove the insectoid's too."

Gabe was taken aback. He should have seen that coming. Brenda wanted him to give up and yield. That ruse wasn't going to work on him. Gabe gulped and then approached the insectoid carefully, eyeing his head covered by the helmet which was attached to his body by a copious amount of tape. He peeled some of the tape carefully, and the insectoid hissed as the tape's removal left an abrasion on his exoskeleton.

"Almost done," whispered Gabe, as he removed another strip, again eliciting a hiss. Gabe could see the insectoid's eyes flaring a furious green under the helmet.

With all the eyes turned to them, nobody paid much attention to the only two persons in the watching crowd that weren't silent. They were two reptilian aliens, an adult and a child, covered in gray scales, their long, prominent jaws were filled with tight rows of pointy fangs. As they stood in the second row of the crowd, the child became agitated: "Mommy, I can't see!"

"Shut up, this is getting good," said the reptilian child's mother.

"Can I have a hot dog, mommy?"

"Shush! Not now!"

"I'm hungry!"

The reptilian mother ignored him, her eyes locked on Gabe and the insectoid. And then, she suddenly roared in pain, as her offspring bit her backside, digging his small yet sharp fangs into her flesh. The growl was loud enough to make all the heads turn toward the source, including Gabe and the insectoid. The furious reptilian mother lifted her offspring: "Did you just bite my ass?"

"I'm hungry and I'm gonna eat you!" said the defiant offspring.

"Not before I eat you first, you brat!"

Gabe noticed Brenda and the other security guards producing their batons and immediately stepping toward them.

"Boss, I dealt with a similar situation earlier today! Let me handle this!" said Gabe, who then turned his attention to the reptilians without waiting for Brenda's leave: "Excuse me, Ma'am."

"What?" said the angry alien.

"Are you going to…actually eat that child or is that…a cultural thing?"

Now, the reptilian species native of 12 Vermillion 3 are known for eating their own under two particular circumstances. One of them is during periods of widespread famine. The other is for educational reasons. Instead of answering to Gabe, the reptilian nonchalantly bit off the arm of her own child. She'd have done the same to the other one if the security guards hadn't tackled her. Gabe was speechless.

"I take that your approach has… failed, Mr. Chagas," said Brenda with a venomous grin, "You are fi—"

"Wait!"

Brenda grunted at the sight of Wendy rushing in the company of a man clad in a red hat that read "Make Earth Great Again". That was too trashy even for Brenda's xenophobic standards. Wendy didn't waste time and shoved a form into Brenda's face: "I have here a legal order that allows the insectoid family to stay on Earth as permanent residents!"

Brenda snatched the form with impatience and scanned it: "'Residents of economic relevance'? How come? All those roaches do is eat iron!"

"Yes, and it just so happens that through their digestion they can convert the iron they consume into gold!"

Wendy showed the solid object she found amid the goo at S Wing. It turned out to be a golden, nuggety piece of crap.

"I know the law. They'll need a sponsor for their residence!"

"Clem here will be glad to host them. He happens to own a junkyard full of scrap metal!"

"And potties! As many potties y'all fellas need!" said the man in the red hat.

Brenda rubbed her head. This was another long and chaotic day at Terminal 3 and, for once, she thought that things would wrap up without surprises. No such luck: "My head is hurting," she moaned.

Suddenly a big claw popped up in front of her face, offering a flask of Advil. Brenda snatched the flask and stomped away.

Gabe eagerly approached the insectoid and removed the helmet from his head. "Did you hear that! You guys are free to stay on Earth now! Isn't—"

The insectoid's eyes went green and Gabe was hit by a psionic blast. His last memories were of happiness for the outcome of his effort and of blood cascading from his nose.

***

Gabe slowly opened his eyes, but all he could see was a fuzzy whiteness.

"You owe me fifty credits, Chip," said a voice that sounded familiar to Gabe.

His blurred vision slowly drifted to clearer shapes. He was in the infirmary, lying in a cot placed beside others occupied by security guards that survived the confrontation with the insectoids, although with injuries. José was checking on the other patients and supervising the caretaking operations of his team of robotic nurses. That's what Gabe could see in the cracks between Chip, Sue, Wendy and Brenda, who were standing by his cot.

"Am I fired?" asked Gabe.

"It doesn't matter, the important thing is that you are alive!" said Wendy.

"Shut up, Wendy, you only talk smack," said Brenda, "The actual important thing, the only one that I expect from my team, is to solve problems, instead of creating them."

"So I am fired," concluded Gabe.

"I was going to fire you, but then I thought it through. The insectoids would have done whatever it took to stay on Earth," said Brenda, "We'd need to escort them all the way to the closest hub to their homeworld on the fucked up side of the galaxy. That'd be a week long trip, assuming that the pirates infesting that quadrant didn't raid the ship. You... solved a problem, Mr. Chagas."

"Am I... hired?"

"Not quite. I still agree with Chip's understanding that this job is not for you."

"Sorry little guy, just trying to do what is best for you," shrugged Chip.

"That's why I'm extending your probation period for one week, and Chip will supervise you. Use this time to prove us wrong."

"What?! Ma'am I don't have time to babysit this shrimp!" protested Chip.

"Make the time," said Brenda, as she walked away while waving, "And if he's hurt again, it will be on you, Chip. See you tomorrow."

"Welcome to the team, Gabe!" said Wendy, as she clapped her hands happily.

"You are not part of the team, Wendy," pointed out Sue.

"Now that I am part of the team, do I get to have a locker?" asked Gabe.

"Nope," said Sue. "I hoarded all the insectoid crap I could find in the available lockers."

"Maybe we can share a locker, partner!" said Gabe to an annoyed Chip.

"First, I'm not your partner, second, if you touch my locker, you die."

"But if I die, you are fired," reminded Gabe.

"I will write down Chip's locker password for you, Gabe," said Sue.

"How the hell do you know my locker's password?"

Before Sue could answer, José approached them with a stern look on his face: "Visiting time is over, this patient needs to rest in order to have a full recovery."

"Am I gonna spend the night here?"

"Don't be ridiculous. This is not the 21st century, you will be good to go in a half-hour."

Gabe eyed his new co-workers walking out of the infirmary, and then looked around. Nobody else was paying attention to him. He touched his holophone, and played the message he had received one month ago, to be sure that it was real and he had not imagined it. The message was conveyed by a deep, ominous, masculine and somewhat muffled voice that said: "If you want to know the truth about Cida Chagas, meet me alone at LA Spaceport's Gate 665."

INTERLUDE

Personal Diary of The Bailiff of the Time Court, Human Division.

July, 5^h 2119, the day of beginning of the Slow yet Irreversible Great Collapse of the Universe.

It started in a simple fashion, at least as simply as dealing with reality in its quantum aspects could be, with me pushing my left foot toward the solid ground ahead of me in space, but behind in time. That was the easy part. I let the queasiness of having a foot in 2119 A.D. and the other one at the End of Time sink in. It was not my first rodeo, after all. It was my second one. My second chance after screwing up my first mission and being forced to undergo mandatory disciplinary training on time travel risk and quantum harm reduction.

It was my duty to address and rectify the anomalies in time. I blamed The Secretary and whomever she had been working with when assigning my first and only mission - until now - for my mistakes. If I had been briefed properly about who was the element I had to track, capture and extract, I'm sure that the mission would have gone smoothly. Instead they kept me in the dark until it was time to act because of some asinine non-disclosure clause. It was only reasonable to know, beforehand, that my first mission rectifying the loose ends of the thread of time also involved the loose ends of my life.

Okay, I'm losing my focus here. Where I was? Oh, yes, I was describing my travel to the past. I took a deep breath and then used my left calf muscle to push the rest of my body from the End of Time. It was easier this time. First, I was not in a rush. I had all the time in the universe. Literally. Not that I didn't also have all the time in the universe last time, when I screwed up royally. Second, the movement was easier precisely because of all the mess I left behind. I was traveling to the same location of my first mission, although years later. The shattered fabric of time in that space was within my reach, giving me leverage and demanding less effort from my muscles and the quantum armor that protects them.

And soon I was entirely back to 2119 A.D., this time without breaking anything. I remember sighing in relief under my cybernetic helmet after the crossing was over. The feeling of time flowing through my cells as they resumed aging was now palpable. I knew I was alive because my body is dying very slowly now that I'm back to normal spacetime. One can feel it, you know? It feels good to have such certainty for a change, as one could never be sure about his ontological status at the End of Time.

After that, I scanned the surrounding area. Empty space transportation companies' check-in desks, abandoned luggage carts, dust, so much dust. A mess of my own making. When I activate the quantum visor in my helmet I can see the same desolation, but also the dangerous areas with entropic anomalies that are invisible to the normal eye. An even bigger mess of my own making, as I can see now the actual unstable quantum nature of space instead of the mere Newtonian smattering of abandoned, broken objects it delusively appears to be.

As I went through my first exploration of the abandoned terminal, I could notice that the windows were covered by planks and tarps and only the few still active emergency lights barely illuminated the mostly dim vastness of the space. I passed by a food court filled with overturned tables and a shop alley where the shelves that once displayed their merchandise were now bare.

The advantage of being an Agent from the End of Time is the awareness that everything in the Universe is meant to end at some point. That thought comforted me, since it implied that my mistake just precipitated something that was meant to happen somewhere, somehow, sometime. The only difference was that, thanks to my action, what was meant to unveil through a few millennia took place in the span of a few seconds. No biggie. After all, depending on your perspective, some of the blinks of my eyes at the End of Time had lasted longer than that time discrepancy.

And then I finally reached my destination: Gate 665. Now I just have to wait. I'm writing these words as I wait. I don't know for how long, but it doesn't matter. How long never mattered. I have all the time in the universe. And I shall have my redemption when Gabriel Chagas will be shown to his place. And time.

DAY 2

CHIP REALIZED THAT HE WAS IN FOR a long day when he saw, just a few minutes after waking up that morning, a text message on his holophone. Nobody but his hook-ups and Sue knew his number, and they both only messaged him at the end of the day.

"Care for a drink later this evening, pal?" said the message.

Yup, definitively neither his lays nor Sue. The former would skip the drink and get to action, and Sue would just show up with the booze: always uninvited, always welcome. The sender identification solved the mystery: "Message by Christopher Davis". Of course, who else would call him his 'pal'? Chip typed his answer: "How the hell did you find my new number?"

The counter-answer came in a blink: "I asked your girlfriend, Sue"

"She's not my girlfriend"

"Phew, that's good, you can do better. Anywho, see you at 6pm at Glorgon's"

Chip thought about making up something, but he decided not to bother. It's been almost a month since he had seen Christopher, and he knew that he would get relentless and hound him if he felt ignored. Better have a stupid drink with him and pretend to listen to his nonsense so he would get his attention fix. That'd be enough to give Chip a reprieve of one or two months during which Christopher would temporarily forget about his existence.

Chip put a breakfast burrito disk inside the rehydrator and waited for it to be ready while looking at a street of Covina through the window of his apartment's kitchen. The street was filled with trash, both in the form of litter and in the form of persons who strolled with brooding faces along the sidewalk and past the facades of closed shops. A blue humanoid, whose long limbs glittered like a sapphire with the sunlight, disrupted the morose decay of the streets of Covina when he stepped out of the Maglev station, looking around in confusion. Chip sighed at the sight. Yup, you came to the wrong neighborhood, turn around while you can. A group of thugs approached the alien. Too late. They talked to him in what seemed to be a polite conversation. They were just assessing their prey before they pounced. BEEP! The burrito was ready.

Chip snatched the burrito quickly and turned his attention back to the window. The thugs were dragging the alien to a back alley, probably grunting about how they would make him regret coming to Earth and that he should go back to the Fucked Up Side of the Galaxy where he belonged. Which is ironic since nobody from the Fucked Up Side of the Galaxy would ever venture into Covina. Aliens from there were looking for a better life, and Covina looked way too much like the worlds they left behind. And they were streetwise enough to know that they weren't and would never be welcome to this part of the city. Nope. The aliens that would land here were from the Fabulous Side of the Galaxy and had stepped out in the wrong Maglev station. They didn't know that Covina was for human trash only. The kind that would rather see stores shutting down and jobs dwindling over accepting aliens in their neighborhood. Chip hated this freaking neighborhood and would be happy to move if this apartment weren't the only thing his mother had left to him. That and the memories of a fairly decent childhood in the same streets he was seeing now. When Chip was a kid, Los Angeles was in its final years of recovering and rebuilding, decades after the One Day War. Life could be hard for some, but even though there was lots of trash on those streets back then, it was not rotting nor stinking. Chip finished eating his burrito and licked his messy, meaty fingers.

Chip left his apartment and walked to the Maglev station. He saw the alien from before, now battered and probably robbed. He was hobbling back into the station, realizing by now his mistake. He turned his watery, translucent eyes to Chip for a moment and then limped faster toward the Maglev platform and away from him. Chip thought about saying something, but he shrugged. He couldn't blame the alien for thinking he was human trash, after all he walked, looked and smelled the same as his attackers. He was from and in Covina. His head and heart might be somewhere else, but even if he moved out of that neighborhood he'd always be human trash from Covina. And even if he tried to deny such facts to himself—which he didn't— he would be reminded of them as soon as the Maglev train stopped at Covina station.

The passengers already inside the train would make way for the incoming ones. The braver passengers would throw a spiteful glare at the boarding Covinan and risk getting into a brawl. Most would just look away. No such averted looks today as the passengers noticed the battered blue alien boarding the train and quickly understood what Covina had meant for him. Chip could feel more angry glares at him than usual. Of course, blame the brawny guy. It wouldn't be the first fight he found himself dragged into on the Maglev train because of what the thugs of Covina had done. It'd be their loss: he knew how to kick ass, his muscles weren't only for show. He tensed, waiting for it to come, as the train had fallen into brutal silence.

"Hey, buddy!" said a merry voice behind Chip, who clenched his fist, ready to punch, "Can't believe we are on the same train!"

Something was off. That voice was way too cheerful to be an attacker. And it was familiar. When Chip turned around he saw the friendly face of Gabe staring up at him.

"Do you live in Covina?" asked Gabe with innocence.

Usually that question would not be about the literal geographical location of his home, but about whether or not he was human trash. The right answer to that question usually wouldn't be a yes, but a sucker punch to the mouth of the asker. Chip decided to trust Gabe's innocence, even if he found it somewhat unsettling. He'd feel more comfortable if it was a coded calling to start a brawl.

"Yes, but I'm not an alien hater!" said Chip, louder than he intended, but at the same time noticing that some of the disapproving glares at him faded away after that.

"I know you are not, buddy," said Gabe, cheerfully.

Chip liked to hear that. He knew what he was, but having someone confirming it instead of questioning his certainty about himself felt good. And in such a nice way. Damn, Gabe was cute. He wished that cuteness was closer to him. Or further away. He could punch that cuteness away and get back to the way things were. He decided to try something in between: "Don't call me buddy."

"Sorry, partner."

"Don't call me partner either."

"But we are partners, remember? Brenda said we are gonna work together."

Chip was relieved. Being reminded of that made it easier for him to dislike Gabe.

"It wasn't my choice to babysit you. Which doesn't make me your partner. Just your coworker, and we are not on the clock."

"Yeah, sorry for bringing up work stuff like that. I will try to remember that since we will be taking the same train every day."

Every day? That was way too often, way too close. Chip wanted to punch him and order him to leave at the next station. He could even ask him to never take this train again.

"I'm in Pomona, we are almost neighbors," said Gabe.

Pomona and Covina may be relatively close to each other, but being referred to as neighbors was a utopist stretch. Chip let that go since he had already asked Gabe not to call him buddy or partner.

"Yesterday I took another train that went straight to Terminal 1. I like this one better."

"The Express to Terminal 1 is cleaner and faster," said Chip, "The only reason I don't take it is because those jerks at Terminal 1 don't let us go through it to get to Terminal 3."

"There is nobody on that train. This one is cozier."

At this moment one of the arms of the battered blue alien detached from his body, oozing a crystalline substance that smelled like ozone. And although for humans the scent of ozone isn't particularly stomach-turning, it seemed that the smell was nauseous to half of the aliens in the train, who started puking copiously. And their combined vomit was nauseating to the rest of the train. Chip threw up in the ground but felt a gooey splash in his face. It was Gabe. Gabe had thrown up on him.

"Sorry, neighbor!" said Gabe.

Chip knew that this day was going to be bad when he saw Christopher's text just after he woke up. He should have called in sick.

***

It didn't take long for Chip to understand that Gabe couldn't shut up. At some point Chip just zoned out and let the smaller man go on with his inane babbling while he just grunted something unintelligible when Gabe paused in his talking. The pauses meant that Gabe had asked a question, and Chip's grunts were close enough to answers, which prompted him to restart his monologue, either undeterred or satisfied with Chip's primal pretenses of retort. As Gabe and Chip exited the Maglev train at the Spaceport's Terminal 3 station, Chip tried to walk faster than Gabe, but his colleague would just rush and catch up. Then Chip decided to walk slower than Gabe, and for a few seconds he could see the talkative rookie leaving him behind and the sight made

Chip daydream for a moment about reaching out to his thin neck and snapping it to make him shut up. These reveries wouldn't last long as Gabe would quickly notice that Chip wasn't next to him, which would prompt him to stop in his tracks and wait for his mentor to catch up. In one of those moments, however, Gabe stood in front of Chip, blocking his way. His mouth was moving and it took a moment for Chip to realize that Gabe was insisting on a question where his mere grunting wasn't a satisfying enough answer. He finally gave in and actually listened to what Gabe was saying.

"Where's Gate 665?"

Chip frowned. That was a weird question. There were so many gates in Terminal 3, more than he could keep track of.

"I don't know, check the map. Now move it or we are gonna be late."

Gabe resumed walking next to Chip through the spaceport's always busy main lobby, but without relenting on his question: "I checked the map. I couldn't find a Gate 665. It just goes up to 610 at P Wing."

"Then you got your answer," said Chip, too eager for the conversation to end to wonder why Gabe was interested in a gate that didn't exist.

Chip wiped the sweat dripping from his forehead. The rookie really got him all worked up, or was it hotter than usual in the Terminal?

Chip and Gabe arrived at the security guards' headquarters and headed to the locker room to change into their uniforms. To Gabe's delight, he found a locker with his name on it containing a clean uniform fit for his size.

"Guess someone is getting some respect around here," gloated Gabe.

"Guess Sue took pity on you. Try to stay on her good side," advised Chip, as they headed to the conference room for the shift change with the guards working the graveyard shift.

Sue had been his charge of the graveyard shift and when Gabe and Chip took their place amid the other guards, she started her report under Brenda's oversight: "So, nothing much to say. It was a very uneventful night. We lost two security guards and three were injured because we got some raucous eighteen foot tall aliens coming for the first time to Earth all the way from Delta Ganesh 2, unaware that our atmosphere contains nitrogen. And, according to our resident doctor José, for them, breathing nitrogen is like getting high on a mix of alcohol, cocaine and nail polish for humans. Any questions?"

Gabe raised his hand: "Isn't it hot in here?"

Many mumbling sounds of agreement could be heard in the room.

"Ah, almost forgot," continued Sue. "The Terminal's maintenance crew reached out to us concerning the sudden disappearance of almost all their AC guys, in the last 12 hours. Told them that it wasn't our problem."

Gabe turned an alarmed face to Brenda whom, to his surprise, gave Sue a nod of approval.

"Isn't…people disappearing…a security issue?" asked Gabe.

"Only if it's our people," shrugged Brenda. "Although most of the time they are just quitting without letting us know, so we don't bother with that either."

"But… if they asked for our help. We should do something, right?"

"Oh, do you want to do something about that, rookie?" asked Brenda in a mocking, condescending tone.

"No, he doesn't, Ma'am!" intervened an alarmed Chip.

"I mean, I would be happy to investigate the case if I have your leave to do so, Ma'am," continued Gabe.

"Very well, Mr. Chagas. That's your chore for the day," said Brenda with more than a hint of sarcasm. "And obviously your mentor will be in charge of supervising the progress of your investigation and will be held accountable for its outcome."

***

Chip and Gabe headed to R Wing as soon as the shift change meeting was over. Chip pondered for a moment making a little detour to D Wing, more precisely to Gate 102, where the rocket from the Alicante 8 cluster had just landed. These rockets would also bring on droves of the predominant species in that quadrant: large feathered aliens whose lower bodies vaguely resembled those of ostriches, but with larger sinewy, muscular legs. They also had the tendency to disembark from the rockets in sprinting, stampeding droves. Nobody would blame him if Gabe happened to be in their way when that happened and got trampled to death. There were actually hundreds of different ways Chip could get away with murdering Gabe and most of them were going through his head as they continued walking to the maintenance crew headquarters.

"Are you okay, neighbor?" asked Gabe as he patted Chip in the back.

Chip leered at Gabe and his smiling, friendly face. Dammit. Why couldn't Gabe's face be just as pathetic as his actions? Chip looked like a Covina guy and people expected him to act like a Covina guy. He once had a hook up with a sociologist who told him that, in human history, men like Chip used to have different designations depending on the part of the globe they were born: chav, bogan, redneck, trailer trash, just to refer to a few of those originally in the English language. Human trash was just an evolution of those derogatory terms. Chip skipped the lube when he fucked that pedantic little shrimp's ass. But Gabe... Gabe didn't look like he was from Pomona. Pomonans were like Covinese without the alien hating – at least not blatant alien hating. Chip could very well have been a Pomonan. The fact is that Chip couldn't pinpoint what Gabe was. He could only judge him by his actions. Gabe's smile and his gentleness made Chip uneasy. His eagerness to go beyond his mandate in this stupid job while dragging him along made Chip angry. Chip was used to unease and anger, but not at the same time. His moments of unease were usually short-lived, as they'd either deescalate to apathy or lead to anger. Chip didn't particularly appreciate feeling angry, preferring his moments of apathy, but he could deal with it. What he didn't like was that his current anger was not shooing the fleeting unease away, as it'd usually do. Instead the two emotions were merging, becoming something new and unfamiliar. And every time something new and unfamiliar showed up in Chip's life, it only caused him sorrow. As they arrived at the maintenance crew headquarters, Chip regretted not taking the detour to Gate 102.

Chip and Gabe entered a vast room filled with mechanic paraphernalia, in the middle of which four maintenance workers, each dressed in a blue jumpsuit, were seated at a table playing poker. Unlike the rest of Terminal 3, where the temperature kept rising, the air conditioner seemed to be fully operational in here. They either didn't seem to notice or pretended not to notice the two security guards standing next to them. With Chip being there only reluctantly, Gabe decided to take the initiative: "Excuse me, gentlemen, can I please speak to your boss?"

"Jamil disappeared," answered one of the workers. "Check."

"I see. Who is in charge, then?"

"Nobody is in charge," answered another worker. "Check."

"If there is no one in charge, who is doing the terminal's air-conditioning maintenance work?"

"Nobody," said a third worker, as he put some chips on the table. "I raise my bet to ten credits."

"So, can you guys take me to the place where your boss... Jamil, disappeared?"

"Nope, I just answer to Jamil. He's not here," said the fourth and last remaining maintenance man as he put his cards down. "I fold."

Gabe turned a distraught face to his mentor: "Do you have any questions for them?"

"Sure," said Chip. "Hey guys, can I join the game?"

"Sorry, closed game," said the first worker. "I fold too."

***

A frustrated Gabe left the maintenance headquarters, followed by an apathetic Chip. Witnessing Gabe's failure had been surprisingly soothing for Chip, maybe because such failure was neither new nor unfamiliar to him. "Hey Chip, don't you think those guys were a bit...off?"

"I do. Who the hell could say no to another player bringing more money to the table?"

"No, I mean... They were a little... indifferent?"

"Ah. No, that's normal."

"But... it's already getting super hot in here. It could be a hazard if nobody fixes the Air-Conditioner in the Terminal."

"Well, that's how things go here."

"You don't seem very worried."

Chip sighed. He didn't have the balls to get rid of Gabe, it'd be like killing a puppy with a sledgehammer, which would be beneath his standards, even if they were not particularly high. Instead, Chip decided to educate Gabe into his ways of apathy and indifference.

"Follow me, shrimp," commanded Chip.

They walked a few steps toward another one of Terminal 3's support facilities: the firefighter squad headquarters, which was a room similar in dimensions to the Air-Conditioner Maintenance headquarters, although the absence of shelves hoarding all sorts of paraphernalia made it look bigger. The large vault, instead, had only a small red vehicle not much larger than a hockey rink Zamboni to which a large hose was connected. At this moment the hose was in the hands of an extremely muscular man clad only in his orange underpants who was releasing a jet of water toward two other equally muscular men dressed with the same minimal attire and two athletic women wearing red lingerie. Those guys looked like lifeguards, not firefighters.

"Chip!" said the firefighter holding the hose, who immediately turned the water jet toward the two arriving security guards, drenching them.

Gabe thought about protesting, but he realized that it was quite refreshing as it was getting too hot inside the Terminal.

"Hey, Vick," greeted a soggy Chip.

"We are just getting a little refreshed before we start to play. Why don't you take off those soaked clothes and join us."

Vick turned his face to Gabe and his smile turned into a scrutinizing frown: "Hey Chip, I'm cool with you bringing guests, but we have standards here. That guy is a shrimp."

"Actually I...This time I won't be joining you guys," explained Chip. " I came here to ask for a favor."

"Anything for you, bro!"

"Can you tell my ne... colleague Gabe over here about that time we had to deal with the new smoking regulations?"

"Sure thing, bro! When was that again? Last week?"

"More like last year."

"Oh yeah, right! So, the Spaceport's administrators were concerned about cigarette smoke being bad for the health of certain aliens and shit—"

"Huh, cigarettes are...bad for humans too," pointed out Gabe.

"Don't interrupt me, shrimp," scolded the firefighter. "Anyway, they decided to make the spaceport a smoke free zone. The problem was that some aliens are made out of gas and shit, so they had to be walked around the terminal inside canisters to not trigger the fire alarms. But lots of those airheads were ignoring the rule and that was getting on our nerves. So we decided to give them a hand and we broke all the fire alarms."

"What if... there is an actual fire?" asked Gabe.

"Then we are all gonna die," said Vick as he picked a pack of cigarettes from a shelf and lit one. "That's why we try to enjoy life and shit. You should too, shrimp. Even if you are ugly and I would never tap that scrawny ass of yours."

"Is the spaceport's administration aware of this?"

"Wanna file a complaint? Feel free. Their office is at Terminal 1."

"I think I'm not welcome there."

"None of us are, not even me and I'm hot as shit."

"Why... did you bring me here, Chip?"

"Because there is nothing you can do to change things," answered Chip, as Vick walked back to his peers/lovers, "All you can do is prevent things from staying the same, and nobody wants that. Then just do nothing."

"Yesterday we did something good."

"Don't get used to it."

Gabe shook his head, more disappointed than surprised. Dealing with Chip felt like peeling an onion, a new layer every time. During that morning many things started making sense when he saw Chip stepping into the train from Covina station. Covina people had a… reputation, especially in Pomona. Gabe felt like at some point he and Chip could be friends, even though he never had someone whom he could call a friend. But at that very moment what he needed was to be a bigger man than Chip and not let him drag him into the hole of apathy where he was settled. At least not until he found Gate 665.

***

Historians, sociologists, cosmographers and exoethnologists of the many academic institutions on Earth and beyond can't agree on why some of the arms of the galaxy host planets are economically thriving, politically stable and socially fair to those lucky enough to be born there, while other arms are a complete, absolute mess of poverty, desperation, corruption and tyranny. Consensus only exists regarding the terminology: there are two sides, one of them being the "Fabulous" side, the other one being the "Fucked Up" side. Some scholars tried to use the term "underdeveloped", but were immediately ridiculed by the majority of the academic community both from the left and the right: their detractors from Berkeley University's Institute of Social Sciences called them "well-intentioned yet condescendingly misinformed", while the ones from Duke University's Ayn Rand's Fraternal Lodge referred to them as "social justice pussy asses" – although, to be fair, they used that wording to anyone that didn't look like their reflection in a mirror or Ayn Rand.

According to the scholars from Berkeley, the "Fabulous" side of the galaxy has always economically exploited the "Fucked up" side, and that imperialism caused the gap in levels of development. According to the scholars from Duke, the creatures from the fucked up side aren't naturally inclined to democracy, only being able to live under either anarchy or despotism. The only fact that both institutions agree upon is that the fucked up side of the galaxy is a terrible, horrible, really bad place to live. Some planets simply depleted their natural resources and their populations live in constant poverty. Those are the lucky ones. The ones that still have an abundance of natural resources usually fall prey to the many neighboring tyrannical empires, which happen to be at constant war with each other.

All that is crucial in order to understand why Gabe and Chip, who never went to Berkeley nor Duke, were taking longer than usual to walk through the aisles of Terminal 3. Going across the Terminal could have its own hazards, even for security guards. Although guards would be spared of the scourge of thieves and muggers that roamed the corridors and preyed on the distracted and weak, they were the main target of those who nurtured resentment against institutions and those who carried their banners. That was the case for most passengers coming from the fucked up side of the galaxy. Some came from colder worlds than Earth, others from warmer planets and satellites, but all of them gauged the functionality of their homeworld's institutions on the capacity of their spaceports to keep the inside temperature different from the one outside. An artificially climatized spaceport meant that, even if the homeworld was fucked up, it was at least trying to save face. If that didn't happen, it meant that their worlds were too poor or too ravaged by war to afford to keep their front gates running properly. It meant that it was time to make plans to get the hell out of there for good since there wasn't anything left of value that would justify a minimally functional turnstile.

It was July in Los Angeles, and the AC was out. As Gabe and Chip went through the agitated droves of aliens, they were unaware that thoughts of riots were brewing in the many minds of aliens and humans that were transiting through that space, triggered by their survival instincts and their cultural expectations of proper room-temperature. The only person aware of this was the resident exoethnologist Wendy Lin who, after being kicked out of the security guard headquarters by Brenda Roy when she tried to convey her concerns, was back in her office venting her frustration to her co-worker and best friend, Doctor José. He wasn't very sympathetic to her struggle.

"You are a coward, Wendy," said José, while sipping from a straw inserted in a cubic purple fruit.

José had ditched the scrubs for a bikini bottom and top despite his species lacking the protrusion most female humans have on their chests that justified the attire.

"Come on, José, I am just another sentient creature in this Terminal whose mind is torn between the voice of reason and reasonably tamed instincts of survival. And hell is going to break lose in a few hours."

"I am not signing your demand for a sick leave. You are not sick."

"First, it is my right to use my sick days as I see fit!"

"The human arrogance and proneness to self-assessment never ceases to astonish me," remarked José with what would be a frown if he had the muscles to perform a frown.

"Second, I pointed out an upcoming social issue. The unrest is brewing and there are hundreds of reports of that phenomena occurring all across the galaxy. As soon as the AC systems go down, the spaceports collapse! It always ends in carnage and mutual annihilation. Trust my assessment as a fellow scientist!"

"Gotta pitch harder than that soft science exoethnology mumbo jumbo."

"I went to Berkeley!"

"I went to Medical School. Show me someone who is actually sick and I can do something about that."

"I could show you some trampled people in a few hours, but I'm afraid we will be one of them!"

José sighed and reluctantly signed a form that was laying on his desk: "Fine, there's your sick leave, Wendy."

"Thanks, José," said Wendy, relieved. "Let's get out of here."

"I'm not going anywhere."

"Wait, didn't you—"

"You did not convince me. I just signed it because you are my friend and you really wanted me to do that for you."

Wendy looked at the sick leave form in her hand and started crying.

"Are you in pain?" asked a puzzled José as he noticed the tears on Wendy's face.

Wendy's answer was to hug him.

"I... acknowledge, although will never understand, your species' cultural need of physical contact, Wendy, but the current air temperature makes that sort of body contact hazardous. And what's your motivation for the human hug thing this time?"

"My motivation is that it will be an honor dying next to a good friend like you," said Wendy, as she let José go, tossed the form in the garbage can and sat at her desk, resigned to her upcoming doom.

A few seconds later Gabe entered the room.

"Gabe! Nice to see a friendly face before death!" said a cheerful Wendy as she grabbed a box filled with an assortment of pills of different colors and shapes from a drawer. "Would you like to get super-ultra-high with me?"

"I... Not really, thanks. I'm working. Are you... dying?"

"She's not," said José.

"Not clinically, but we will all be dead in a few hours," said Wendy as she popped a handful of pills.

"What do you mean?"

"Take a seat," said Wendy.

Wendy shared with Gabe her take on the upcoming riot triggered by the AC failure that would result in the death of anyone without astonishing survival skills. She then started listing those who were, in her opinion the most likely to survive, with Sue on the top of the list and Gabe at the bottom. And then she passed out.

"Wendy?" asked a puzzled Gabe when Wendy suddenly stopped talking and her head crashed onto her desk.

"She's probably fine," said José. "I will run a scan just in case she took the wrong combo of pills again."

"You don't seem very concerned about what she said."

"I'm a physician. People will suffer from the heat and I will be here if they dehydrate or display any other kind of physiological reaction to be expected from an abnormal environmental temperature change. But I cannot stop anger triggered by the symbolism of a broken institution conveyed by the elevated temperature, or whatever hippie crap Wendy would say about that. However, there's one thing I can tell you for sure: there is nothing I can do for this situation that fixing that AC system wouldn't do better."

"Can you do something about a person… with an injured… part?"

"Part? Like an arm?"

"Sort of. Lower than an arm."

"Like a leg?"

"Above the leg. Like, right… in that area…"

"Yes, probably, but what does that have to do with the broken AC?"

"Nothing, but it does have to do with the reason I came here in first place. You see, my partner Chip likes to come to this wing because of the… action at the restrooms. And… apparently the person who was giving him a… you know… got a bit… heated… and… bit down."

"Ah."

"So, I was wondering if you could do something about that?"

"Sure, bring him here.'

"Well, that's the issue, it's a bit embarrassing for him."

"Why would it be embarrassing to be seen in public with a bleeding crotch that suggests that one customarily seeks sexual relief through the intimate exposition to moody strangers by cruising in public spaces?"

"Can you help him or not?"

"Fine, I will go meet him in the restroom," said José as he stood and picked up a suitcase, but not before opening a drawer to remove a syringe containing an orange liquid and giving it to Gabe. "But you keep an eye on Wendy and use this if you think that she is going to die. It's a universal psychotropic blocker."

"Why not use that on her now?"

"Because she might be having a really good trip and it would be a dick move to interrupt that. Plus, the side effect if used too early is a slight yet persistent headache that prevents any enjoyable intercourse for up to one week. I don't think Wendy could go more than three days without sex."

"Ah, does she have a boyfriend?"

José walked out of the office with his suitcase and without answering the question but with an amused cackle that Gabe found puzzling.

***

Gabe stayed in the Assistance to Passengers and Staff Office, observing Wendy intently and being sure that she was breathing. After a few seconds he felt like a creep, as he often did when he looked at a woman that he wanted to know better, which would never happen, since such woman was a stranger and their existences were just briefly happening at the same space and time only to be diverted again, forever. Gabe couldn't stop thinking that Wendy, unconscious before him, was quite pretty. Much prettier than the few women he had some sort of connection with during his whole life and tended to be abusive toward him due to his physical and emotional shortcomings.

Gabe knew that there was something in him that would just stir either ire or pity in people. Sometimes he thought it was his scrawny physique and five foot, six inch height in a world where most men were genetically designed to be six feet, two inches. Geneticists justified the prescription of the height of six feet, two inches as ideal, since a man this height would be tall enough to reach up to the luggage compartment in space transports without having their knees turned into mush on the long-haul space travels in economy class seats. This recommendation came just after humanity had reached peak genetic manipulation advancement at the same time they were invited to join the Galactic Confederation that, despite the name, was exclusive for planets on the Fabulous side of the galaxy, thus becoming aware that they were not alone in the universe.

Gabe had never left Earth and he was sure as hell that he was not genetically manipulated during his embryonic stage to be six feet two inches and non-asthmatic like most men. That meant he was the product of a woman's unplanned pregnancy, and he was too young to ask his mother any questions about that before she disappeared. Most of the other human kids in the foster care home weren't planned and genetically enhanced either, although they were all taller than him. As one of the physicians that followed up with him during his days at the foster care home explained, humanity's natural genetic tendency was to grow taller than the past generations, and five feet, six inches was a very normal size for men during the 20th Century—and the same applied to his slightly below average intellectual capacity. Programming genes to allow men to grow to six feet, two inches was actually a deterrent, and that's why Gabe knew that Chip, at the height of his six feet, eight inches was also the outcome of an unplanned pregnancy. The kind of big guy in his foster care home days to whom he wanted to be a sidekick but always turned out to be a punching bag, especially that night when he didn't yet understand that the sock on the door handle meant that he was supposed to sleep in the hallway, as his roommate was busy with a girl and didn't want him witnessing all the action like a little creep. And there he was. Looking at Wendy and wondering if she would ever pay him any attention if they were not coworkers of sorts. Staring at her sleeping form. Like the puny little creep he was now and was doomed to remain.

Wendy suddenly jerked her body up to her feet and turned her attention to a surprised Gabe with glazed, wide-eyes: "We need to save the day, Gabe!"

Gabe put the syringe containing the universal anti-psychotropic in his pocket but kept his fist around it. She was not dying, but she was acting weird.

"We have one hour and forty-four minutes before chaos breaks lose! Follow me!" commanded Wendy.

She then bolted outside the office with Gabe following suit. Actually trying to follow suit. Whatever she took was giving her a lot of stamina as she was running much faster than him, sprinting toward the main lobby and apparently unbothered by the sultry, stale air inside the Terminal.

TERMINAL 3

Gabe stopped in his tracks when he reached the main lobby. It was crowded and hectic. That could be normal. The lobby had been crowded and hectic since the moment he was tossed into it by the security guards of Terminal 1. What was not normal was the fact that the lobby had turned into a giant brawling arena with larger creatures squashing the smaller ones. And Gabe was very aware that he was on the smaller side. As he scanned the lobby, Gabe was dismayed to notice the relatively small Wendy dodging stomping columns of flesh covered in scales, feathers and rough skin. Gabe's attention turned to an alien that looked like a bipedal bovine with long, thick tusks instead of horns charging toward Wendy, his boulder-sized shoulders readied to drag her with him. Gabe gulped and scurried through the ordeal of stomping ungulates, non-ungulates and semi-ungulates paws and feet, his mousy form almost being trampled many and many times by those moving pillars of flesh that made him momentarily lose sight of Wendy in their swinging and thumping movements. When he crossed the lobby, to his relief, he noticed that Wendy was sauntering toward the access to M Wing and the bovine alien now had his tusks embedded into the concrete wall.

Gabe was out of breath when he finally reached Wendy. She was standing in front of a door with a sign that read:

Maintenance Employees Only

"What are we doing here?" asked a panting Gabe.

"This is the location of the Terminal's central Air Conditioner. I thought it would be a good place to start investigating the disappearance of the maintenance workers."

"I... never told you that the AC personnel disappeared."

"Oh, really? I guess I read your mind without noticing," shrugged Wendy.

"Wait, you can read minds?"

"Not usually, but when I take my combo of the random pills José gives me from his leftover stash eventually weird shit happens. Most of the time I just get knocked out or have a really good trip. But other times I die and a few times I get these weird powers for a while."

"That… sounds dangerous."

"Don't be a square. Anyway, I just realized that I also have X-Ray vision, and there are people in there."

"Should I call reinforcements?"

"No, I'm cool," said Wendy as she tore the door off its hinges with her mind.

"Wait, you can do telekinesis too?"

"I guess I got a lucky draw!" said Wendy as she manically barreled into the room.

When Gabe walked inside, he found the large central air conditioner of the spaceport being dismantled and boxed by a dozen maintenance men, who gave a lingering, mistrusting stare at Gabe and Wendy.

"I…I thought you guys were missing," said Gabe.

"Not us," said one of them. "Just the boss and…. a few others."

"So, you are trying to fix the AC?"

"Nope, taking it apart and transporting the parts to Gate 440."

"Why?"

"Boss orders."

"I thought Jamil had disappeared."

The maintenance worker scratched his head as the others stopped their activities.

"You can't lie for shit, Oleg," said a particularly burly one, as he grabbed a steel pipe.

The workers, now displaying a more threatening demeanor, started surrounding Gabe and Wendy.

"Sorry, man. I think we are gonna need to get rid of you. Nothing personal," announced the one they called Oleg.

"I wouldn't do that! I am a trained security guard!" warned an unconvincing Gabe, eliciting some chuckles from the workers.

The burly maintenance worker raised the steel pipe, ready to strike Gabe. However, he didn't hit him with it. Wendy suddenly sprinted like a bolt toward the worker and kicked him in the balls. She quickly snatched the pipe midair and hit three other maintenance workers with a barrage of extremely fast swings. She moved frantically, like a poisonous wasp stinging a herd of bulls. One by one the maintenance workers were falling to the ground unconscious. Wendy was about to knock out a very battered Oleg when Gabe intervened: "Wait, Wendy! I still have questions!"

Wendy, who had a hold of the man twice her size, dumped him on the ground.

"Why are you guys doing this?" asked Gabe.

"They got Jamil."

"Got like in kidnapped?"

"Yes, but they also offered better employment conditions if we shut down the AC, along with a bigger salary, paid maternity leave, better union, you know the drill."

"I... don't think security guards have a union. But I know for sure that what you guys are doing will land you a place in jail, not work benefits."

"We wouldn't be staying on Earth. We'd all be moving to Kappa Hortence and taking the AC equipment with us."

Wendy slapped her own forehead as she reached a breakthrough, which left a big red mark: "Of course, how could I have forgotten about that! Kappa Hortence 4 is going through a major global warming due to their sun's expansion! They are known for smuggling every AC device in the universe they can get their hands on to counter that. They also like to enslave maintenance workers to operate them."

"Enslave?" asked Oleg.

"Yeah, can't see much of a Union for you guys if you go with them," said Wendy.

"Where are they?" asked Gabe.

"I sincerely don't know and wouldn't tell you if I knew. I wasn't lying when I said they have the boss," said Oleg.

"Kappa-Hortencians have mimetic abilities, so they can blend anywhere," said Wendy. "But they are also very vulnerable to the heat and would wither if exposed to a temperature greater than eighty degrees Fahrenheit."

"Wait, the maintenance headquarters still had their AC on!" remembered Gabe.

"Fine, let's get there then!"

"It's chaos out there, Wendy! We are gonna get trampled if we—"

Wendy touched Gabe and they suddenly materialized at S Wing, in front of the AC maintenance crew headquarters.

"Did you just teleport us?"

"I guess! Man! This combo of pills is awesome, I wish I had paid attention to what I was swallowing!"

"Not sure about the swallowing, but you are swelling!" said an alarmed Gabe.

Wendy's face was bloated and pink. And before she could answer, she passed out, crumbling onto the ground. Gabe felt her pulse and realized it was extremely faint. Without having any other choice, Gabe picked out from his pocket the syringe with the universal psychotropic blocker José gave him and injected the orange liquid in Wendy's bloodstream. Although she remained unconscious, it seemed to work, as the swelling reversed and she was back to her normal skin color. Gabe dragged Wendy to her office and then returned to the AC maintenance office's entrance, this time alone. He then opened the door.

The room looked exactly like before, with four maintenance workers playing poker and ignoring him. It felt exactly like before too, still having a comfortable temperature that contrasted with the scalding sauna that the rest of the terminal was becoming.

"Drop the act," challenged Gabe. "I know that you kidnapped Jamil and were trying to steal our Air Conditioner. Guess what, you got busted!"

The four maintenance workers immediately stood up and turned to Gabe in an almost choreographed fashion. Gabe gulped when he realized that he was outnumbered.

"Why don't you show your real faces and surrender before I...do something like...kick your asses?" nervously bluffed Gabe.

TERMINAL 3

The Maintenance men started to dissolve in front of him. The rough features of the four burly men deflated until they each revealed their true shapes of two foot tall, red creatures whose bodies were a thin worm-like cylinder from which sprung four pairs of rickety arms on the sides, two slender legs on the bottom and a long head on top, ornamented with a pair of fractured, shiny compound eyes and two small feelers. There were hundreds of alien species living on Earth and almost none were smaller than Gabe. But it turned out that the Kappa Hortencians were not only smaller than him but also totally scrawny wimps that made Gabe feel big for a change and, as a result, confident for the first time in his life.

"Very well, shrimps, you better surrender or I'm gonna kick the hell out of you!" said Gabe in a cocky tone that had never passed from his mouth until this moment.

However, instead of surrendering, the four aliens quickly rushed toward Gabe and leaped upon him. He tried to slap them away, but that only resulted in pushing them back for a second until they pounced again. And then they started getting bitey. The Kappa Hortencians had small mouths with little pointy teeth that were barely perceptible at least until they tried to rip someone's flesh. And that's precisely what they were doing with Gabe, gnawing relentlessly as Gabe pirouetted in frantic, clumsy despair around the room, succumbing to the assault by the four tiny tenacious aliens. He might be bigger and stronger even if outnumbered, but he was still not a fighter.

Gabe had come to terms with the prospect of a slow and painful death when the sharp pain of the tiny bites from the four itsy-bitsy mouths started to relent, one by one. When the last Kappa Hortencian mouth was dislodged from his flesh, Gabe noticed that Chip was back. Instead of his uniform pants, his crotch was clad in bandages that looked like something between a loincloth and a diaper. In each one of his big hands he was holding two squirming Kappa Hortencian by their feelers.

"Man, you really are a total shrimp," said Chip.

***

It didn't take too long for Chip and Gabe to find the head of the maintenance department, Jamil, inside a crate that was headed to the next cargo flight to Kappa Hortence 4 in the company of a dozen of his coworkers. Once rescued, they were more than happy to reassemble the central AC machinery with the help of their colleagues that Wendy had beaten and José, subsequently treated. When Gabe sought José's advice on how to deal with the bite marks along his skin, he got a prescription for over-the-counter baby oil, which made Chip laugh non-stop until they boarded the same Maglev train back to their homes in the Eastern suburbs of Los Angeles.

"Maybe those bites were dangerous! Who knows what kind of bacteria they might have in their mouths," said Gabe, defensively.

"It's not too late to quit, you know," said Chip, taking a serious turn.

"That again, look—"

"You don't know how to fight. This job is so shitty that they don't screen whoever is hired, but you need to at least know how to punch and kick if you are a security guard."

"I know how to punch," said Gabe.

"Go for it," egged on Chip, opening his arms broadly and approaching Gabe. "Punch me."

"I don't want to hurt you."

"Punch me or I'm gonna punch you."

Gabe punched Chip. A little, pathetic pat on Chip's chest.

"You don't know how to punch." assessed Chip with a shrug.

"I know how to take a pounding and then stand up."

"Those bites were nothing."

"Fine, punch me."

"I ain't gonna punch you, shrimp. I'd destroy you."

"You will. And then I will stand up again," said Gabe with a determination that gave Chip goosebumps. It was hard for Chip to witness confidence, although he was not really sure why.

"Let's leave that for another day," said Chip, as the train stopped at the filthy Covina station.

"Hey Chip, wanna have a drink? On me," offered Gabe, as the train doors opened.

For a moment Chip thought about answering yes. He could use a drink in the company of someone whose face he didn't want to punch. And at this moment he realized, with surprise, that he no longer wanted to punch Gabe. Or hurt him in any other way.

"Have plans," muttered Chip as he exited the train without looking back.

Chip followed straight to Glorgon's, which used to be a Z Chamaleontis-owned pub in Covina until the riots of 2084 evicted all the aliens that lived in the area. They kept the name, though, the same way the Anglosaxons kept the name Covina when they kicked the Spaniards out in the 19th century. Inside, Glorgon's was as filthy as the streets of Covina and had nothing alien. The smells in the air were of very human piss, sweat and vomit from their very human patrons. Chip was early for his appointment, so he approached the bar were the owner and only employee of Glorgon's was standing. His name was Maury, and he was born in Covina at the same time as Chip. And, like Chip, he stayed. They used to be childhood friends, but their lives took different turns and lead them to different interests. Where Chip had buffed up, Maury chubbed up.

"What are you gonna have tonight, Chip?" asked Maury, as he dried a couple of glasses on his dirty apron.

"Draft beer," answered Chip, knowing that he didn't need to give him any more instructions, as Glorgon's had only one tap that would spit a light-yellow liquid into the glass which always came with a complimentary hefty cloud of foam on top.

"Been doing anything fun?" asked Maury as he filled the glass.

"Not really. Just here to see Christopher."

"Cool. Wanna hang out later tonight when you are done with your old man?"

Chip looked at Maury's face. It was round and flushed. Very different from the boy he had his first kiss and lost his virginity to many years ago. It still had a charm, a different kind of appeal that was at the same time rugged and cushy. He wouldn't object to a bit of cushiness in his life for a change. "Maybe. What do you have in mind?" asked Chip.

"The boys are gonna come over after I close and then we'll see," answered Maury, as he put the now full glass on the counter with a beefy hand.

Chip noticed that the skin of Maury's knuckles was flaking off due to abrasion. Those knuckles certainly weren't cushy. Chip's incipient interest faded away and, almost at the same time, he heard a voice behind him: "Hey, son."

Chip didn't turn. He kept his now morose eyes locked on the glass in front of him. Chip didn't know why he still came to Glorgon's to meet his father, always ordering a glass of draft beer he wouldn't even sip, as he preferred taking his alcohol in patches. At the moment he had two tequila patches under his shirt, and he felt that he might need a third one as he realized that he might be stuck in that filthy pub for the night and in Covina for the rest of his life.

"What do you want, Christopher?" asked Chip, still as a statue.

A big man sat on the barstool next to Chip. His body had the type of brawn that comprised both Chip's muscles and Maury's fat. He could have been the father of both – the kind of father that went out to buy cigarettes to never be seen again: "For starters, a beer."

"Right away, Mr. D!" said an eager Maury as he drafted another pint of his vile beverage.

"Thanks, Maury. You are looking good! Have you been working out?"

"Gee, Mr. D. Not really," answered Maury, flattered.

"Boxing counts," pointed out Chip in a wry tone as he glanced at Maury's knuckles.

"I guess," said Maury with a chuckle as he punched the air with his free hand. "Someone around here needs to keep them aliens out of our hood."

Christopher and Maury talked for a moment about banal topics while Chip endured their conversation. The pub started filling up with the early evening patrons: locals, low-tier human sex workers having a drink before their shift started and their upcoming customers arrived. That movement took Maury away from them.

"Okay, now that the meatloaf has stopped bugging us, let's talk."

"You know that the 'meatloaf' worships you, right?"

"Can't stand the fat fuck."

"His dad died in the riots when we were kids."

"Couldn't stand the fat fuck's father back in the day either."

"What do you want, Christopher?"

"Just my son's company!"

Chip activated his holophone and opened his checking account: "How much do you need this time?"

"I could never accept your money!"

"You do accept it, every freaking time you come crawling in here begging."

"Well, I did accept sporadically a loan from you, and I intend to repay it today!"

"Cool, just transfer the credits to my account and let's get this over with."

"I was planning to repay it… after a little service."

"Crap."

Christopher put an orange metallic cylinder on the counter. It looked like an old-fashioned flashlight, the kind you could find in thrift stores in Los Feliz.

"Thought buttstuff was my thing, not yours, Christopher."

"Don't be rude, son. Here's the deal. Ten thousand credits if this device can be retrieved inside A Wing by 9am tomorrow."

"Fuck off, Christopher," said Chip as he stood up and stomped away.

Christopher shrugged. He noticed that his glass was empty and helped himself to Chip's, which was still full. That's how most of his meetings with his son ended. He was sincerely trying to repay the debt he had with Chip. Last time he tried they had a fight, just because he proposed to his son to let him sell the apartment Chip's mother left to him on his 18th birthday, just before she flew to whatever part of the galaxy whores travel to. But the kid was hopeless. His mother clearly pampered the brat way too much after the divorce and destroyed his mind. It looked like he would need to call his other contact to do this job, and get a much smaller commission than he would get had he persuaded his son to do his biding.

Christopher fidgeted with the cylinder. It had just one small button. Surely it was not a weapon. It probably belonged to some rich guy who wanted to throw a prank. He pointed the cylinder toward Maury, who was serving two sex workers, and pressed the button. Maury started chuckling, and then laughing, hysterically. Christopher turned the cylinder away from him just as Maury moved his hands to his chest. He didn't want the meatloaf to have a heart attack. He was not done drinking for the night.

INTERLUDE

Personal Diary of The Bailiff of the Time Court, Human Division.

July, 6^h 2119, 1 day after the beginning of the Slow yet Irreversible Great Collapse of the Universe.

I spent most of my time patiently sitting on one of the few dusty benches that hadn't crumbled, arranged in a row in front of the discolored vinyl walls of Gate 665. The chair winced under the considerable combined weight of my body and the cybernetic armor, but it held up. The last hours allowed me to observe the terminal's strange environment. The damage in the fabric of time wasn't noticeable per se without the technological help of the quantum visor in my helmet, but some attention to details such as gravitational alterations that I could detect after hours of observation gave me a subtle yet crucial clue on the patterns of the time fractures.

The areas of the terminal where the debris or pieces of furniture were hovering in the air or sticking to the ceiling had zero or inverted gravity. In that area, time would run terribly fast - or terribly slow from the perspective of whoever would make the mistake of stepping into that zone of anomaly. That poor fool would age years or even decades in just a matter of seconds from the perspective of an observer outside the entropic anomaly. On the other hand, areas without furniture that displayed shattered pavement and debris were also extremely dangerous, but for the opposite reason. The entropic anomaly in those areas slowed time, which meant that whoever entered that zone could, theoretically, cross it in a blink from the perspective of someone observing that person from outside. That is to say if the person crossing the damaged area had a body capable of resisting a gravity dozens to hundreds of times greater than Earth's. The observer would just see whoever entered the zone being reduced to pulp in the neatest of ways, as the gruesome process of compaction of organic and inorganic matter would seem to happen in a relatively stomachable fraction of seconds and a whole body would appear to almost instantaneously become a compact disc surrounded by the outfit the person was wearing. I tested these effects sometimes during my waiting, by throwing small shards of glass into the areas just to see the effect of the entropic anomalies on them, but soon stopped as I found it pointless. I have all the time in the universe, and having that much time is dangerous for someone in my position if I start becoming impatient or, even worse, bored. Impatience leads to uncalculated action, while boredom conveys deliberate irresponsibility. I can't have either of those. I can't screw up again.

I tried to refocus my attention to the teachings from my training sessions with my mentor, back where there was no time, as all the time of the world had ended. And yet, my training spanned through centuries – or at least felt that way. My mentor taught me that having just a little of something desirable makes one value what they have through the virtue of temperance. Having none makes you either lose the need for it or wish it with the most absolute greed. I had no time before, and now I had plenty. And between none and all, there was the time and place where I would capture my prey. I can smell him. Gabriel is close. Gabriel was looking for me. It will take a moment for his below-average brain to figure out the location of Gate 665, as he is not only looking for a point in space, but also in time, even if he doesn't know that yet.

The most beautiful thing about time is that it can often be wrong, but sooner or later, a time will always be right. I will be there for both the rightness of time and a time of rightness. I have all the time in the universe, a universe that is infinite, at least until time will be over. And I felt lucky for that, as space and time couldn't be dissociated. It was such a shame that my prey didn't abide by that notion... Because I have plans for my prey. As soon as I get a hold of Gabriel Chagas, I will use my two instruments of choice to deliver an overdue comeuppance. One is time. The other is space. And they are actually one. It would be better if my prey was aware of this. Oh well, I need to accept that I can't have everything I want. At least I still have the whole time of the universe.

DAY 3

IN THE EARLY 21ST CENTURY, SKID ROW used to belong to the homeless. Then the struggling artists started pouring over that corner of Downtown Los Angeles, either coopting the homeless into their lifestyle or shooing them away to Inglewood and beyond. Some of those artists became wealthy, which brought other wealthy artists to Skid Row in droves. These well-to-do artists and their push to turn the cheap dive bars into expensive avocado-and-almond brunch establishments forced the remaining struggling artists out of Skid Row and turned the decrepit buildings that hosted all manners of art experimentations into white-walled art galleries. Edginess and risk and its rewards for a curious, sensible soul turned into the kinds of convention and zeitgeist that are dully entrenched in secured, brokered money-transfers – no paper, no plastic, only crypto, sorry-not-sorry.

During that time, the skyscrapers that laid siege to Skid Row, the only enclave of relatively small buildings in Downtown Los Angeles, started growing past an average of three hundred stories in height, built with the finest, most durable materials in the world. Materials resistant enough to withstand the nuclear blast of the One Day War. Luckily for Skid Row, the skyscrapers shielded them from harm. The regional economic crisis at the aftermath of the war, however, made the art galleries close their doors. Fortunately, the powers that be left behind a gift to Skid Row: a virtually irrevocable art-fostering city ordinance that prevented the demolition of any of the existing buildings. That's when the restaurants arrived, small ones popping up within the existing real state along the relatively narrow streets of Skid Row and catering to the executives in the surrounding skyscrapers that were hungry for food and for the increasing corporate profits of a recovering economy. Most of the patrons were humans. There was something intimate and soothing for a human who slaved his days away for one of the big corporations headquartered in Downtown Los Angeles to go to a small restaurant, nested in a building with walls built with actual bricks that had been made many decades ago through pottery techniques that were now outdated and forgotten, and eat human food made by human hands. Some of those eateries even stayed open until very late at night for the white-collar employees that had to work extra hours. That was the case of Curry Castle, a restaurant that served South-Asian food and had a good reputation among local gourmets for its Gujarati dishes. Curry Castle was inconspicuously furnished like a basic American diner, with a smattering of tables and chairs and a counter with a row of stools for those eating alone.

It was past three in the morning and Curry Castle had just closed for the night. The owner/cook/waiter/dishwasher/maitre d', Manohar Patel, swept the floor behind the counter. He was a bald, mustachioed middle-aged man, short yet sturdy. He was alone but for a young woman clad in a Terminal 3 security guard uniform. She was seated on a stool, dozing with her head on the counter and a conspicuous liquor patch glued to the back of her neck.

"Sunanda, we are closing," barked Manohar.

She didn't budge. He poked her head with the tip of his broom, and she mumbled something unintelligible, but still not budging.

"Wake up, Sunanda!" he insisted, as he peeled the liquor patch from her neck with a swift move. By the smell, Manohar realized it was highly-concentrated tequila.

"It's Sue, dammit," said Sue, as she lifted her head from the counter and glared at Manohar.

"Sunanda is such a beautiful name. You should be proud of it," he said, as he turned his attention to the old holocomputer on which he ran the books.

"Sue is simple," said Sue, as she stood up. "How much do I owe you?"

"Five hundred credits."

"For the drinks? That's a rip-off."

"This isn't a bar."

Sue looked around confused: "Didn't realize I was home."

"This isn't your home. You owe me five hundred credits for the rent."

"Come on, Manohar, cut me some slack this month."

"I only do favors for family."

"Come on, *uncle* Manny."

"I hate when you call me that."

"Uncle?"

"Manny. That's the guy who runs the taco place down the block, not me."

"Manny is simple."

"Not everything in life is simple, Sunanda."

"Why don't you pour us a glass and we can talk about that?"

"You've had enough drinking for the night and, again, this isn't a bar."

"But I know that you keep a bottle under the counter."

"Go to bed, Sunanda."

"Fine!" growled Sue.

She used her right arm as a support to lean over the counter and give Manohar's bald head a smooch. At the same time, Sue reached for a bottle of whisky hidden under the counter with the left arm.

"Are you going to pay for that?" asked a frowning Manohar.

"This isn't a bar, remember?" said Sue, as she strolled to the exit door with the bottle.

Sue walked down the Skid Row street just the few steps that were necessary to get from Curry Castle's entrance to a side door of the same building. This door opened to a narrow set of stairs leading to the two small apartments above the restaurant. Manohar lived in one and Sue occupied the other. It was a one bedroom apartment and very affordable considering that she was several months late in rent. Manohar was being really nice by only asking for the five hundred she owed for the last month.

Sue wasn't particularly tired. She had been the head of the graveyard shift the night before and slept during most of the day. When night came she got hammered until she passed out. And then, for some reason, woke up at her uncle's restaurant. Her day shift would start in only a few hours. At least she had the bottle of whisky to keep the boredom away until it was time to leave for work.

"Aren't you going to pour me a glass?" heard Sue as soon as she opened the door.

She hated her twin sister's sultry voice, but even if she hadn't said anything Sue would have known that Pree Patel had broken into her apartment again by the stench of expensive perfume that would linger in the air wherever she was.

The similarities between the two twin sisters ended at their shared appearance. Sue was tomboyish and carefree, while Pree was nothing short of a dolled-up vixen eager to seduce and manipulate in order to prevail. Right now Pree was dressed in a deluge of pink silks that enveloped her body with an unexpected lean elegance given their clear excess. The perfume always matched the color of whatever she was wearing, hence this time it had a rosy hint.

"I would ask how you managed to get through the new locks, but I don't think you'll give me an answer," said Sue to her twin sister, who was graciously seated in the armchair that was one of the few pieces of furniture in the small apartment's living room.

"The answer is finesse, Sue," said the visitor, as she flashed her pearly whites at her sister.

"Get out of my apartment, Priyanka."

"Priyanka? Since when are we so formal?"

"Since you almost got me killed the other day when you stole my Terminal badge for your smuggling and amusement needs."

"We were partners in crime."

"For starters, to be a partner in crime I should have been aware of the crime. Also, never got my cut."

"I have a proposal for you. Full disclosure this time, and your cut will be fifty percent."

"Not interested."

"Really? Heard that you are struggling to pay rent to Uncle Manohar."

"One day I will find the microphone you planted in his diner."

"Please don't, they are expensive and you'd need to tear down the whole building, although when we pull our next job, money won't be a problem anymore. You will even be able to move out of this shithole."

"This place is fine. Surprises me that you come here at all since you have such a poor opinion of it."

"I'd come more often if I were welcome."

"Can't blame Uncle Manohar for hating your ass after what you've done."

"Talking about you, not about the old fool. You and I have very... complimentary skills, you know. We would be unstoppable if we worked together."

"Terminal 3 is hiring."

Pryianka released a haughty laugh: "Why don't you pour us a glass of whatever cheap booze you have in your hands right now so we can start discussing your way out of that grubby job?"

"Sure, Pree! Here, have a sip on me!" said Sue, as she hurled the bottle toward her sister, who deftly bowed. The bottle flew over the armchair and crashed against the wall.

"Thank you for the drink, Sue," said Pree, as she stood up. "next time you see me, either get out of my way or don't miss your shot."

And before Sue could ask another question, Pree rushed to an open window and faded through it in a whirlwind of wavy, pink silk.

Sue cursed. Every time her sister would show up in her life, problems would arise. Sue didn't consider herself a particularly honest person but, compared to Pree, she was a girl scout headed to sophomore year at nun prep school. Pree was a criminal mastermind, the kind that got through all her schemes without ever being caught, and considered that her only failure in life was her sister's lack of interest in her illegal activities. All Pree got from her sister were hints of anger, the kind you obtain for being an inconvenient stalker instead of a formidable, insidious foe. Pree wouldn't mind if Sue were her competitor, even though she would prefer having in her sister an ally. Instead, whatever Sue felt for her seemed very close to indifference, and Pree feared that if she just vanished from her life she would be forgotten. She wouldn't stand for that. In her criminal life, Pree was competent at erasing all her footprints. With her sibling, it was the opposite: she needed to resurface from time to time and give Sue the slightest nudge in order to hold claim to their sisterhood.

Sue laid on her bed and tried to sleep. She couldn't. Pree's smug smirk kept showing up in her mind, and with it the prospect of problems. Plus, the lingering smell of rosy perfume was nauseating her. Whatever Sue felt for Pree certainly was not the indifference that her criminal sister feared. Sue decided to take a shower while opening all the windows, hoping the smell would go away. The water felt good on her body, giving her a sobering comfort. As soon as Sue acknowledged that effect she turned off the shower. She was not ready to get sober yet.

After putting on her security guard uniform, Sue leaped through her apartment's window and climbed the rusty emergency stairs to find her most treasured possession: a hovering race bike. When upset, Sue relied on two fixes: one was alcohol, the other was high-speed at great heights. She climbed onto her bike and drove it up to the skies of Los Angeles, past the skyscrapers, riding from the coast to the San Gabriel Mountains and back again, all the while dodging vehicles coming in the opposite direction and evading air traffic patrol, as the fees for her bike were late and she was obviously speeding beyond the legal limit. She rode her bike until sunrise, then she headed to Terminal 3.

***

Sue arrived unusually early and entered the meeting room to wait for the shift change. To her surprise, Gabe had already arrived and was there alone, eating what seemed to be small rolls shaped like horseshoes pinched on one end.

"Don't you have a life?" Sue asked.

"I thought I should arrive early and observe things a little, in order to learn and... hey, you arrived early too!"

"Are you suggesting that I don't have a life? That's rude."

"No, but since it's only the two of us, maybe you could answer some of my questions."

Sue thought for a moment about saying something particularly nasty to Gabe, but then she realized that she hadn't had breakfast yet.

"What are you eating?"

"Ah, have you ever had Brazilian cheese rolls?"

"Yup, and they are round. Why do those have that weird shape?"

"Because they are a cheese roll variation from central Brazil, harder and more like a cookie than a roll. They are called *biscoito de queijo* and—"

"Let's make a deal. Stop being a nerd and keep me fed. As long as I'm eating I will answer whatever questions you have."

Gabe eagerly gave the bowl with his breakfast treat to Sue, who started chomping down on them eagerly. They tasted like Brazilian cheese rolls, although they were more floury and less sticky.

"Where's Gate 665?"

"There's no Gate 665," answered Sue, with her mouth full.

"There must be a Gate 665."

"Not in Terminal 3."

"I checked, Terminal 1's gates stop at 650."

"Maybe Terminal 2?"

"I tried to look into it, but there's not much information. The access gate is closed."

"Yup, there was a creepy ass accident in there many years ago."

"Tell me more about that."

"I don't know much, just that Terminal 2 had to close after that accident. And then they had to rush-build Terminal 3. Brenda was there, ask her."

"I... don't think she would answer my questions. What if—"

"Ah-ah," interjected Sue, as she showed the empty bowl.

"Come on, last one."

"Fine, but I want you to tell me where you bought these rolls—"

"Cookies."

"Whatever, they were delicious."

"I made them. My question is... how do I enter Terminal 2?'"

"You don't. I told you they shut down that place. There's stuff in there that's dangerous. Why are you so interested in freaking Terminal 2?"

"Oh, I just want to... be good at my job."

"Don't. Just go through your day and get paid at the end of the week."

"Maybe there's more in life than going paycheck to paycheck."

"Not in our line of work."

Before Gabe could argue, Brenda and a woman clad in black sunglasses and a black pantsuit swaggered into the room.

"That's all you have, Brenda?" asked the woman as she raised her sunglasses, nervously scanning both Gabe and Sue.

"I told you that the shift change starts in a half-hour."

"Fine, we only need two anyway," said the woman bending over and scanning Sue attentively, her eyes only inches from her face.

"Hello and... what the fuck?" said Sue.

"Sorry, I forgot to introduce myself. I'm Thadie Zulu, deputy operations director at the Department of Homeworld Security. There is a very important task ahead related to the arrival of the Trade Emissary of the Ifritian Empire, and we will need two volunteers from Terminal 3 security staff to work with our team."

"I volunteer!" said Gabe eagerly.

"I don't," said Sue.

"I'm afraid we don't have the time to be picky here. There is actually only one skill that matters. Are you... funny?"

"I'm the most humorless person ever," stated Sue in a dead-pan tone. "Really."

"How humorless?" asked Thadie, as she continued to invade Sue's personal space while scrutinizing her attentively.

"I don't know a single joke, laugh tracks are my favorite part of any sitcom because I find them poignant. One day I tried to make a sad child, who had lost a soccer game, smile and since then he wears a bag over his head."

"Perfect, that's what I'm looking for."

"Wait, I thought—"

"We are seeking humorless, surly people."

"I'm not sure if I will fit," said Gabe. "People in my foster care home used to say that I was funny, especially when they pulled my pants down."

"No son, you are the most pathetic human being I've ever seen," said Thadie as she studied Gabe's face and body with undeterred, fascinated revulsion. "Like, you have those extremely creepy baby-sized hands that barely have the strength to lift your baton. You make me want to cry and, believe me, I'm not used to crying. Two years ago I was on the Secretary's security detail during his state mission to Iota Crucis 6, and our whole staff of more than fifty persons was literally eaten from inside-out by the paragenetic parasites on that planet, except for me and Bob. Actually, only half of Bob, since I had to drag the upper half of his body with my teeth as I was also carrying a suitcase containing sensitive intel. And then, when I finally got myself and half of Bob's ass onto the spaceship, he died. Do you know how many tears I shed for Bob and the other agents I lost that day?"

"None?" guessed Gabe.

"How dare you?! Do you think my heart is made of stone? I cried one tear. See?" Thadie produced a tiny little flask containing a drop of water. "And I'm on the verge of dropping another one in this flask just because I can barely control my emotions when I look at your face. Why would you even hire that poor, clearly disabled young man, Brenda?"

"I'm not disabled," pointed out Gabe.

"Is it some sort of sick, twisted joke where you keep this abnormally short, mentally challenged man as a mascot or something?" continued Thadie.

"If it was a joke you wouldn't feel sad for him," asserted Brenda.

"Good point. We can do sad for this mission, son. Your sad ass is in."

***

As Gabe, Brenda, Sue and Thadie exited the security guards headquarters they noticed that the Terminal's main lobby was less hectic than usual, and the reason was obvious: a detail clad in suits and ties was attentively controlling the circulation of passengers, in particular the ones directed to A Wing. Thadie stopped in front of a few of the agents: "Give these three the access badge."

It became clear that the agents were under Thadie's command, as one of them approached Gabe, Brenda and Sue and pinned a small holographic badge to their lapels.

"This will give you access to A Wing, which was locked down for the envoy's arrival. I have some issues to discuss with my personnel, why don't you go ahead and brief your guys, Brenda?"

Brenda was happy to oblige and she followed with Gabe and Sue to A Wing. The briefing started as soon as they were at a safe distance from Thadie: "Okay, rookie, here's the deal. From time to time there's a VIP landing in this terminal. Most of the time they are persons of interest headed to prison and connecting on Earth after they were captured by the galactic police, which is normal since every major high-security prison was built on the fucked up side of the galaxy. Rich and powerful fucks usually use Terminal 1, as private flights always go there, even those coming from the fucked up side of the galaxy. Now, the VIP who is about to arrive is the trade emissary for His Highness Morgubin the Second, Head of the Ifritian Empire that conquered something like one tenth of all the habitable star systems in the fucked up side of the galaxy. And even if they are a brutal tyranny, they don't want to send the wrong message to their people and cause unnecessary unrest by using the terminal that their regular citizens are not allowed to. That's why we will use the VIP gate at A Wing."

"And what kind of business would we want with those dicks?" asked Gabe.

"They are brutal, they are rich and they sell all sorts of minerals for much cheaper than we currently buy from the Fabulous side of the Galaxy."

"Because they come from mining colonies that use prisoners of war as a work force," said Wendy, who had been listening their conversation behind them without being noticed until now.

"I don't want you here, Wendy," said Brenda. "Shoo!"

"Not your choice this time, Brenda. Ms. Zulu herself asked me to be here as an advisor," explained Wendy, as she proudly showed the holographic badge pinned to her lapel. "I must say that it feels good to have my hard work recognized for a change."

"Rookie, Sue, ignore her," ordered Brenda. "As I was saying before I was interrupted, our government needs those minerals to make Earth's manufacturing industry competitive on an interstellar level."

"And our job is to protect the emissary," concluded Gabe.

"Wrong as usual, rookie. Our job is to nod politely, answer if someone asks for directions to the restroom and let the agents of the Department of Homeworld Security do all the heavy lifting as we stay out of their way and, of course, most importantly: don't be funny!"

"Yeah, about that, what's the deal with being funny?" wondered Gabe.

"The Ifritians don't like comedy," said Brenda with a shrug. "And I kind of get them. People trying to be funny make me want to punch them."

"Actually, it's more complex than mere unresolved anger issues like yours, Brenda," said Wendy. "The ruling species in the Ifritian Empire are literally allergic to humor. They will swell if exposed to a high level of comedy, although most run-of-the-mill jokes will only make them uncomfortable. If in doubt, just start talking about the weather, but avoid metaphors. They find the idiom 'raining cats and dogs' particularly hilarious for some reason."

"Nobody asked you," said Brenda. "But yeah, what Wendy said sounds right. Anything else you would like to add?"

"Are you asking for my input, Brenda?"

"Don't make me regret it."

"Well, I just would like to say that it's an honor to finally contribute to the security guard team and get to know you guys better. By the way, your sister is lovely, Sue."

Sue immediately widened her eyes, approached Wendy and took a whiff.

"Shit," muttered Sue, as Wendy frowned.

"Anything wrong, Sue?" asked Brenda and they reached the line for the security access to Wing A.

"No Ma'am!" lied Sue.

As soon as Brenda turned her back to Sue, she approached Gabe and whispered in his ear: "Okay, we might have a problem but I don't want Brenda to know. Will you help me out?"

"Sure, partner!"

"Don't call me partner. Okay, so that twin sister of mine whom Wendy just mentioned, she is trouble. Might be nothing, but can you please keep an eye out for her?"

"Of course, Sue! What does she look like?"

"She... is my twin sister."

"Oh yeah, right."

"She also... smells like she dresses. It's hard to explain, just take a whiff of Wendy."

"I don't think Wendy will—"

"Just do it!"

Gabe approached Wendy and whiffed the air around her, eliciting another puzzled frown from the exoethnologist, and then he returned to Sue.

"Smells like... roses... pink roses... not sure how I know the color, but—"

"Yeah, she is dressed in pink silks."

The people in line were being processed quickly by the Department of Homeworld Security detail that was scanning the badges. Brenda, Sue and Gabe got their leave to pass, but when their device scanned Wendy, it beeped.

"Something wrong?" asked Wendy.

"This badge you are wearing... it's counterfeit."

"That's impossible, it was given to me by Thadie Zulu herself. Brenda, tell them!"

"I don't know her," shrugged Brenda. "Why don't you escort that person to the security guard headquarters in the main lobby and I will handle this issue as soon as we are done here?"

The Homeworld Security Department's agent nodded and dragged a squirming Wendy away as Brenda grinned at the sight. Then she followed into A Wing, leaving Sue and Gabe behind.

"Sue, do you think—"

"Yup, Pree stole Wendy's badge. She's in here somewhere."

"I think we should tell someone."

"Please don't."

"Why not? This might be dangerous."

"Look, my sister is... special. She's not only a criminal mastermind who has never been caught. She... is also an overly dramatic type that has an unhealthy need for attention. I feel pretty confident that she just got this job to poke me. If we create a scene because of her, that will just encourage her to come back more often, hoping that I will acknowledge her or something."

"Not if she is caught and sent to jail."

"She won't get caught no matter what we do. She's the slickest fish in the barrel."

"Look, I'm not in your shoes and I never had a sister, but—"

"Then stop right there."

"But—"

"I'm telling you about my family. Nobody in this freaking job knows about my family and probably doesn't care, which is good. For some reason that I already regret I trust you more than anybody here. Maybe it's those puppy eyes of yours, dunno. Just… trust me back, okay?"

"Okay."

"Okay? That easy?"

"You sound like you know what you are doing."

"Nobody…ever said that to me before," muttered Sue.

Sue wanted to punch Gabe for daring to be not only so damn nice to her, but for saying what she wanted to hear for so long, from her uncle, her sister, and even her mothers, wherever they could be hiding. It turned out that the rookie she only recently met said the right thing at the right time. No, not the right time. An acknowledgement that Sue knew what she was doing when she managed the chaos that was her life was long overdue.

"Let's get to the gate and wait for this circus to be over," said Sue, and Gabe nodded.

***

When Gabe and Sue arrived at the only gate within Wing A, they found two dozen Homeworld Security agents ostentatiously displaying their weapons – from laser pistols to bazooka-sized, high-density beam projectors. They were in every corner of the hall, scanning everyone and each other from behind their sunglasses, their gaze only relenting when they noticed the holographic badge fixed to their lapels. A table next to the gate contained an assortment of human and alien finger-food and beverages, and Brenda was feasting on the bounty. Gabe remembered that Sue ate his breakfast and approached the table.

"What would you... suggest, Ma'am?" asked Gabe, as he studied the diverse assortment of snacks.

"Anything made by and for humans," said Brenda while munching a tiny croissant.

Gabe ignored her recommendation and helped himself to a snack that looked like a blue ball of yarn.

"That's really good," he said, as he tasted the tangy sweetness of the alien snack, whatever it was.

"We'll see how good it is when you get food poisoning or an allergy."

"I appreciate your concern, Ma'am."

"Sue!"

Sue, who was scanning the wing looking for her sister, turned to the table.

"Since Chip is not on this mission, Gabe is your burden for the day. Anything that happens to him is on you. For starters, don't let him eat any alien food."

Brenda walked away from the table.

"She hates my ass," said Gabe.

"No, Brenda only hates aliens. When it comes to humans she's indifferent, but that's clearly not the case for you. Weird as it is, she cares about you. What do you have on her?"

"I have nothing! I never met that woman before my first day of work here!"

"Well, try to figure it out, it's becoming annoying for Chip, and now me."

The agents aligned along the gate under the lead of Thadie, ready to welcome the trade envoy from the Ifritian Empire. Considering the bellicose reputation of the Empire, Gabe pictured the emissary as a large, scary, beastly alien with claws that could shred steel and a breath of fire. He was slightly disappointed when, a few moments later, a small, ocher slug slowly crept its way through the gate. The Ifritian trade envoy couldn't be more than 4 feet tall and displayed a sullen, gelatinous face with a couple of green blobs of eyes that didn't seem to focus anywhere in particular.

"On behalf of the Department of Homeworld Security I would like to welcome you to Earth, your Excellency!" said Thadie, "Please follow me. A motorcade is waiting outside the Terminal."

"I just hope you will do a better job than your people did for my two predecessors."

"I am the very best, your Excellency! You have nothing to worry about."

"I hope so, since I took a cautionary measure in case you fail. I injected an extremely potent explosive chemical in my blood stream that will be activated in case I reach a lethal level of laughing."

"With all due respect, I don't think I can allow you to leave the grounds of this Terminal if you pose such a risk."

"Is that a joke?!"

"What?! No! I meant—"

"I don't like jokes, Ma'am."

"I know you don't—"

"Jokes can kill me. And you. And everyone else in a radius of 10 miles. Just do your job and take me to the Ifritian Consulate so I can negotiate with you human vermin fair sales terms for our minerals."

Thadie flinched for a moment, but released a resigned sigh. Her background in risk assessment was much too advanced to allow her to even consider a solution other than abiding by the trade envoy's diabolical ploy. She turned her attention to her crew and commanded: "Let's get the envoy safely out of here!"

The Homeworld Security agents flanked the trade envoy from both sides as he slowly, very slowly, advanced toward A Wing's exit.

"Your Excellency, would you mind if one of my employees carried you?" offered Thadie, "That would make things move faster."

"I am no child, Ma'am, and even if your offer wasn't condescending, when non-gelatinous creatures touch me with those dry, crispy paws of yours, I get ticklish."

"Suddenly one of the agents in the front row turned to the envoy and pointed a gun at him."

"What are you doing, Suzuki?" asked an alarmed Thadie, but it was too late.

The agent pulled the trigger, but instead of a lethal laser ray, the gun squirted water onto the envoy, who chuckled. Thadie immediately tackled the agent and apparently pulled at his hair. A second take revealed that she was pulling off a mask from his head: the agent was actually a clown. Not a simple clown, but a native of 69 Zegma 4, a planet where their literally colorful natives were born with a naturally ludicrous propensity and went through life with Dionysian humor and a lightness of heart. That is, until their planet was blown up by the Ifritian Empire. Now all they wanted was revenge on the destroyers of their civilization.

"Security breach!" yelled Thadie.

Another agent, this one holding a large bazooka, pointed his weapon at the envoy with one hand as he removed his mask with the other, revealing a thick crust of clownish makeup. He pulled the trigger, and a cloud of multicolored confetti showered over the envoy, who chuckled again, this time harder, his ocher, gooey skin now becoming slightly orange. Sue immediately darted toward that clown and punched him hard in the belly, interrupting a juggling performance he was about to start.

"What do you think you are doing, you imbecile?!" reprimanded a distraught Thadie. "Everybody knows that nothing is funnier than a clown being punched! All agents! Cover the line of sight of the envoy and pull the hair of the agents next to you until you are sure they are humans, not Zegman clowns!"

Gabe, Sue, Brenda and the agents formed a circle around the envoy and started painfully tugging at each other's hair. None seemed to be another clown hiding behind a mask.

"Ma'am, this one here is bald as an egg," said Gabe as he pointed out a hairless agent.

"Hehe, bald as an egg!" chuckled the envoy. "That's hilarious!"

"Shut up, Gabe!" commanded Brenda.

"I thought this deformed guard of yours wasn't funny, Brenda!" complained Thadie.

With the Zegman terrorists arrested, the convoy followed for a few more yards, and the envoy seemed to be slowly returning to his usual plague-ocher color. They were all scanning the surrounding area as they slowly gained ground. However, none of them were looking up. If they did, they would have seen a large, creeping creature crawling above them. The creature had a certain similarity to Earth's spiders, that is, if spiders had long, flexible, black and white tentacles instead of legs. Suddenly six of those tentacles lunged down, wrapped around two agents each and tossed them against the wall. The spider creature then crashed onto the ground in front of the envoy, whose line of sight was now unobstructed.

"Is that another alien clown?" asked Gabe.

"No! That's much worse than an alien clown! That's a space mime!" yelled a distraught Thadie.

Nobody knew where space mimes came from. They seemed to travel from planet to planet, showing up unannounced in public gatherings to bring joy to the children and cardiac arrest to the elderly who would literally laugh to death. Some believed that they were genetically designed by enemies of the Ifritian Empire, others thought they spawned from the confines of the universe where dark matter prevailed. In their current situation, a space mime was the last kind of creature they needed in Terminal 3. And indeed, as soon as the creature found its footing in front of the envoy, it started a humorous routine. A human mime would take their time to use two arms and lots of facial expressivity to convey an action or show to his audience the limits of invisible walls or the shape of unseen objects. However, a space mime, like the one that disrupted the convoy, needed only half of their many arms to perform a refined yet stridently humorous routine on galactic politics, by using their movements to convey the shape of the galactic parliament building as well as many of the prominent politicians both from the ruling party and the shadow cabinet, all the while using the other half of its tentacles to keep the Homeworld Security agents at bay, who were trying to interrupt its routine. The space mime did this by grabbing the agents by the waist and hurling them away every time they tried to charge. The combat had to be physical and direct, as the agents were concerned that their weapons had been replaced by comedy props by the Zegman clowns which would, if deployed, just strengthen the pervasiveness of the dangerous hilarity they faced.

The frenetic assertiveness of the space mime's visual comedy was taking its toll on the envoy, who was cackling out loud at the sight of the mime ridiculing his political adversaries from the fabulous side of the galaxy, through a series of unflattering, silent portrayals. And it was not only the envoy that found the mime's performance hilariously endearing. The security guards who hadn't been knocked out by the space mime's tentacles soon became hypnotized by the comedic narrative and found themselves laughing. That was also the case for Thadie and even Brenda. Only Gabe and Sue seemed to be immune to the mime's contagious hilarity.

"Is the mime illustrating how the General Secretary of the Galactic Confederation is trying to convince 2 Gloriana 2 to raise their share of taxable contributions?" asked Gabe, who was struggling to follow the themes tackled in rapid and perfectly timed succession by the mime's performance.

"I think so," answered Sue. "But by using stereotypes of the Glorianese as cheap and greedy. See, now the mime is showing them preferring to drown in pools filled to the brim with their surplus of metaplasma instead of allowing the Confederation to use it to fuel their rockets."

"Oh, I get it now. It was a little funny, but too specist for my tastes. Hey, the mime moved on already, what is—"

"You are too dumb and slow to get the jokes."

"Sorry."

"That's a good thing, at least for now."

"I didn't see you laughing either, Sue."

"Oh, I was not lying when I said I'm humorless. I was mostly observing the envoy."

"He's orange now."

"I'm not a specialist, but my guess is that when he turns red he will explode."

"That's very observant. You were really observing him."

"I was also observing what makes him laugh. He frowned and became a little less orange when the mime mocked his own species. So I have a guess that he doesn't like deprecating jokes that hit too close to home. Let's try to get the envoy's attention with that!"

"I... I don't think we are a match for the mime. As you said, I'm too slow for comedy, and you are humorless, and that mime looks like it went to both space Juilliard and space West Point."

"Oh, I was trained too, trained in the Skid Row school of Bullying!" said Sue, as she took a confident step toward the envoy, getting close but not too close to him. "Hey, you freaking slug! Look at me!"

The envoy, who was almost out of breath, turned his attention from the mime to Sue with a frown, taking a breather from his non-stop laughing. The Mime immediately saw the threat that she represented. Despite all the sophistication of its performance, it knew that it was disadvantaged when facing the crude usage of sound for humorous purposes. Worse: it's hard to be funny, but it's easy to be mean, and that's precisely what Sue was doing.

The mime charged toward Sue with a tentacle. However, Sue was athletic enough to keep her distance from the mime's insidious tentacles and, now that she had the envoy's full attention, she doubled-down on her taunts: "That's right, someone gimme some butter and herbs! Yum yum! I'm in the mood for some escargot for lunch!"

The mime relentlessly crawled toward Sue, who kept baiting the performer/terrorist and dodging the battery of expressive tentacles targeting her until she reached her starting point at Wing A: the disembarking gate, where the table of welcome snacks set for the envoy still stood. Sue grabbed one of the silver plates now emptied of the appetizers that were dully devoured by Brenda and tossed it to Gabe as if it was a Frisbee.

"Time to serve the entrée to the French, Maitre D'!" said Sue, this time driving the envoy to his original ocher color.

"I will file a complaint with my consulate for your derogatory wording!" protested a now sullenly yellow envoy.

Gabe held the plate in confusion, until Brenda snatched it from his hands.

"You really are slow, aren't you?" Brenda said as she grabbed the envoy, who giggled with the contact.

"I told you physical contact makes me ticklish!" protested the envoy.

Brenda's hold on him was short-lived, as he was slammed on top of the plate. "I must tell you that, despite my appetizing appearance, I am terribly poisonous!"

"Nobody is gonna eat your gooey ass."

"Better not, because this feels awfully like a take-out."

"More like a delivery," said Gabe, as he rushed with Brenda to the exit of Wing A.

"Godammit, rookie," said a grumpy Brenda. "Go easy on the cologne. I can smell your flowery stench from here."

Gabe was about to answer that he didn't us cologne, but despite his proneness to slow-reasoning he was very aware of the possibility of meeting Sue's evil twin and her warning about Pryianka's perfume matching her outfit. He did smell roses, and indeed, a groomed version of Sue wrapped in layers of pink silk was standing in their way. That didn't deter Brenda, who kept rushing in her direction carrying the plate containing the envoy.

"Sue? Why aren't you wearing your uniform!" asked the puzzled commander. What Brenda didn't notice was that Pryianka had produced a cylindrical, orange device from underneath the pink fabric of her outfit. She steadily pointed the cylinder toward the envoy. Nothing visible happened, but it was too late. The envoy was stricken by an induced laughter attack.

"My mother disappeared when I was nine and I was raised in foster care!" yelled Gabe.

"What are you doing, rookie?"

"Trying to make him sad with a sad story?"

Gabe's attempt was clearly unsuccessful. The slug was literally laughing to death, the shade of his grimy skin had already changed to orange and was becoming redder by the second. And this time, the flaps of his body were also inflating. When Brenda looked back at the direction where Sue's doppelganger was, she was gone. Brenda was confused, but it didn't mean that she was unaware of the fact that she had only a few minutes left to deal with the problem she literally had at hand. Brenda pushed the plate containing the envoy at Gabe: "Follow me, rookie, and don't screw up this time!"

Gabe was more than happy to comply and they quickly rushed to the exit of Wing A, going through the security line set by Thadie's detail. They were back at the spaceport's main lobby, which had been cleared of passengers probably by Thadie when she became aware that the Envoy had infused his blood with explosives. Brenda rushed to a large gate that seemed familiar to Gabe. It looked pretty much like the one he was ejected from by the staff of Terminal 1, except that it was situated in the opposite side of the lobby and had a big red sign that read:

TERMINAL 2
SPACETIME HAZARD AHEAD
ACCESS FORBIDDEN FOR NON-AUTHORIZED
PERSONNEL

There was a small keyboard by the side of the gate and Brenda typed a password. The door immediately opened.

"Stay behind me and follow closely if you don't want to fall in a gravity or temporal deathtrap," said Brenda.

"Ma'am, I'm not sure if we have much time, he's getting red and round like a ball!"

"Then don't drop the ball!"

***

TERMINAL 3

Brenda and Gabe, with the envoy on a plate, rushed through a concrete corridor that was similar to the one that Gabe went through on his first day of work. This one, however, had a dankness in the air and displayed infiltrations and cracks on its wall that were less akin to the neglect of the brutalist concrete structures of Terminal 3 and more to complete abandon. They soon reached another metallic gate, but this one was open and lead to the dark, dusty lobby of Terminal 2. Gabe noticed that an effort to bring on an architectural and interior design signature was developed here, although in a very different way from Terminal 1. Where Terminal 1 had high-ceilings sustained by elegant, curvy, white pillars which gave plenty of space for the lights of its abundant windows to permeate its lobbies, wings and aisles, Terminal 2 was more intimate, having low ceilings decorated with metallic lamps and vinyl boards painted in funky colors which had lost most of their coloration. If Gabe was not totally ignorant of architecture he would know that the inspiration for the interior design of Terminal 2 had come from 1970s Italy and France, and Terminal 3 was a grotesque and rushed version of it. However, the neglect in Terminal 2 and the fact that the only lights still working seemed to be a few emergency ones by the vinyl-clad walls gave Terminal 2 a claustrophobic, eerie vibe. The flying furniture that he could spot in certain areas of the main lobby didn't help. His contemplation was short-lived, as he focused on the envoy, who couldn't stop laughing, and was clearly in his final moments. He was now totally red and round and started to glow.

"We need to toss him inside the men's restroom. If I remember well, the path to it is clear as long as we go in a straight line," instructed Brenda.

"Okay, I can see it," said Gabe as he noticed the large sign above the two doors leading to the restrooms.

Gabe realized that Terminal 2 was indeed old since the restrooms were separated by genders instead of the texture of the users' excretions. Gabe rushed in their direction, but suddenly halted, as he noticed Brenda didn't move. When he turned back, he realized that his boss was staring at a corner of the hall where a table and two chairs seemed to be glued to the ceiling. A second-take allowed Gabe to notice that she was actually looking past that particular area of the lobby. Brenda's expression was totally different from her usual permanent frown, as her eyes were glazed. Brenda's usual grumpiness had turned into pure anger with a hint of fear.

"Ma'am?" perused Gabe, but she ignored him.

Brenda took a step, and then another, and then started rushing toward the direction at which she was looking. Brenda took maybe ten steps until a baton hit the back of her head, knocking her out. As Gabe turned his head, he found the person who tossed the baton: Sue, standing at the entrance of the lobby.

"Why—"

"No time to explain, we need to get rid of that bomb!"

As usual, Gabe took a moment to understand what she was talking about, until he realized she was referring to the envoy on his plate, on the verge of exploding.

"She told me to take him to the restroom," pointed out Gabe.

"Then do it!" urged Sue.

Gabe was happy to comply, immediately sprinting to the men's restroom while carrying the envoy. He flinched for a moment at the doorway, baffled by the unexpected sight. The bathroom was nothing but exposed concrete, cracked in many areas and covered by pulverized fragments of white ceramics. He saw what seemed to be clothes and shoes in a corner, stained in red and totally flattened, as if there was an invisible force pressing them down. Gabe was just about to take a step inside the room when he felt a tingle at the tip of his toes, and then remembered that Brenda's order wasn't to carry the envoy inside the restroom, but to toss him. And so he did, with difficulty as he almost burned his hands when picking up the envoy from the plate and realized that he was as hot as a kettle.

The envoy flew in the air for a fraction of a second at the same time the first signs of an explosion appeared, fire bursting from the cracks on his round surface. No ordinary human eye could have detected an explosion, and Gabe was as ordinary as it gets. And still, the explosion was unveiling in front of him in slow motion, as was the movement of the envoy bursting in the air until it came to a sudden halt. The envoy hovered still for a moment, and then, somewhat, compressed into itself, becoming just a shiny dot that suddenly slammed onto the ground, where it stayed.

Gabe tried to take a step back, but the tingling in the toes of his left foot intensified. To Gabe it felt like his toes were taken in a bear trap. He yanked his left foot back hard, feeling his bones click without cracking, and after some excruciating seconds he managed to free himself from the edge of the spacetime trap or, as he perceived and understood it, from that weird ass room.

Gabe exited the restroom and found Sue dragging the now unconscious Brenda to the access gate to Terminal 2.

"We need to get out of here."

"Why did you attack Brenda?"

"She was running in that area to her death," Sue pointed at the zone with the chair and tables glued to the ceiling.

"How—"

"You are too dumb to understand. Here, let me show you…" said Sue, as she patted Brenda's pockets until she found a stash of snacks collected from Wing A.

Sue hurled a mini-croissant toward the area where Brenda was running before she was knocked out. Gabe's first thought was that Sue would make a great baseball player. Not only for hurling that baton precisely at Brenda's head, but also the elegant angle with which she pitched the croissant. But those thoughts were suddenly interrupted when the flying croissant reached the area underneath the suspended table and chairs, becoming green for a split second and then disintegrating.

"Time runs faster inside that area, if Brenda entered it she would become an old woman in one second, a skeleton in two and dust in three."

"I thought… you didn't know anything about Terminal 2."

"I know what Brenda told me, which was not much. Just enough to understand that it's part of my job to keep people the hell away from this place. That's why we are getting Brenda out of here and closing the door behind us!"

Gabe nodded at Sue's command and helped her carry Brenda back to Terminal 3. However, on his way out, he passed by a wall map of Terminal 2. Gabe couldn't help but notice that Terminal 2 had a total of 665 boarding gates.

***

When a person spends a long time in a busy, vast space such as the Los Angeles spaceport's Terminal 3, the experience of that space is progressively shaped in ways that fit their individual needs and urges. That's particularly true for Terminal 3, where any intended functionality of the vast building as a space of transit for passengers was sabotaged by its architectural shortcomings caused by the rushed process in which it was built as well as the perennially low-budget and callousness-inducing chaos. The passengers are just passing through, but those tasked to ensure their flow, such as the security guards, with time became more than persons that populated that space: they turned into permanent fixtures, with their own preferred subspaces of choice. For Chip that would be the restrooms at R Wing. For Sue, it was a small concave hole in the concrete outside C Wing. That was the best place in the entire spaceport to not only see the rockets taking off, but also hear the booming noise of their engines. Sue liked the noise and how it would deafen any thought that dared to hammer itself into her mind when she was feeling the blues. Sue liked even more the minutes of silence that would follow the noise after the rocket was well up in space, maybe even hyperspace. And then more noise would follow, in a crescendo, as the next rocket in line started its own procedures to take off.

This had been one of those days where Sue needed all the alternation of noise and silence she could get. The only person who knew about her small personal space was Chip. She saw him only briefly this day after dropping a still knocked out Brenda at Dr. José's infirmary. Chip told Sue that she looked like a Pomonan dumpster fire, which probably only made sense if you were from Covina or Pomona, since Chip laughed alone at his own joke and Gabe gave him an insulted stare while calling him alienphobic. Sue knew that Chip was aware of her secret place because whenever she had a really bad day, she would always find a hard liquor patch on the concrete ledge where she sat to watch and listen to the rockets. This day wasn't different. She immediately glued the patch to her neck and enjoyed the high of the strong alcoholic flux to her bloodstream and the surrounding noise. Shortly after the last rocket took off, its noise dissipated and the smell of burning fuel evaporated. That's when Sue detected the odor of roses.

"Get the fuck out of here, Pree," growled Sue, which prompted Priyanka to immediately appear from behind the ledge.

"Are you sure? This is quite a rad place to have a final showdown. We can wait for the sunset, just for the dramatic effect."

"You almost killed us all today."

"Maybe you should have followed my advice and teamed up with me."

"It was not advice, it was a demand. And your demand was denied. Also, you failed."

"Still got paid, though."

"Who would pay you to explode the envoy?"

"The guys who currently supply minerals to Earth and don't want competition, the association of run-away slaves from the Ifritian Empire's mines, the Galactic Guild of Comedy Performers, whoever pays more or, all of them, as long as they are not aware that they are all paying for the same service. That's lots of money, Sue. Enough for both of us. You can leave your shitty job and that shitty apartment in Skid Row."

"I like my shit."

"Our mothers wouldn't have us raised by Uncle Manohar. They knew that loser would induce us to be mediocre."

"That 'loser' raised us just fine after they were gone. Maybe you should appreciate more the effort he made instead of obsessing about how our lives would have been if our mothers were still around."

"You know… I wonder if you work here because of them."

"Our moms died at the Terminal 2 attack, but I'm—"

"They are still in there, did you know that?"

"That's impossible."

"I'm gonna give you two things today. One you already got: the drink you are having through that patch which I left for you. The other is our mom's whereabouts: check inside the women's restroom in the main lobby."

Sue stayed quiet for a moment, processing what her sister had just said.

"Well...thanks for the brandy, Pree," said Sue, as she patted the patch on her neck.

"Your favorite," said Pree with a wink before walking away as another rocket prepared to launch.

Sue couldn't help but chuckle bitterly at her sister's total lack of shame. The patch on her neck was vodka, not brandy. That could have been only a distraction, all liquor patches looked pretty much alike and maybe Pree had bought the wrong one. Alas, Sue's favorite drink was tequila.

INTERLUDE

Personal Diary of The Bailiff of the Time Court, Human Division.

July, 7^h 2119, 2 days after the beginning of the Slow yet Irreversible Great Collapse of the Universe.

There he was. Gabriel Chagas. Standing in the middle of the Terminal's lobby. This could have been so easy. Just fetch and go. But he was not alone. That was uncanny... Gabriel Chagas was supposed to be a loner, how was he gathering a social entourage in just three days? The broader an individual's social network, the more likely the extraction process could cause ripples in time.

Chagas was carrying what seemed to be a dying citizen of the Ifritian Empire at their territorial apogee. The Ifritian seemed to be organically infused with some sort of potent explosive on the verge of being activated. I started gauging the odds of such an explosion interfering with the entropic anomalies scattered in the area when I realized that the other person accompanying Gabriel Chagas seemed to be looking straight at him. At first I thought it was a coincidence, after all my quantum armor keeps me invisible as long as I don't take any effective action in the time I'm transiting on. But there was no doubt. That person, a sturdy, middle-aged woman wearing a security guard uniform saw me. With recognition. Of course she recognized me. If she noticed me despite my quantum armor, it meant that she had peeked inside the Schrödinger box before. We had already met somehow, somewhere, sometime.

It took me a moment until I recognized that woman. She was there in my first and only mission before the current one. What were the odds of that woman being there again? That was bad, very bad news. The Quantum armor couldn't erase memories, but it could suspend them from any witness of my last incursion. All they could remember were rudiments of what happened and feel an ongoing emotional malaise as a side-effect. But a second chance to witness what had been shielded from remembrance would irreversibly overrule the unpredictability's safeguard from the entropic alloy of my suit. She saw me. Twice now. Two is a dangerous number when dealing with Quantum physics, as a double-take is enough for a Heisenbergian uncertainty to become a very Newtonian fact. She saw too much, even if only my armor.

And then, to my surprise, she seemed to be charging toward me. That… was convenient. My job was to solve issues that could not steer themselves to a temporally stable outcome. Often that involved a simple nudge to correct the wrongdoing of an individual breaking the natural evolution of spacetime. Not that I had the chance to be subtle before. My first mission had been accidentally conspicuous, and my second one, the one going on at that very moment, was compromised. But she was charging toward me, and on her way there was an entropic anomaly. The accelerated kind, that would make her age and die in a matter of seconds on the spot. The woman seemed to be too emotionally invested in reaching out to me to notice the visual hints about the anomaly. But then a flying club knocked the woman out before she entered it. Bummer. I would need to do something about her, but that would involve research. A fourth person appeared. Another woman, younger this time, as Gabriel Chagas seemed to have moved toward another entropic anomaly. The deaccelerated kind, concealed in Terminal 2's lobby restroom. That would be dangerous, even my abilities and my armor's capabilities couldn't remove the remains of a person trapped in a pocket of high-gravity and deaccelerated time. And Gabriel Chagas had to be extracted, even if all that remained of him was a mush.

For a moment I felt like simply breaking the cloak of my Quantum armor, capture Gabriel Chagas and eliminate everyone else. From an entropic perspective, that locale was already doomed. If I had to add a few more anomalous ripples in the same space by killing some individual before their time, then that was the perfect place-and-time. However, I decided to ignore my urges. And soon Chagas came back to the lobby, this time no longer carrying the Ifritian that was on the verge of exploding. I saw Gabriel Chagas and the second woman drag the one who recognized me out of Terminal 2. I would need to be stealthier if that woman waltzed in there again. But I had a feeling that Gabriel Chagas would come back. Alone. And then, he will be mine.

PART TWO

TIME

"Don't we all have a certain number of images that stay around in our head, which we undoubtedly call memories and improperly so, and which we can never get rid of because they return in our sky with the regularity of a comet - torn away also from a world about which we know almost nothing? They return more frequently than comets do, in fact. It would be better, then, to speak of them as loyal satellites, a bit capricious and therefore even troublesome: they appear, disappear, suddenly come back to badger our memory at night when we cannot sleep. But, little as we may care to, as our hearts tell us to, we can also observe them at will, coldly, scrutinize their shadows, colors, and relief. Only, they are dead stars: from them we shall never grasp anything other than the certainty that we have already seen them, examined them, questioned them without really understanding the laws that the line of their mysterious orbits obeyed."—Marc Augé

DAY -3,533

BRENDA ROY GOT DRESSED IN HER tank top, sneakers and shorts and left her apartment exactly at 6:47 am. She went straight to the Southern Santa Monica boardwalk for her daily morning jog. Brenda hated jogging. The Roy Family used to be an institution of American powerlifting starting in the 2040s. Powerlifters were known for their lack of cardio exercise and for dying early. That's one of the reasons why powerlifting competitions were banned in 2072. The other being that strenuous effort was no longer necessary to achieve the physical results that had previously relied on weightlifting or cardio exercises. Muscular hypertrophy could be triggered with a single pill by any couch potato. Unclogged arteries could be obtained through one shot of the right medication. And still, Brenda ran, puzzling those she passed by. She ran with heavy stomps, as one would expect a burly woman like her to run, puffing and sweating, like a bear chasing a doe. The doe was ahead of her. Also clad in a tank top, sneakers and shorts. The doe was slender, gracious, not even remotely sturdy like Brenda. Brenda quickened her pace. She wanted to pounce on the doe. Instead she started running alongside Cida Chagas, who acknowledged her with a shy smile.

"Enjoying your cardio?" asked Cida in an almost demure tone, as she noticed how Brenda stared at her with intent.

"You know that with one shot of Neathrosine 4 you can skip cardio for 6 months, right?" pointed out Brenda, who was almost puking due to the extreme physical effort.

"I like to do things the old way."

"The old way is gonna give me a heart-attack."

"The secret is to find the right pace," said Cida as she flashed the politely snarky smile that would make Brenda melt every damn time.

Cida then bolted ahead, being kind enough to avoid glancing back so Brenda could save face as she halted and caught her breath. She hated cardio.

Brenda strolled to her destination, which laid just after the border between Santa Monica and Venice. The open air gym was a staple of Venice from a time when effort was the main reason muscles would expand, and whatever drug one would take back then, would be just a nudge in that direction. It's true that this nudge could push the weightlifter to an early death. It did just that to the entire Roy clan except Brenda.

In the first years of the 22nd century, vintage physical effort could only be witnessed from the edges of the open air gym. For the passerby, those weightlifters were a picturesque curiosity. Brenda didn't mind, exhibitionism, or at least tolerance to being stared at, was part of the drill. She was fully aware that she was just entertaining a tradition, and traditions need to be acknowledged by others in order to exist and persist. Ironically, traditions also must be often updated in order to remain authentic to their roots. Weightlifting in Venice's open air gym at that time was only for those who wanted to inflate their muscles the hard way, without the nudge of old-time drugs that would eventually cripple or kill the users. The entrance to the open gym had a turnstile with a spittoon attached to it. The spittoon had a built-in scanner that would detect any sort of artificial muscle-enhancement product in one's saliva, and block the turnstile if it read positive.

Once inside the gym, Brenda found Cida lifting the smallest weights available in a rapid, frenetic pace.

"You ain't gonna get very big with that routine," said Brenda as she picked a large dumbbell and started repeating the same movements that Cida was performing, except in a much slower pace.

"I'm aiming for something different here."

Brenda knew that. She found Cida's body the hottest since the first time that doe waltzed into the open air gym. But still, she was afraid that if she didn't say anything she would lose Cida's attention. Hence, she couldn't be blamed for saying the exact same thing every morning, could she? Especially when Cida didn't seem to mind answering to the same question with the same answer. Every damn day. Their conversation was a loop, just like their morning exercise routine. There wasn't much she could do to change that, the repository of small talk between them had dried up many months ago, and for some reason they both struggled to talk about anything deeper, even though the chemistry was obvious. After that same initial answer, Brenda would follow up with the exact same question, to which Cida would counter with a yes. The question was: "Lunch later?"

But this morning was different. Brenda was tired of saying the same bland, old things to Cida. She liked repetition, particularly the physical part of her routine, but not the conversational one. After months of seeing Cida almost every day, she wanted more. And to get more, she had to say more than she usually did: "Dinner tonight?"

Cida dropped her small weights with a frown: "You mean, lunch later?"

"No, I mean dinner. Steak. Wine. Candles. No tank tops nor uniforms. Maybe a nice dress. Or no dress at all would be nice too."

"I... I have a kid, Brenda."

"I know. There's this thing called robot-nannies. Look into that."

"I don't trust a machine to look after my kid," said Cida as she moved to another workout station. "Let's have lunch later, okay?"

"Okay," mumbled a defeated Brenda.

That morning, Brenda lifted larger weights than she usually would. At the end of her routine her muscles were sore and Cida was gone. Brenda was in so much pain she had to grab a cab for the six block trip back to her apartment. A triple-dose of muscle relaxer and a shower got her ready to leave for work.

It was a very short drive from Southern Santa Monica to Los Angeles spaceport, she did not even need to take the airway route. After arriving, Brenda went straight to the security guard quarters which stood in a secluded employee-only wing. She cheered her co-workers who were already dressing in their gray uniforms that displayed, at the right shoulder, the silvery badge that read "T$_2$". The employee perks and the ease of the work routine made the job appealing, creating a merry atmosphere in the locker room as they dressed. With the corner of her eyes, Brenda noticed Cida changing in one of the few secluded spaces in the room, far away from the conversations between her coworkers. She had no clue why Cida was so prudish and she still remembered the first time she talked to her, in this same locker room. Cida blushed at having her nudity acknowledged and covered her exposed breast and crotch. At first Brenda thought that it was a rude, over-the-top way to display her disinterest toward her, even if she was not being particularly flirty – only slightly. Brenda only saw the appeal in Cida after many months as her co-worker. Cida was shy, yet assertive when necessary, both toward the passengers and her co-workers, and seemed to have an infinite repository of patience, while Brenda tended to become blunt as soon as the situation they were facing turned slightly sour. That made the pair a good duo, as some situations required Cida's soft approach, while others could only be disarmed through Brenda's callousness. When Brenda asked Cida how she managed to always keep her cool, she said that she had a son. That was the first time she mentioned her child, the second one being that very morning, in Venice's open air gym.

***

That morning work started on an uneventful note for Brenda. She tried to give Cida some space, as she felt that she had hit a wrong button when asking her out for dinner. That's why Brenda decided to patrol the customs area of the Terminal by herself. Just when it was about lunch time, she sought out Cida. Brenda found her in the main hall, which was built with concrete in a style reminiscent of the edgy architecture of the 1970s. The ceilings had metallic lamps and framings. The tables, chairs, check-in counters and some of the walls were all made in vinyl, always in the most garish shades of yellow, pink, green and blue seemingly borrowed from highlighter marker pens or post-its. Cida was standing next to a small water fountain, tending to a group of twenty agitated refugees from 58 Teal 3, each one commanding a towering, hairy body that would be intimidating if their voices weren't high-pitched, their manners weren't mild and their meaty fingers weren't prone to a nervous, slightly comical fidgeting. Cida was accompanied by Terminal 2's resident exoethnologist, Amir Pahlevan, who was doing his best to reassure the nervous yet extremely polite aliens that their papers were in order and they would be sent to the refugee shelter that had been prepared for them.

"I've been thinking," said Brenda, as she approached Cida.

"Can't you see I'm busy with these passengers?"

"Let brains deal with them."

"I—"

"I screwed up this morning."

"No, I—"

"I shouldn't have said steak. I should have said sushi. So, sushi tonight. With your kid."

"I said no, Brenda."

"Fine, sushi now, let's go."

"I already had lunch."

"You… always have lunch with me."

"Well, not today. Sorry."

"What the hell are we?"

"Coworkers?"

"With benefits?"

"Not here, Brenda."

Brenda turned and noticed that Amir and the hairy aliens were silently following their discussion. "Could you take the zoo out of here? We are trying to get somewhere in our relationship."

"Mind your choice of words, Ma'am," said Amir, as he gently nodded to the refugees to follow him.

"What the hell is wrong with you? Amir could report you for mistreating the passengers!"

"Screw them and this job! I need to know what we are!"

"Brenda… It's complicated…"

"Explain to me!"

"Being with you… feels wrong."

"Bullshit. You know that I can push your button down there just right until you can see stars, but it would be much better if I could do that on a bed instead of the terminal's toilet stall."

"See…That's the problem," said a blushing Cida. "I…I was not raised like that."

"Look, I get it. You came from somewhere in Brazil, where people were not very integrated… For godsake, you still speak English with an accent. Who the hell has an accent these days?"

"Is my accent a problem?"

"Your accent is perfect! You are perfect! I want to date you and get to know your kid, because that's what people do when they want to get serious."

"Well—"

"Excuse me, can I ask for information," asked a woman passing by Brenda and Cida.

"Not now, we're busy," said Brenda.

"Brenda, come on. We are on the clock here," said Cida, as she turned to face the woman. "How can I help you?"

Cida's smile faded as she noticed that the woman was accompanied by another one. They were dressed in matching pink saris and covered in golden jewelry.

"We are supposed to board the next rocket to Beta Cancri, but we can't find the gate and there is no mention of it on the departure screens."

"Oh yes. That's because it's a chartered rocket from..." Cida checked her holotablet, "...the Intergalactic Daughters of Sappho."

"I heard about you guys!" said Brenda effusively. "You are the lesbians that go on retreats across the galaxy."

"Couple retreats, to be more specific," pointed out one of the women, "have you two been to one?"

Cida gulped and started to answer: "We are not—"

"—going this year! But maybe next! Isn't that right, *sweetie*?" said Brenda.

"Well, it all depends on *our* son, *darling*," said Cida. "It's not like we can leave him behind and fly half way across the galaxy. That would be *irresponsible*."

"We left our two girls with my brother Manohar," said one of the women. "Don't you have any parents with whom you—"

"Sorry to cut you off, but your rocket leaves soon," interrupted Cida. "And it's a bit of a walk to Gate 540."

"Oh my! I really need to go to the john."

"There is a restroom just behind you, but I would try to move fast," advised Cida.

"Thanks! You two are cute, hope to see more of you!" said one of the women before they both sprinted to the restroom.

"You shouldn't have lied to them about us being a couple."

"Dinner tonight?"

"Brenda..."

"Wherever you want. We can take your kid to Chuck E. Cheese's for all I care. I just want to get closer to you. Please!"

Cida sighed, and yielded with a tired smile: "Fine. See you at my place. I'm cooking."

"Are you going to make that *galinhada* dish you can't shut up about? Or maybe—"

Brenda stopped midsentence as well as everyone else who was talking. Those who were walking stopped in their tracks, as any sentient creature could detect, through their different sensorial outlets, something unsettling in their surroundings. The aliens that relied on their tactile sense noticed that the air suddenly turned crispy and dry. The ones that privileged their auditory organs, noticed a static humming that gained intensity every second. The creatures who oriented themselves predominantly through their sight, saw a half-dozen purple dots appearing in scattered areas. The dots began to elongate, becoming lines. At the same time the humming sound turned into a very distinctive sizzling that could now be heard by any creature that wasn't completely deaf. The sizzling became a deafening crackling noise when the lines started branching out in many directions and unpredictable ways. These were cracks. Spacetime cracks. And then, on top of the water fountain, an entity clad in a metallic armor started to materialize. His gauntlets displayed five fingers and his booted feet were narrow and long, like a human's, although his race couldn't be determined. If he was a man, he was on the taller side. He seemed to have been there for a while, but when the spacetime started cracking he had no choice but to make himself noticeable. After Brenda realized all the weirdness that was happening in Terminal 2's main lobby, as well as the strange man in the armor, she noticed that he seemed to look, from within the dark confines of his helmet's visor, in her direction. Wait. No! He was not looking at her!

"Get out of here, Cida."

"We need to evacuate the passengers, we can't—"

"I said get out! That—"

Too late, the armored man leaped from the top of the water fountain with a certain grace and ease, which was contradictory, considering his great height and apparent heaviness of his armor. As soon as his metallic boots touched the ground, the real ordeal started. The purple cracks and the deafening noise vanished, as both transitioned from their initial electromagnetic nature to gravitational. The vinyl furniture as well as the persons standing next to them rose in the air or crumbled under a massive, sudden weight. The sight of these people trapped in the former type of entropic anomaly aging and becoming dust and the bloody mess in the latter was terrifying for those who were observing from outside. The surrounding crowd turned into a panicked throng that desperately ran for the exit. The exception was Brenda, who quickly unsheathed her baton and charged toward the armored man. With a swift move of his left hand he repelled Brenda without touching her, hurling her many feet away. With his right hand he snatched Cida by her collar. And then they both disappeared.

Brenda, who was now standing up, double-checked the area where Cida and the armored man were just moments ago. She vanished. And so did he. He who? Brenda scratched her head. Not he. She. Cida. Yes! She was just there, and then all that chaos started, and that… something, was on top of the water fountain. No, there was no one on top of the water fountain. There was just her. And then there wasn't anymore. She wasn't… was… no more. She… who? The more Brenda thought about what happened right in front of her eyes, the more she forgot. It was as if her memory of that very moment was sand inside an hourglass, doomed to slide, grain by grain, to the lowest point and remain there, forgotten, at least until someone turned the hourglass upside-down. Or broke it.

PRELUDE / POSTLUDE

Personal Diary of The Lawyer of the Time Court, Human Division.

Untraceable Date, sometime after the end of the Slow yet Irreversible Great Collapse of the Universe.

Back in the days when I was growing up, especially in those fiery moments when I was assaulted by the urgencies and appetites of my teenage years, my mother would say, with the most condescending of tones, that there was a time and a place for everything. That was the informal motto of the foregone House of Lambilly, or at least of its late matriarch. Then there was a time of revolution in that very place where I had had my upbringing. A place called France.

The guillotine was set up in many locales in that place called France that were very public, and at certain times heads would roll. France had become a place of terror during those times, but one could say that I was lucky as I was no longer a girl being tamed by my mother during the Terror. I was a woman, a married one, living with my husband as a refugee in a place called England during the worst of the revolutionary wave, although I had to face the trials of its aftermath when my husband and I made the mistake of returning to our homeland thinking that it was safe again for provincial nobility such as us. Compared to the Jacobin Terror that preceded it, what we faced was no more than a miniature caricature. And still, that caricature could hurt and kill. That's when I had no other choice than to stand up. That's when I became a lawyer before becoming The Lawyer at the End of Time.

I was amid a process where I had to follow my mother's instructions. Not the ones related to time, those were ignorant, unaware that History's tides could not only change suddenly, but also History was doomed to end as time itself would. The instructions I was following were the recipe for the pastry that would always have a place on our breakfast table in Brittany. The Bailiff had gone out to fetch my new client and I would be acting very poorly in my mandate as an attorney if I didn't have something for him to eat upon his arrival.

Baking could be particularly challenging at the End of Time. Although I had access to any ingredient I may need, the art of pastry making, as any other, consumed time. And at the End of Time, obviously, there was none. Everything could be/has been, and nothing was. The pastry I was baking would only exist in its potential, as both a series of uncombined ingredients and a pastry that had been duly chewed, swallowed, and conclusively annihilated in my client's digestive tract. The pastry was, at the same time, unmade and eaten, as everything and nothing were simultaneous. Which meant I was not baking for an upcoming client to be extracted from his timeline by The Bailiff. I already had met him, he had already gone through his trial, and a verdict had been delivered. Except none of that hadn't happened yet. I still had my work to do, both as an attorney and a pâtissier. *Noblesse oblige.* And in the interstices of the same things that had and hadn't happened, I was baking a plan, which would be triggered by the Gabriel Chagas' trial, but with consequences far beyond my client's life or the Time Court's mandate.

I could smell the fragrant fumes of my sugary *kouign-ammans*. They were ready. They've always been. Except they were not. They had never been, as they had been pastries that, once consumed, are no more. The important question now was: should the *kouign-ammans* be served with milk, tea or just plain water?

DAY 4

GABE AND CHIP EXITED THE MAGLEV station at Terminal 3's main entrance at the same time Wendy Lin stepped out of a ramshackle car.

"Oh, hello Your Highness!" teased Chip, "Looks like someone is too good for public transportation."

"Oh, hi guys!" said Wendy in a defensive tone, "That's not my car, it's a Suber."

Gabe and Chip looked at the car's windshield and it indeed displayed the Suber logo. It also featured a driver with the appearance of a serial-killer at the wheel.

Suber was a ride-share system run by drivers that either failed Uber or Lyft minimum requirements or botched their test, catering to clients willing to take the risk of using a service known for being less reliable and more dangerous in order to save a few credits. A Suber ride would ensure the client an exciting experience of contact with a driver that would either try to steal their wallet and harvest their organs, talk them into joining a cult (the most popular one involving a ritual that required the acolyte to surrender their wallet and organs), or force himself on you sexually and then bury you in the desert with only your eyeless head sticking out of the rocky ground (the eyes duly sold on the clandestine organ market). Many found this appealing. Others would just endure the experience since, at least, they didn't have to use the only alternative cheaper than Suber: the Maglev public transportation system. No Maglev commuter would assume that someone riding a Suber was better than them, so Chip immediately stopped teasing Wendy and, as soon as the threesome entered Terminal 3's main lobby, they parted ways: Gabe and Chip headed to the Security Guards headquarters to start their day and Wendy to her office at R Wing.

As usual José was already at his desk when Wendy arrived. She enjoyed the company of her best and only friend in the Terminal. When José didn't have to deal with his share of sick travelers and injured personnel, he always had something to say, ask or discuss during the times they were in each other's company. Wendy, unlike José, was almost always idle. The security guards rarely sought her counsel, passengers were carefully misinformed by the security guards about the services she could provide to them in the spaceport and, even when there was room for her intervention, something would always botch it. Like, the day before, when the Department of Homeworld Security asked for her assistance, she saw her access blocked as the security badge they gave her seemed to be counterfeit. Probably more of Brenda's shenanigans. The head of the security guards never liked Wendy since her first day of work in the Terminal. Wendy knew that Brenda wanted her to quit, and she would seriously consider doing that at least once a day.

"Good morning, Wendy," said José, as soon as Wendy crossed the doorway. "You have a request for assistance from one of my patients today. She is waiting for you at the infirmary."

Wendy was delightedly surprised that someone other than José had an interest in seeing her this morning, and darted to the infirmary adjacent to her office. Wendy assumed it was Gabe again, as in the last days it seemed that he was getting in trouble and dragging her with him. Not that Wendy minded, on the contrary. Two days ago, during the AC incident, she felt useful, even if she could barely remember what kind of role she played because of all the pills she had ingested. No, it couldn't be Gabe. She had just seen him arriving at the Terminal at the same time she did.

Wendy was taken aback when realizing that only one of the many cots in the infirmary was occupied by no other than her nemesis, Brenda Roy. "I... I think José made a mistake. He told me that someone in here wanted to talk to me."

"That'd be me," said Brenda.

"But you never want to talk to me. Or let me talk. Or listen to me. Or—"

"Shut up."

"See?"

"I need your help."

Wendy couldn't help but emit a joyful shriek. Earning the respect of the head of the security guards had the potential to be a turning point in her career in Terminal 3. She would finally be allowed to intervene and help and feel useful for a change. "Anything for you, partner."

"Don't call me partner. Here, check this out," said Brenda as she handed a holotablet to Wendy.

The holotablet displayed a rough sketch drawing of a humanoid apparently clad in some sort of armor.

"Does this mean anything to you?" asked Brenda.

"Not really, maybe—"

"Scroll through it."

Wendy obliged and went through two dozen similar drawings of the armored humanoid. Some focused on details of his attire, such as his helmet or his gauntlets. "A little context would help, Ma'am.'"

"Does this mean anything to you or not?"

"No, but I can investigate as an exoethnologist. I can run those drawings through the galactic sartorial catalogue and see if there's a match. I could also—"

"Do whatever you need. Any input will help."

"Understood. Can you at least tell me where these drawings came from?"

"I made them over the last few hours."

"So you saw this... individual?"

"I need to rest. My head hurts," said Brenda, as she laid her head back on the pillow and closed her eyes.

Wendy thought about insisting on answers to her questions, but she decided to relent, so as to not get on Brenda's bad side again. Wendy had her assignment, and she intended to give her best to deliver results and earn Brenda's respect.

"Why is she here?" asked Wendy to José as she stepped out of the infirmary and back to the Passengers and Staff Assistance Office.

"She had a mild concussion yesterday and was brought here by some of the security guards," answered José. "It would have taken me two minutes to fix her up and let her go but I noticed that she has been a *pendeja* to you for a while and decided to keep her here so you can exact your revenge."

"I...I'm not seeking revenge, José. But thanks, I guess?"

"Are you sure? Humans have a very particular tendency to steer their contempt toward vindication, I noticed."

"Not me."

"I can make her suffer in hundreds of different ways and you could watch the ordeal."

"Please don't."

"Okay then, I will just let her go."

"No, wait, José!" said Wendy, as she took a look at Brenda through the door's crack, "I think she could really use the rest."

"Whatever. So, I got a new medication for dementia that took me on a very cool trip," said José as he displayed a small green pill in his hand, "Wanna help me figure out if humans without major neurological diseases will get high too?"

"Not now, I have work to do."

***

TERMINAL 3

Wendy typed on her holotablet as she trotted to Terminal 3's main entrance. She was calling her Suber ride. However, she was not using the official, phishing-prone app to do so. She was sending a message to a private number. A message that read "Need a ride now. Meet me at the entrance." And as soon as Wendy exited the Terminal's main lobby, the very same ramshackle vehicle that had dropped her at the premises was waiting for her amid the hectic traffic of cars trying to find a parking spot to either drop-off or pick-up passengers. Wendy entered the vehicle and the driver had no trouble breaking through the chaotic traffic around him thanks to a series of well-timed, offensive driving moves, after which he propelled the car up into the skies of Los Angeles. The unpredictability of the local traffic was one of the reasons why robotized Ubers or Subers weren't allowed in Los Angeles, although those were certainly not the moves of an average driver.

"Leaving earlier than usual, Miss Lan," said the driver.

His face was as expressionless as his voice, covered in a pale, pasty bald skin clad with watery blue eyes, a small, almost bridgeless nose and a pair of thin, purple lips.

"Not going home, Krause. Take me to UCal."

Through a light arching of his spare white eyebrows the driver frowned in surprise, this being the expressive limit his constant phlegmatic stance allowed him. "I wish I was informed beforehand that you would be traveling."

"It's just Berkeley, a half-hour from here if you take the Free Airway."

"Still... out of town."

"Should I sign a form or something?"

"Well, you are within your work schedule Miss Lan, and I am here just to facilitate whatever do diligence you may have. But I'd like to accommodate you in a different vehicle."

"Come on, that's a waste of time," protested Wendy.

"I understand that a woman in your position must rely on a decoy to be safe from harm in your... work station. But since we are headed to a prestigious University, you ought to have a ride that conforms to your social status."

147

"I really don't need that bullshit."

"I insist."

The ramshackle car entered a mega-garage building along the part of Rodeo Drive where Beverly Hills was so rich that the local restrooms never ran out of gold leaf toilet paper, as nobody would bother to clean their own asses and would rather hire someone to do that for them. It soon stopped in front of a massive limo. Krause stepped out of the vehicle and opened the door to Wendy, who sighed. She headed to the limo, with the Driver rushing ahead of her and opening the passenger door.

"Can you please not do that?" asked an annoyed Wendy. "I know how to open a door by myself."

"I would be violating the terms of my contract as your driver, butler and security guard."

"Could be our secret."

"There aren't any secrets between you, me and my employers, Miss Lan. You know that very well."

Wendy stormed into the limo and slammed the door behind her before Krause had a chance to close it. He shook his head with the slightest smile on his face. Miss Lan amused him sometimes, even if only barely.

The limo darted through the free airway connecting Los Angeles to San Francisco without bothering to slow down at any of the many toll stops. When you reach a certain level of income in California, fines are just another type of taxation. That has been true since the 20th Century.

As predicted the trip didn't last more than a half-hour, and soon they were landing on the leafy campus of Berkeley University, more precisely in front of its Social Sciences Institute. Wendy tried to open the vehicle's door as soon as it halted on the ground, but it was locked. She kept trying to push it open and it only yielded when Krause opened from outside. "At this point, I was hoping you would oblige to certain conventions in our relationship."

"Whatever, wait for me here," said an irritated Wendy. She noticed, from a distance, some undergrad students laughing at the pomp and circumstance of her arrival. It felt like her freshman year all over again.

"I am afraid I will need to stay close to you in order to ensure your safety, Miss Lan."

"Okay, twenty feet behind."

"Fifteen," counter-offered the driver/butler/security guard.

Wendy didn't wait and stormed into the building. She didn't look back but she could feel Krause following her. He had been her mother and father's eyes and hands since she decided to study exoethnology at Berkeley. He was her shadow and although she had managed to persuade her parents to give her a break from his presence inside Terminal 3 during her work hours, she somewhat knew that he was nearby even in there. Discreet, invisible. She liked when he was not conspicuous, like in that very moment, so she could enjoy that stroll through the halls of her Alma Mater. The Institute of Social Sciences hadn't changed much. Droves of pot smelling ethnology students walked through a throng of antidepressant doped sociology students. She used to be one of the former although she was never one amid the crowd. Back then she wasn't Wendy Lin yet, she was just Wen Lan, the heiress of Lan Corp and her shadow would scare her fellow students away. She still did have friends though, the ones that were also high-performing students and were mentored by the same professor as her. His name was on the office door where Wendy stopped.

Professor Amir Pahlevan, PhD
Comparative Ethnology

Wendy knocked at the door and opened it, as Amir had told her the first day they met, years ago, when she stood at that same door, knocking in two minute intervals, waiting for his leave to come in for a good half-hour. Amir tended to be too focused on whatever activity he was developing and a mere knock wouldn't be enough to fetch his attention. Usually it was an endearing read of the first batch of studies from the exoethnologists who dared to be the pioneers in reaching out to the very distant planets in

Andromeda and other galaxies – a life-commitment, due to the distance. This time he was taking notes while watching the holographic recording of a centipede alien stomping its myriad of paws on the ground, in a rhythmic pattern. There was no obvious functional purpose in that motion. He noticed Wendy's presence with the corner of his eyes and a half-smile: "I'm headed to Zeta Horologii 3 to record the natives' coming-of-age ritual tomorrow. Real footage with top-notch equipment, not this amateur crap. Wanna come with me?"

"As your assistant?"

"I have the undergrads for that. I was thinking co-researcher."

"Thanks Amir, but I have a job now. One you referred me to."

"Just quit."

"Also, the centipedes of Zeta Horologii 3 are fifty feet long. Recording their dance *in loco* will possibly result in both of us being stomped."

"You work at Terminal 3, stomping centipedes affirming their adulthood in their matriarchal society is like a swim in the kiddy's pool for you."

Wendy shrugged. He wasn't wrong.

Amir turned off the holographic projection, and the dim office lit up, revealing a hoard of instruments and artwork from all corners of the galaxy and beyond. Amid them there were a few human pieces, all of them Persian which had more sentimental than ethnologic value to him as none of them were priceless artifacts. That was the case for a backgammon board that, among all the pieces in his office, fascinated Wendy the most.

Amir stood up and gave her a big hug. She missed being hugged by a friend. José was culturally averse to physical contact and could only tolerate her hugs without hugging back, so this was a change.

"It has been way too long. How are you doing, Wendy?"

Wendy almost cried. Amir was the first person who ever called her Wendy. An affectionate variation of her real name

Wen. She adopted it for her alter ego at Terminal 3 and he wasn't aware of that. "I'm actually doing fine. Brenda had a request and I thought you could help me out."

"Wait, by Brenda you mean Brenda Roy?"

"Yes?"

"The callous, cold-hearted head of Terminal 3 security, the one that made me quit after Terminal 2 was shut down?"

"Yes, that's her... or was, until yesterday."

"You can't blame me for not having warned you. I gave you a full-disclosure on why I was quitting."

"And I said that I liked the challenge, plus the chance to work close to home."

"You are the only one from the old gang that is still around, you know. Kwame is in Kapteyn 3 researching the local mineral culinary tradition, Jameela is a diplomatic attaché at the Galactic Capital and Teuila is on the itinerant spaceship of Exoethnologists Without Borders headed to Andromeda's Second Arm. By my estimation they will arrive in six months."

Kwame, Jameela and Teuila plus Amir were her only friends in college. And now they were far away while she was stuck as the Los Angeles Spaceport's Terminal 3 Resident Exoethnologist.

"Good for them."

"I don't get it, Wendy. You never left Earth, and you were maybe my best student. Why bother studying exoethnology if you don't want to go out there?"

Oh, she wanted to go out there. She wanted to see it all. See the other planets and breathe in the different airs of their atmospheres. And more than anything, she wanted to see their populations on their homeworlds, and not the scurrying, lost selves they turned into while transiting in the ever inhospitable Terminal 3. But that's something she couldn't be honest with Amir about.

"Well, you are here, aren't you?" said Wendy with a smile that she struggled to draw.

"Barely, and only because I have students to mentor. I spend half of my life in space."

"I'm so glad that you are around today!"

Amir sighed. He knew that Wendy was prone to engage in evasion through cheerfulness. It had something to do with her family, and the shadows under his office's door showing her creepy bodyguard still following her after all those years confirmed that. It was always about her family and he knew that prodding her on that matter would only make her suffer, so he relented: "What did you want to show me, Wendy?"

***

Brenda slowly opened her eyes. That was the best nap she had had in years. She was still at the infirmary by herself. After a few minutes enjoying the quietness she decided to get back to business. Brenda turned on her holotablet and called Sue, who soon appeared on the screen: "How are things going there?"

"Oh, same old. Had some injured guards and F Wing is quarantined due to an alien virus strain."

"Again?"

"Yup. But only two deaths this time, Ma'am."

"I'm in the infirmary, why weren't the injured guards sent here?"

"They resigned when I told them that you were there."

"Good."

"Also, we had an incident with an emotional support pet."

"Something carnivore and predatory, I assume."

"No, it was an emotional support pet rock."

"That's new. Let me guess, was the pet rock made out of crack-cocaine?"

"Chip thought so and tried to smoke it, but it turned out to just be extremely radioactive."

"Sounds like a quite average day."

"Indeed, things are under control and to be honest I'm getting a kick out of bossing everybody around while you are out. So take your time, Ma'am."

"Don't get too used to it, I'm already feeling better and I might ask Doctor José to let me out of here."

"That's a shame... I mean... It will be great to have you back, Ma'am."

"And don't think I forgot about your sister, Sue."

"About that—"

"Not now."

"Thanks, Ma'am."

"Ah, one last question... was... is Gabriel Chagas around?"

"Not with me this time. He's back at teaming up with Chip."

"Good, can you tell him to meet me at the end of the day?"

"Are you gonna fire him?"

"That's none of your business."

"He's a dork, not very smart, but it's always interesting to have a child-sized employee on our staff, we never know when we are gonna need someone small enough to crawl through a narrow space or deal with a tiny alien at eye-level."

"You like him."

"I don't like anyone, Ma'am. I just get used to people and don't like changes."

"You got used to him awfully fast."

"You should try one of his *biscoitos de queijo*."

"Already did."

And before Sue could say something, Brenda ended the call.

Brenda's memories were coming back since the day before, when she saw the armored man. The memories of him and Cida had been just a blur in her mind since the incident. She started working at Terminal 3 as soon as they rush-built this concrete monstrosity to replace Terminal 2. She was the only member of the security guard personnel from Terminal 2 to be willing to work at Terminal 3, hence she became the commander. She hated her job, she hated the aliens, as if every single one of them took something from her that was precious but she couldn't remember what it was. Her stubbornness in clinging to a workplace she hated turned out to be something inside her, compelling her to seek out lost memories through exposure. And the day before, all those years of bitterness and confusion paid off. Cida Chagas. Cida was the gap. She could remember now feeling light-headed and aroused by someone at the open air gym in Venice, and how this someone was her co-worker. And how she smiled and ran so damn fast, like a doe. And how she would bring delicious *biscoitos de queijo* to her sometimes. Before seeing the armored man for the second time, Brenda could remember the love, but not the one she loved. There was a hole inside her, and it hurt even though she couldn't remember what had created the hollowness. Now Brenda did. She remembered everything. She remembered that Cida said that she had a son, a son whom she referred to as *meu anjinho*. His name was Gabriel Chagas and Brenda intended to ask him why he was working at the spaceport where his mother disappeared.

The other memory was of the armored man. In that case the memory didn't mean much. Brenda only knew that he took Cida away from her and, in the process, wiped her memory and turned Terminal 2 into a hell hole riddled with lethal quantum booby-traps. Hopefully Wendy would have some answers for her. And think of the devil, there she was, entering the infirmary with a smile that Brenda always found particularly punchable.

"How are you feeling, Ms. Roy?" asked Wendy.

"What do you have for me?"

"My mentor and I did some research on those drawings, and in fact we found some clues." Wendy gave a holotablet to Brenda which featured the picture of a yellow drawing on a red surface. It represented, in a somewhat deformed shape, the armored man and most of his discernible features. "This is a leather iconography from Olodumare 3."

"So he's from Olodumare 3. Thought those guys were mollusks living in seas of liquid nitrogen. The armor is shaped like a human."

Wendy touched the screen, and another image appeared. Another drawing, but this one much more rustic, in some sort of blue pigment on a piece of paper. But it was, without a shadow of doubt, the same armored man. "And this one was part of a parchment found inside an artifact extracted by archeologists in Tau Cassiopeiae 2." She touched the screen again. This time a carving on rock representing the armored man. "This is from Hwaseong 5, a world protected by the Galactic Federation as most of their sentient population is going through their Neolithic Age. Only researchers are allowed there and need to follow a series of non-contact safeguards."

"What does all that mean, Wendy?"

"The... drawing you showed me... it represents a recurring supernatural entity as registered by a dozen of sentient species across the galaxy. The only trend is that this entity is an unimportant one in the big picture of their respective belief systems."

"Are you saying that I saw god or some primitive superstition like that?"

"I'd say more like... a demon... in the Dharmic understanding of the word. And you did not tell me that you saw that creature."

"Thanks for your help. You can go now."

"Whatever you witnessed has great scientific value! I can put you in touch with my mentor in Berkeley. He—"

"I said you can go now!"

"I... kind of work here. In the adjacent room, actually—"

"Fuck off, Wendy!"

Wendy gulped and reluctantly obliged, exiting the infirmary and walking to her desk. José became concerned when he noticed her distraught expression.

"My offer to torture her still stands, Wendy."

"I... I think I'm going home early, José." said Wendy, her eyes wet, as she rushed to the door.

***

Krause was waiting for Wendy at Terminal 3's main entrance with an oily smirk on his face. She was leaving earlier than usual, which meant that her day had been bad. If there were several days in a row of leaving work early, it meant that she was having a bad time, and when there was a succession of bad times, it meant that her life was hell. Work was just a small piece in the whole picture of Wendy's suffering. Krause was another. The driver/butler/bodyguard was a patient, diligent snake. He assumed that Wendy would crack at some point and just run away to some solar system populated by horny alien junkies where she could get high and laid every day. And, by doing so, she would be breaking the agreement she had made with her parents that listed her as the only heir of Lan Corporation once they both passed away. That agreement had just one clause: do not voluntarily leave the metropolitan area of Los Angeles for more than 48 hours. The agreement had nothing to do with the management of the giant conglomerate. Wendy was not expected to run their trillion-dollar business, as her parents weren't currently making any business decision. Not because they couldn't, but because they didn't want to. Something as big and successful as Lan Corporation ran its course on its own, and their founders reaped the profits. If Wendy ever broke the agreement, her share in the company would go to the loyal butler Krause.

After Wendy made the daily change from the fake Suber car to the limo, Krause drove straight to her parent's manor, an architectural masterpiece of twirling titanium and fullerene plates separated by glass panels perched on the highest street of Bel Air. Wendy stopped seeing this place as her home when she signed the agreement her parents foisted on her when she announced her acceptance to Berkeley's exoethnology undergraduate program. The manor was just a place she had to be due to a contract.

Krause opened the car door for Wendy and announced: "Mr. and Mrs. Lan are aware that you arrived home earlier than usual *again* and would like to dine with you in fifteen minutes."

Wendy nodded and stomped into the house. It was not an invitation; it was a command.

Wendy walked past the luxurious walls of the manor's main hall, ornamented with an array of Chinese antiquities: a canopy of terracotta, lacquer and jade. She respected her parent's taste in art, despite the extravagance. That doesn't mean that she wanted any of it. She had decided that, when they died, she would ship all the artwork across the rift separating Bel Air and the neighboring mountain where the Getty Museum stood. Those Chinese antiquities should not exist only for the eyes of a few.

After her stroll through the hall she arrived at her destination. She called it the mess room. That's where Ji and Mei

Lan, Wendy's parents, spent all their time. It was a circular room with cushioned white walls and a vast red carpet. The ceiling was covered with technological paraphernalia from which dangled wires connected to visors, sensorial patches and other outlets that kept Ji and Mei connected 24-seven to the virtual reality worlds they decided to spend the rest of their lives in. A world they had created and within which they were also the landlords to the billions of people that dwell there as paying tenants. Besides the wires that connected them to that virtual reality, there were also tubes dangling from the ceiling, such as the ones connected to their mouth that would feed their scrawny bodies with atrophied muscles, while another tube attached to their backside and crotch was in charge of draining their excretions. For Wendy the sight of that elderly couple suspended in that circular room reminded her of puppets supported by the threads operated by an invisible puppeteer. It was quite a macabre show she had to witness every day.

A visor and a feeding tube lowered in front of Wendy. It was Krause's doing, she only hoped that whatever he was going to feed her this time was based on vegan protein. She attached the visor to her face and inserted the feeding tube down her throat and soon Wendy found herself no longer in the mess room. She was on a balmy beach at which an amazon of a woman was roasting a pig in a firepit. Wendy gasped when noticing that the tall, athletic woman was completely naked and each one of her breasts was the size of a watermelon. "Mom! Can you please put something on!"

"Hello to you too, Wen! Where are your manners?"

"I'm saving them for when you cover that stuff up."

"You mean my news boobs? Stop looking at my face and look down here at them. That's some quality rendering, huh?"

"That's bizarre."

A voice behind Wendy startled her.

"Wen, do not boob-shame your mother! Especially when you look ridiculous like that."

Wendy turned and saw a bodybuilder approaching her, also naked, also displaying a proneness to exaggeration of his intimate parts.

"That's how I look in the real world, dad."

"That's sad. Can I render something less bland and more appropriate for you? We are having a Hawaiian luau."

"Would that involve me being naked?"

"It's a Hawaiian luau, we should abide by the tradition."

"I don't think people get naked in luaus."

"You can't know that, you aren't Hawaiian."

"I'm an ethnology graduate. You know, I spent years studying cultural traditions and—"

"Boring!"

Wendy sighed and reminded herself that she was there for them, not the other way around.

"Sit down, Wen," said Mei, as she pointed out a table that suddenly appeared by the roast pit.

Wendy obliged to her mother's order, while Ji picked up the pork from the spit and slammed it on the table in a far-fetched and unnecessary macho move. That made Mei giggle and even Wendy smiled a little at the sheer yet harmless stupidity of that act. It felt good to see that those two were somewhat happy, even if in a silly way. Ji started slicing the pork and putting big chunks on plates. Wendy took a bite. She knew it wasn't actual pork and could only taste the non-descript paste that the feeder was pumping in her mouth each time she bit in a chunk of the virtual meat.

"Krause told me that he took you to Berkeley today," said Ji.

"Yes, a work issue."

"Sounds boring."

"Yes, extremely. I will spare you from listening to the boring details, dad."

"Don't be rude to your father, Wen," said Mei.

"Sorry, mom," said Wendy. She knew that she couldn't win with them.

"I really don't understand why you are wasting your time out there. You could just live with us here. There are so many young men that are also permanent residents in LanWorld. They'd love to meet you."

"What can I say... I like my life out there," lied Wendy.

"It doesn't help the company that the heir isn't an avid user of their own product."

"I think Lan Corporation is successful enough and doesn't need any further marketing."

"We built all this for you, Wen. That's your legacy."

Wendy finished eating the last bit of meat on her plate. "I'm full."

"I'm sure that there is still room for dessert. What do you want? You can have anything."

"I think I'm going to my room now, mom." Wendy saw her parents' face contorting in disappointment. "But I'm looking forward to seeing you guys tomorrow. I promise that I will stay longer."

"We are going to have Mongolian barbeque tomorrow. It was your favorite when you were just a little girl."

Wendy smiled. That was true, even if she couldn't stand Mongolian barbeque anymore. She changed. They all changed. "That would be great, dad. And maybe some Mahjong after dinner?"

"Boring!" said Ji.

"Oh, you and your obsession with Mahjong, Wen!" complained Mei, "There are thousands of highly-renderized games on LanWorld. Why settle for Mahjong when you don't even like to play for money?"

"Afraid of losing again, mom?"

"I never lose and you know that very well. Challenge accepted, Wen."

Wendy stood up and approached her mother. She wanted to give her a hug but just realized that the size of her breasts and her nakedness would make it really awkward. "See you two tomorrow, okay?"

And before they could answer Wendy removed the visor from her face.

She was a little startled when she realized that Krause was standing just a few feet ahead of her: "That was an unusually brief visit, Miss Lan."

"Are you keeping track of the time now?"

"Not only now."

Wendy took a look at her parents. The real ones, with their elderly, frail bodies clad in wires and sensitivity plates so different from the over-the-top renderized anatomies they adopted in LanWorld. She couldn't leave them even though she didn't care about the money. Krause could have all of it for all that mattered. But if she left, it would almost certainly be their death-sentence.

Back in Wendy's undergraduate years, Amir implied one day that, as an exoethnologist, she was a great social worker. He hadn't meant that as a compliment. Wendy thought about answering, but then she realized for the first time that, amid the hundreds of cultural artifacts from all across the Milky Way that decorated Amir's office, there was also a very human backgammon board. Wendy asked if he played backgammon. He said that she was changing subject. She let the conversation end there. Later she learned through some quick research that, among Middle-Easterners and Iranians, backgammon was mostly a game played by men in men-dominated spaces. She realized that she was indeed changing subjects when asking him about backgammon, as the topic that Wendy wanted to tackle, back on that day, was family. She wanted to ask him about his family to see if, by any chance, his most cherished memories could be at least slightly similar to hers: a crisp Fall day in a manor overlooking Tahoe. Wendy, only ten years old, was seated at a table with her parents, drinking green tea and playing Mahjong. Her parents weren't going anywhere any time soon. Wendy's father never left his wife's side. Wendy's mother would never stop playing while she was winning. And Wendy had no problems with losing on purpose.

For years now Wendy had been meeting her parents for dinner. It was time for something to change. She decided to call in sick at work the next day, for the first time since her start at

TERMINAL 3

Terminal 3 so she could surprise her parents by showing up for breakfast the next morning. They'd still play Mahjong. That wouldn't change. But this time Wendy would play to win.

INTERLUDE

Personal Diary of The Bailiff of the Time Court, Human Division.

July, 8ʰ 2119, 3 days after the beginning of the Slow yet Irreversible Great Collapse of the Universe.

I haven't slept in the last four days, which wouldn't be a problem back in the headquarters at the End of Time, where one was never sure if they were sleeping or awake, dead or alive, going through time or space. Things didn't have such ambiguity billions of years before the End of Time, and my exhaustion is an obnoxious reminder that, underneath the armor, I am a living, sentient creature that couldn't rely forever on caffeine shots to stay awake. I'm afraid of falling sleep if I dare sit down, that's why I'm standing still at Gate 665. Waiting for him.

I realized that I hate yawning because I've been doing that a lot. Since I can't afford to sleep, I decided to focus my thoughts on the subject that would fill me with fury. Rage is the best wake-up call. I thought about Gabriel Chagas. It's true that my mission is unrelated my personal grudge, and I wished he could have come for me before. But I had to abide by the wish of The Manager, who was so sure and so adamant in his memos, long on commands and short on details concerning the slow yet irreversible collapse of the Universe that started three days ago, and which required to be dealt with in that precise timeframe. I didn't notice anything remarkable in terms of the risks to the fabric of time, except for what I had caused myself: the entropic anomalies in Terminal 2 and now the fact that Brenda Roy was able to see me and had probably recovered access to her memories from my last extraction mission.

I must admit: I wonder if I had failed this current mission as well, even though I am following the procedure and the safety standards expected from me to a *T*. I also wonder, since The Manager is not fond of providing any sort of analytical input in his memos, if the slow yet unyielding collapse of the Universe had been/was being caused by Gabriel Chagas. If so, how and why only now?

I know that my role in the organization I belong is only to be the hand that reaches out, intercepts, extracts, deports. I had my orders and I intend to follow them. I know I am good at his job even if I didn't have the chance to produce results. Yet. My mentor, who was The Bailiff before I replaced him, showed me the ropes of the craft and then went back to the place and time of his upbringing: a remote Pacific Ocean island during the 4th Century. That's where and when he intended to live his final days within the normal flux of time that was needed for a person to succumb to death. I saw my mentor as a friend, the only one I truly had since that weird night in early 21st century São Paulo, when I accepted his invitation to be his successor at the Time Court and shared with him a meal of taro pudding. And yet I don't miss my mentor.

TERMINAL 3

My mentor and I are quite similar in nature, despite being originally from different centuries and continents and, at the time of our first encounter, me being just over eighteen years old while he was physically almost a century old. We both knew how to fight, even if one had his training grounds in the seasonal tribal skirmishes on certain Melanesian islands, the other in the dog-eat-dog reality of a stray kid in the streets of an early 21st century third-world metropolis. Another point of convergence between us was that both my predecessor and I were deeply unhappy, although my mentor sacrificed his own happiness over the importance of his mandate to ensure cosmic stability. This didn't mean that he ever stopped longing for his original life. My mentor would spend hours talking to me during my training time about the sandy beaches, the turquoise sea waters and the perfumed flowers of his home island in his home time. I certainly couldn't relate to the longing my mentor nourished, as my favorite fragrance from my original time was from the rotisserie chicken ovens placed on the sidewalks in front of São Paulo's small grocery shops. Back in my teen years I would watch, as in a trance, those chickens spinning slowly, sometimes with a dog or two watching as well next to me, until a red-faced grocery shop owner stormed out to shoo us away. Customers didn't like to shop in places where stray kids and abandoned dogs lingered.

Like my mentor, I knew that I would age very slowly, only during the moments I spent outside the End of Time while performing his missions. Like during this exact moment as I write down whatever comes to my mind while fighting sleep deprivation. It would take a long time, extremely long, but at some point I will be too old and frail to carry on my missions. By then I would need to fetch an apprentice and train that person like my mentor did. And then I would return to my time and place of origin to die as well. I already made plans for that. I'm gonna shoot myself in the head as soon as I'm back to early 21st century São Paulo. Unlike my mentor, I hate my place and time of origin. And I hate Gabriel Chagas for making me have an upbringing on the streets of that huge, heartless city. Without love. Without a mother. Without anything but my damn guts. Guts that back then craved rotisserie chickens and now have a totally different kind of hunger. I can feel that hunger burning inside me right now. That's good. That will keep me awake.

DAY 5

CHIP BOARDED THE THIRD CAR OF the Maglev San Bernardino-El Segundo line at Covina station. Usually he wouldn't be bothered with what car he chose to ride in on his Maglev journey, day after day, to Terminal 3. That is, until three days ago, when he and Gabe discovered, in that same car at that same time of the day, that they would be taking the same Maglev train to the same workplace. Chip traveled in the third car two days prior, but Gabe was nowhere in sight. He just shrugged. The shrimp probably had quit or was in another car. But it turned out Gabe had arrived earlier than usual to the spaceport and had his own run-in with Sue. And then, the day before, Gabe and Chip were at the same car at the same time. They spent the whole day together, including a few hours in a decontamination chamber that smelled like old farts due to a radioactive pet rock they had found. The shrimp wasn't annoying him anymore, on the contrary, Gabe would cheer him up even if Chip didn't let it show. Gabe didn't need to be inside that foul-smelling decontamination chamber as Chip was the one who tried to smoke the radioactive rock, but Gabe decided to tag along anyway. Gabe's jolliness was unrelenting, no matter the bluntness with which Chip would react to his colleague's pestering enthusiasm.

After scanning through the crowd on board the third car of the Maglev train, Chip saw Gabe standing in a corner. He shoved other passengers that were in his way until he reached Gabe and then quietly stood next to him, pretending to ignore him, waiting for the rookie to greet him. Chip didn't want to give away that he cared. However, after a few seconds, Chip realized with a frown that Gabe didn't acknowledge his presence. With reluctance he looked down and noticed that the shrimp's eyes were looking distant, in a morose daydreaming way with an obvious hint of sadness. Seems like not everything was rosy in Shrimpland. Chip felt like a fool for thinking that this fireball of enthusiasm wouldn't have a bad day and decided to let his alpha pride make a concession for once through a grunt. The guttural sound was sufficient to startle Gabe and catch his attention.

"Oh, hey Chip," said Gabe, with the saddest smile creeping on his face.

"What's wrong?" asked Chip, just to bite his lips in regret.

Chip blamed himself silently for not having talked about some innocuous subject first before trying to steer the conversation to Gabe's mood. Now the shrimp would know that he was concerned.

"I… I got fired yesterday," he answered, with a shrug that was more akin to Chip than Gabe.

Chip was taken aback. Gabe had been working at Terminal 3 for five days now, the few rookies that lasted that long would stick around, at least until they found a better job. Almost nobody got fired, they'd just quit, more precisely stop showing up. That couldn't be right. Chip wanted to ask Gabe questions about what happened, and make plans to talk to Brenda directly on his behalf. He was sure that Sue would side with him. She seemed to like having the shrimp around too, although in a different way. And maybe they could scheme with Wendy as well, Chip was sure she could pull some strings from outside. Wendy didn't fool anyone about the influence she was hiding when she got a visa for the roach… insectoids. Yes, insectoids. Chip was trying to do better. There were many possibilities for the shrimp. Gabe didn't need to quit. Gabe wasn't going to quit. Gabe couldn't quit. And Chip wanted more than anything to let Gabe know that.

"I guess you don't have what it takes, shrimp," said Chip, startling himself with his own callousness.

"I guess not. I'm just gonna empty my locker today," said Gabe.

For the first time since Gabe's second day of work, Chip wanted to punch the shrimp. Maybe if he punched Gabe he would put up some fight and tell Chip that he was wrong, that he belonged at Terminal 3 with him and Sue and Wendy. Chip barely knew Gabe, why did he care so much? He shouldn't care. Yes, caring is a choice. Just don't care. The conversation was over. Chip pushed other commuters out of his way as he darted to the opposite side of the car. He needed to loathe himself alone, and nothing is lonelier than being amid a crowd of strangers.

Gabe was disappointed yet not surprised by Chip's unsympathetic attitude. He thought he was doing well at Terminal 3, but clearly Brenda thought otherwise. The same apparently applied to Chip. Gabe imagined he was developing a friendship with his mentor, but it turned out he was discarded as soon as the professional bond between them vanished. Gabe didn't matter, he never mattered to anyone in his life since his mother disappeared. The last five days made him think otherwise, but it was just a delusion.

Not mattering is not entirely bad. At the foster home, invisibility was an asset, as he would only have problems when the bullies noticed his discreet presence. It was by trying to be invisible and scurrying through life that Gabe thought he earned a pass to be nothing but mediocre during his whole life until he started at Terminal 3, although most would say that a security guard at Terminal 3 was a mediocre job. And by losing it, Gabe failed at being mediocre. He was maybe just bad at being human.

***

Sue was the one that told him to meet Brenda the day before. He had just walked in Brenda's office when she went for a straight shot, not even giving him the time to have a seat: "Why didn't you tell me about Cida?"

"I... How—"

"She used to work at Terminal 2."

"Did you know her, Ma'am?"

"So you are Cida's son."

"Yes—"

"You should have told me."

"I didn't think my background mattered."

"Did she tell you... about me?"

"Not that I can remember, Ma'am. Why are—"

"So... You never forgot about her."

"How could I forget my mother?"

"I'm wondering that too."

"You... are not making sense, Ma'am, what—"

"Did you take this job because of her?"

Gabe flinched. He couldn't tell her about the message he received urging him to go to Gate 665. Especially now that he knew that the Gate was actually at Terminal 2. "I was very young when she...disappeared—"

"'Disappeared' is a way to frame it."

"—but I remember she liked working as a security guard at Terminal 2 a lot, Ma'am. I kinda looked up to her and wanted to be a security guard too."

"I understand..."

"I am sorry for not telling you, Ma'am."

"Working here won't bring her back, rookie."

"I never thought it would. I just thought—"

"I think you are way too personally involved with this place to be part of our team. I... I'm afraid that I should let you go."

"Ma'am, please—"

"I think there's a form or something for you to sign, not sure, I will check that. So go home now and come back tomorrow."

Gabe left without arguing. He was not the confrontational type and was completely unaware that Brenda would rather die than see the son of the woman she loved cling to this horrible place as she did, or worse, fall into the clutches of the same armored man that took Cida away from them both. For Gabe it was just another moment when the world was screwing him over, even though this time it was because he was a somebody instead of a nobody. Same difference. Same indifference.

This could be the last time Gabe ever went to Terminal 3. He intended to sign whatever forms Brenda wanted and leave on good terms. That's why, the following day, he had brought a huge bucket filled with *biscoito de queijo* with him, which he had baked the night before. These people may not want him around, but he would leave a good impression before fading away forever.

***

When Gabe was about to enter the security guard headquarters he almost bounced against the expansive belly of Mason. Gabe didn't know him well and could only remember him from his first day, when he asked Brenda what a galaxy was. Seeing Mason dressed in his uniform meant that he was the last rookie from the orientation session that had lasted, as Gabe couldn't remember seeing any one else sticking around.

"Look where you are walking, squirt," said Mason.

"Brenda was right, you clearly have what it takes to be a good security guard, Mason."

"Hey, I remember you... you work here too, right?"

"I used to."

"You mean, you bailed out or found something better?"

"No. Got fired. I'm just here to sign my termination papers," said Gabe, impatiently, trying to dodge Mason, but the chunky man used his mass to block Gabe's way.

"What kind of loser can screw up in this job?"

"My kind of loser, can I pass?"

"What's that smell?" asked Mason, eyeing Gabe's bucket filled with *biscoitos de queijo*.

"Some farewell snacks I baked for you guys. Do you want one?"

"I think I'm having all of them," said Mason as he grabbed the bucket with his chubby paws.

Gabe tried to hold on to the bucket but, as usual, he didn't have the energy to put up a fight. He looked around and noticed the other security guards snickering at his ordeal. Oh no. It was the foster care home all over again. No. Gabe wouldn't have that. Not this time.

"You don't deserve a *biscoito de queijo*, Mason," muttered Gabe.

"What was that, squirt?" said Mason, as he was ready to help himself.

"None of you deserve it!" yelled Gabe with an anger that he had never felt before.

Gabe's small dexterous hands acted without thinking when they snatched Mason's holstered taser and, in a blink, blasted him with electricity. Mason immediately went down, crumbling like a heavy bag of potatoes. The taser fell out of Gabe's now shaky hands almost at the same time. That was maybe the first fight he had ever won in his whole life, and yet, he was feeling terrible, as if he had betrayed everything he was, or used to be. He didn't want to spend another second in this place. He didn't belong here and did not like what it had made him do. He picked up the bucket with *biscoitos de queijo* from the ground and scurried out. Gabe wanted to talk to someone. Someone who he was sure wouldn't be indifferent or aggressive towards him.

***

When Gabe arrived at the Assistance to Passengers and Staff office he found that only José was at his desk. And he seemed to be whimpering. "Good morning, Doctor. Can I ask you where Wendy is?"

"That's a good question," said José in a dry tone as he turned his attention to Gabe, who noticed that the tiny alien's hexagonal pupils seemed to be dilated. He was either high or very, very angry.

"I just wanted to say—"

"That she sucks? That she's useless? That she is worthless? Because that's how all you morons from the security staff feel about my friend Wendy!"

"I would never—"

"Oh, yes, just pretend that you are not like all the others!"

"Is Wendy okay?"

"She called in sick!"

"I hope it was nothing serious."

"She never calls in sick. Sometimes she did consider calling in sick but I always managed to change her mind. But this time, she just said that she had some business to attend to."

"I—"

"I blame you! I had it easy with Wendy before you started working here. She always thought that there was something more than she was actually delivering here, but you made her actually go out of her way to seek that. And that was a mistake, because she called in sick!"

"Maybe she is actually sick and will be back tomorrow."

"Or maybe she's gonna quit and leave me all alone!"

"I…would you like a *biscoito de queijo*?" offered Gabe as he picked up one of the snacks from his bucket and offered it to José.

José grabbed the snack and tossed it at Gabe's face.

"Ouch!"

"Can I please have another one?" asked José.

Gabe was happy to oblige, but José just threw it at him again, this time aiming at Gabe's forehead.

"I think…I should go," pondered Gabe.

"Yes, you should."

Gabe walked out of R-Wing with a new found purpose. He did want to follow in his mother's professional footsteps, but he also had a greater objective and it was time to act on it.

***

Gabe was surprised to find Sue in front of the locked access gate to Terminal 2 at the main lobby.

"I have a bucket full of *biscoito de queijo* with me," said Gabe from behind Sue, startling her. "I know how you like them and I will give you the whole thing if you walk away and forget you saw me here."

"Maybe you should be the one walking away. I'm busy."

"Let me guess. Brenda ordered you to keep an eye on me so I won't enter Terminal 2."

"What?! No! I...wait, you want to get in there too?"

"Yes. So, you aren't here because Brenda asked you to?"

"No. Why do you want to get in there?"

Gabe flinched. During the incident with the Ifritian Empire envoy, he had a chance to listen to Sue share something personal about her family. Something that even Chip, who couldn't shut up when he started talking about himself, never did. Gabe wanted to enter Terminal 2 for a family matter, after all, due to the message he received about his mother. But again, why trust a self-proclaimed bully with the most important decision in his life? She would probably just react like Chip, with indifference. Or worse, she could act like Mason. Better keep it to himself and avoid another disappointment: "I... I have my reasons. You?"

"It doesn't matter. I can't crack the entrance code anyway."

"I may have a guess, Sue," said Gabe, as he approached the console.

He typed the word "Cida" on the keyboard. Access denied. "Cida Chagas". Access denied. "Aparecida". The door opened.

"How did you know that?"

"Doesn't matter."

Sue shrugged and the twosome walked through the corridor until they reached the gate to the dusty, worn Terminal 2.

"Gimme a *biscoito de queijo,*" said Sue.

"It isn't time for—"

"Just give me one without yapping, dammit," insisted Sue.

Gabe begrudgingly produced the bucket. Sue helped herself to a handful of *biscoitos de queijo*, but instead of eating them, she tossed one in the direction where the floor seemed worn. The snack crashed onto the ground, pulverized by the high-gravity anomaly.

"Yeah, I wouldn't go down that path," she said before turning her back to Gabe and heading to the restrooms.

Sue moved carefully, always tossing a *biscoito de queijo* ahead of her to be sure the way was clean. Gabe thought about telling her that the path to the restrooms was probably safe, as he had learned during the incident with the Ifritian Empire envoy, but he decided to stay quiet, as he couldn't know if the areas with spacetime anomalies shifted. Besides, Sue seemed not only to know what she was doing, as usual, but also eager to find whatever she was seeking. Gabe was puzzled by Sue's unusual aloofness and secrecy about her business at Terminal 2. But he couldn't blame or query her, as he had his own secrets, although he wondered if, like him, she had received a message about a missing parent. Gabe knew that he was maybe going way too far just because of a simple message he received. It could be a prank from one of his former tormentors at the foster care home, who called him crazy for claiming that his mother had disappeared. But the fact was that he had nothing to lose by following a clue that could finally solve the biggest mystery in his life and track the source of his unhappiness since the age of nine. Worst case scenario, if it was a prank, it would just be another humiliating experience on an oh so long list. Nothing that he couldn't deal with.

Gabe took Sue's cue on how to safely navigate within Terminal 2, and used his *biscoitos de queijo* to discern walkable paths from the ones that were rigged with anomalies. After a few detours, he finally reached Gate 665. It was just a boarding gate in a particularly secluded wing of the terminal, not much different from the ones from Terminal 3 except for the broken glasses and the dust. He saw no signs of life.

And then, there was a blunt pain in the back of his head immediately followed by darkness.

TERMINAL 3

INTERLUDE

Personal Diary of The Bailiff of the Time Court, Human Division.

Untraceable Date, sometime after the end of the Slow yet Irreversible Great Collapse of the Universe.

I think it was euphoria. I read about it, but never experienced it until the moment I stood over Gabriel Chagas' unconscious body on the ground, laying by my metallic boots. For a moment I was afraid I had punched him too hard and turned my prey into damaged goods. That would be a problem: Gabriel Chagas needed his full mental faculties for what was about to happen. I decided to not overthink that and stick to the mission. I picked Gabriel Chagas up and dumped him on one of my shoulders like a bag of potatoes, a small bag at that, to my surprise, as I expected my nemesis to be much larger

I had attained my goal and there was nothing else to do but go back to headquarters. Without further ado, I pushed myself through the limits of time. It was harder with luggage. I squeezed Gabe hard against my shoulder with one of my gauntlet-clad hands. The last thing I needed now was to lose my catch in the gaps of space and time. And then I felt my right boot cross through the limits of the 22nd century, finding footing in the inconsistent grounds that lay beyond that border. When I entered Terminal 2 a few days ago, I had to pull myself with the leg that first emerged in that time. Now, on the way back, I had to push myself with the leg that was still in 2119, with all the soundness of its temporal normalcy. Carefully, again, as to not shatter anything. And then, slowly, my luggage and I drifted entirely away from 2119. I was back to the End of Time.

An overwhelming feeling of numbness took over my whole body as the aging of my cells halted. I was surrounded by darkness except for a disk of light around me no wider than a few feet. Home sweet home. I was alone but for Gabe on my shoulder and The Secretary. She wore a floral taffeta dress and had a clipboard in her hand, eyeing me from behind her thick-framed glasses. She bore the affable smile that would never leave her round face, topped by a very large, blond beehive hairstyle carefully erected with the help of many cans of toxic hairspray from the 1950s. She allowed herself this indulgence as carcinogenic toxins couldn't kill anyone at the End of Time, as time itself was dead.

"Subject Gabriel Chagas extracted from 2119 AD," I informed The Secretary, in accordance with the manual's guidelines.

"You look tired and hungry, sugar," said The Secretary, what was not the answer that she was supposed deliver to me according to the manual but had her signature sweetness that always felt to me awfully close to flirting. "I just baked a batch of chocolate chip cookies, why don't you go get some in the break room and then rest a little?"

"I don't need food nor rest."

"It would feel good to lay down and munch something sweet, though. You—"

"What am I supposed to do with the defendant, Dottie?"

"You can drop him right here," said The Secretary. "I will inform The Lawyer that her client arrived. By the way, The Manager is very satisfied with the way you handled the situation this time. Good job, Miguel."

DAY ∞

GABE WOKE UP SLOWLY. NO. HE WAS not waking up. He was recovering his awareness, which was a quite confusing process when one wasn't even sure if he was breathing or breathless, standing on his feet or dangling upside down, sleeping or awake, alive or dead. Somehow, it felt like both and none. He wasn't even sure if his eyelids were open or closed. He decided that he wanted to see, and that decision allowed him to do so, although the whole process didn't seem like opening his eyes at all. In the slowest blink of an eye, Gabe realized that he was in a space completely dark and empty but for a small lit circle in which he stood next to a pink marble table. On the square table there was a crystal jar of water, two empty glasses and a basket filled with small round cakes that smelled as buttery as croissants but with a large dash of sugar. And, on the other side of the table, there was a woman who had a polite yet assertive smile on her face. She seemed to be in her early forties, her head clad in a white crepe bonnet ornamented by blue bows. She was dressed in a blue satin dress topped by a tight, white lace corset.

"Take it easy and focus on the smell, *mon chéri*."

"What… is this?"

"They are called *kouign-amman*, they are a pastry from my homeland."

"I mean, what the hell is *all* this?!" yelled Gabe, who would have been hyperventilating if he knew for sure if he was breathing or not. "Am I dead?"

"You really should have a *kouign-amman*."

"I'm not hungry…I think…I mean…I think I'm not hungry."

"It's not about your appetite. You don't need nourishment in here, but it will help anchor your senses instead of letting them warp away by the chaotic flows of entropy."

"I'm dizzy, may I sit down?"

"You are already sitting down."

Gabe noticed that he wasn't standing anymore, he was in a chair facing the woman with the table between them. He wasn't sure if he had been standing at all.

"What is… all this?" asked Gabe as he nervously flailed his arms.

"This is the end of time."

"Where is that?"

"At the end of space."

"At the… end of space?"

"Yes, at the end of time."

"End of time or end of space?"

"That's what I said."

"I'm confused."

"Eat some *kouign-amman*. I just baked that batch, although, since you are American, you might prefer one of those awful chocolate chip cookies Dottie makes. Would you prefer that?"

"The end of space and the end of time?"

"They are the same thing."

"So we are at the end of spacetime?" guessed Gabe.

"I am so sorry, *Monsieur*. If you don't mind my blunt honesty, I'm not particularly versed in the vernacular of the 22nd century and its limitations, not the most interesting century on the board. In order to make this experience more accessible to you, I will try to make my language more pleonastic from now on. Would you like a glass of wet water?"

"I will have the koui... kou—"

"*Kouign-amman*," said the woman, as she pushed the basket with the pastry toward Gabe. He helped himself to one of the snacks. It did taste like an ultra-buttery and very sweet croissant.

"Is that a pastry from the future?"

"There is no future from here, we are at the End of Time, remember? There are only the past and tatters of present time."

Eating wasn't doing much for Gabe; he felt like the chewed food was just being pushed through his digestive tract without undergoing any sort of transformation in the process. Tasting, on the other hand, was calming and he felt slightly less estranged to his current situation. His taste buds could detect a certain flavor: sweetness. Not sourness. Not bitterness. No doubt. Only the unquestionable, inexorable certainty that a pound of sugar corroding his pancreas in a flimsy association with butter and flour could have.

"What am I doing here?"

"You mean 'here'?" asked the woman as she stressed the quotation marks with a little tilt of her index fingers in the air.

"Yes?"

"Now you are asking the right questions! I said that my *kouign-aman* would help. You've been extracted from the 22nd century and will be screened by the Time Court where you'll face a trial for deportation to the time the Court deems appropriate for you. By the way, I'm your attorney."

"I... just want to go home."

"Of course, and we are here precisely to assist you with that."

"I mean, to LA."

"22nd or 21st century LA?"

"22nd century! I was born there! My life is there! Why the hell would I want to go to the 21st century?!"

"Calm down, *Monsieur* Chagas, you were doing well, let's not ruin it. Here, have another *kouign-aman.*"

"I don't even know you, Ma'am. How can I have you as my lawyer?"

"Well, I'm here to answer all your questions you may have. I'm on your side, believe it or not."

"Fine, who are you?"

"I'm your attorney."

"Do you have a name?"

"I had many, depending on the time."

"Right now?"

"There is no right now, at least not right *right* now. Time ended, remember?"

"But you are an attorney right *right* now, *right*?"

"There are so many variables in that question that it would take years in regular time to answer it. What is doable, but I may need to bake more *kouign-amans.*"

"I... really don't understand this place."

"Time."

"So confusing."

"Then let's focus on you."

"Okay, who's the person that is my lawyer?" asked Gabe, trying to make sense of the cryptic terms of the woman by playing her game.

"Well, I was born Marie-Victoire de Lambilly in 17th century Kingdom of France, more precisely in the province of Brittany, and stayed that way during my run as a *demoiselle*. After that I married and became Countess Victoire de La Villirouët. Then the French Revolution happened and I became a simple *citoyenne*. You might not have heard about me."

"Not really."

"Can you believe that I didn't get my own Wikipedia entry until the 2020s?"

"So, what should I call you?"

"Right now?"

"You said there isn't a right now."

"Just testing. You are getting it. Just call me *Madame* de La Villirouët. That's what almost everybody else at the End of Time calls me, with certain variations."

"Everybody else?"

"Well, we have a staff at the End of Time that administers time justice. Each one has a function. I'm The Lawyer, picked out from my time to assist defendants like you. The purpose of this meeting is to prepare your defense for trial, which will happen sometime before the End of Time, since nothing is conclusive in here. And yes, I know that it might be surprising for some to have a female lawyer, but I can ensure you that I can do the job."

"Ah, there are lots of women attorneys in my time, I think at least... I don't know lots of people."

"There weren't any women lawyers in France until the early 20th century, but I was a pioneer of sorts, as I stepped up to defend my husband who was going to be sentenced to death by those dirty neojacobins from the Directory. It seems that my defense was so poignant, fierce and uncalculating about how rigged the whole process was that, even if I never actually worked as an attorney, The Manager of the time court's algorithm determined that I was the best suited person in the whole of Human history to work here as The Lawyer."

"You must be proud."

"Of my husband's defense? Not really. I wish I had let the Directory guillotine his penis. When I turned 40 he poisoned me because he wanted to marry someone younger and I would be dead if I hadn't been invited to join the Time Court."

"Sorry to hear that."

"Oh, I should be the one who says sorry here. I get carried away when I talk about that bastard, quite unfitting for a woman of my rank. Are you getting more used to your surroundings, *mon chéri*? Maybe a little more pastry would help."

"You did mention that you have chocolate chip cookies, right?"

The Lawyer frowned.

***

Gabe followed The Lawyer out of the illuminated circle in which the desk was located and they dove into the vast darkness of the surrounding area. Gabe couldn't be sure if their walk in the absolute obscurity took them one second or one century. When they emerged from the tenebrous path, Gabe found himself inside a larger lit circle containing three small desks with chairs standing next to a cupboard. Except for the absence of walls it looked like an office's break room. A somewhat androgynous man with East-Asian features was operating a kettle. He wore a brown silk cover robe with vast, broad sleeves that seemed to have three layers of fabric underneath it. His hair was long and tucked between two small, delicate slabs of jade.

"Good End, de La Villirouët *Xiǎojiě,*" said the man with the most courteous of smiles, as he poured boiling water in a delicate porcelain cup of tea.

"Good End, *Monsieur* Lun. Would you by any chance know where Dottie keeps those gastronomic aberrations she likes to bake?"

"Second shelf on the right. I thought you hated American cookies."

"My new client thinks that my *kouign-amman* aren't appetizing enough"

"I wouldn't insult your Lawyer's baking," said the man to Gabe.

"I didn't mean to insult, it's just that I really like cookies."

"Who doesn't?" shrugged the man as he snatched one of the chocolate chip cookies from a tray that The Lawyer took from the cupboard.

"By the way, this is Cao Lun," informed The Lawyer, with a frown, as she saw Gabe eagerly help himself to three cookies. "He is The Prosecutor."

"It is my honor and the mandate bestowed upon me by Heaven to advocate against all selfish personal interests you may nurture within your soul," said The Prosecutor.

"Thanks?"

"He does look like his brother, doesn't he?" pondered The Prosecutor, as he attentively studied Gabe's face.

"I don't have a brother," said Gabe.

"I still haven't addressed that topic with him," clarified The Lawyer.

"Well, isn't that auspicious?" said Cao Lun with a cryptic smile before picking up the tray with cookies and disappearing into the surrounding shadows.

"Sorry about that, *Monsieur* Chagas, I think he took all the cookies that were left. If you want I can ask Dottie to bake more—"

"Do I have a brother?"

The Lawyer sighed. "I was planning to break the truth to you in small doses, bit by bit, but of course that eunuch couldn't lose a chance to make things harder for me. Anyway, first things first. Your biological mother is a woman named Maria Aparecida Silva Chagas, she—"

"—she was born in Brazil, came to LA in her twenties, where I was born."

The Lawyer stared at Gabe in absolute astonishment. "How do you know that, *Monsieur*?"

"Duh, she was my mother. Raised me until I was nine when she disappeared in the Terminal 2 accident."

"Fascinating... What else do you know about her?"

"She had a weird accent that she never managed to lose, she liked to jog and her favorite entree was *galinhada*. I never got a chance to learn how to cook it, but she taught me how to make some snacks called *biscoitos de queijo*. I had a bucket of them with me, but I guess it stayed at Terminal 2—"

"Okay, I see now... You were supposed to have forgotten about her, *Monsieur*."

"How could a son forget his mother?"

"I guess you can't. That may be due to the fact that despite being born in Los Angeles, you were conceived in Brazil."

"I... I don't know much about Brazil other than my mom was from there. She didn't talk much about her past."

"Yes, she was born in the city of Goiânia, on May 5th 1993."

"Wait, that was like… forever ago! Are you saying that my mom and Santos Dumont were living in the same time?"

"Alberto Santos Dumont was born in the 19th century, don't they teach general History to the kids in your time?"

"I—"

"My apologies. I forgot that you were raised in the United States. Did you know that in American schools they used to teach that some Wright guys invented the airplane instead of Santos Dumont?"

"I never heard of any Wright."

"Good! Because they were total crooks who launched an object from a freaking catapult without any witnesses and then claimed that they had invented an airplane, even if nobody ever managed to reproduce their pathetic attempt at aviation."

"Everybody knows that 14-Bis, Santos Dumont's airplane, did fly. It was the first human aircraft."

"Of course, he made it fly in glorious Paris during its apogee no less, not in some boondocks in the mountains of North Carolina were only peasants and raccoons could see. For almost two centuries Americans believed that those Wright crooks and not Santos Dumont were the fathers of aviation. I mean, Americans have a history of falling for local swindlers, like in the Edison and Tesla controversy or—"

"Like when that used cars salesman was elected president in the 2010s?"

"I can see that there's room for improvement in the teaching of History throughout the United States even after our planet joined the Galactic Confederation. The man you are referring to was no car salesman. Using a real estate business as a front, he made his money on a ring of brothels around the globe specializing in Eastern-European prostitutes."

"Okay, can we please go back to my mom?"

"Of course, my apologies for the detour."

"So, my mom was a time traveler?"

"Our job here is to hunt and deter time travelers before they can perform quantum damage, *Monsieur*. Their actions in the timeframes other than their original ones send rifts of gravitational anomalies across space. These anomalies will expand and cause the Slow Yet Irreversible Great Collapse of All the Universe except for what remains in this small pocket of quantum uncertainty where we are. By extracting those time travelers we are delaying the collapse. You wouldn't believe the number of persons that feel entitled to change History according to their views by assassinating someone in the past. I mean, I do wish I could strangle baby Robespierre with my bare hands, stick his tiny little body onto a pole that I would festively parade across France, from Brest to Strasbourg, but I know I shouldn't, I don't have the nerve of those pretentious douchebags!"

"So... my mom was some sort of... criminal?"

"Oh, no, no, *mon chéri*. She wasn't. For starters she was a woman and, for some mysterious reason, all the travelers that deign to try to change History without caring for the consequences of their actions are men thinking with their penises instead of their brains. Second, she traveled to the future, which is much less common and also less harmful for the fabric of time than traveling to the past. And third, it was an accident, as she was dragged by a quantum hole opened by an illegal device that, for reasons we are still investigating, landed in early 21st century Los Angeles."

Gabe nodded with a frown. This was a lot to take in, and The Lawyer seemed to empathize with his confusion.

"It's very complex, *Monsieur,* but the outcome is simple: she was deported to her time of origin after the recollections from her life in the late 21st century were removed from her mind. Some input was added to her memory with a few necessary adjustments that minimized the rifts in time, as she was supposed to have two children, not one."

"So, about that...You mentioned that I have a brother—"

"That'd be me," said a baritone voice from within the darkness around them.

A tall man clad in a heavy cybernetic armor emerged from the tenebrous edges of the End of Time. He held a helmet in his hands, staring at Gabe intently. His light-brown skin, jet-black hair, high cheekbones and narrow, dark eyes were similar to

Gabe's, although they didn't have any of his meekness. Those eyes were fierce and hard, giving him quite a scary look when combined with his advantaged height and the long scar running down from the left side of his forehead and ending next to his chin. He could have been handsome if he weren't so intimidating.

"As an attorney I am entitled to a certain privilege of privacy with my client in this joint!" protested The Lawyer.

"It's not like everybody else isn't listening to this conversation from the shadows." said The Bailiff, addressing The Lawyer although his angry gaze was locked on Gabe.

"Well, then I'd like to politely ask all the other clowns to step out of their tiny little car!" snapped The Lawyer.

The Prosecutor and The Secretary suddenly stepped into the break room, as if summoned.

"Well, let me do some introductions. You already met Cao Lun, The Prosecutor, and then the bimbo over there is Dottie Salvatti, who is The Secretary of the Time Court and the person who bakes those terrible cookies. And finally, there's your brother Miguel Chagas, who is The Bailiff in charge of security and operations. The Judge is probably looking at us from the shadows."

"You know how much she values a big entrance," pointed out The Secretary.

"Also, standing out by their absence is The Manager. We don't know their name or gender or species."

"The Judge told me that she saw The Manager once," said Dottie.

"Yes, she told me that The Manager is a Bald Soprano but it turned out The Judge was just mocking me with some obscure 20th Century literary reference. Anyway, The Manager runs the Court and conveys his orders through Dottie. Any questions?"

Gabe had his mouth agape and didn't answer immediately.

"Still there, *Monsieur* Chagas?"

"I...I...I have a brother."

"Yes, imbecile, you do," hissed The Bailiff. "One that had to fend for himself in the early 21st Century while you got to live in affluence just when all the social problems of Earth were resolved."

"I was raised in a foster home after mom disappeared... wait a minute! Are you the one who kidnapped her?"

"Boohoo! A foster home? How sad! I was deported from the US and struggled in the streets of São Paulo until the retiring Bailiff found me and trained me to replace him! And yes, I did extract mom and deported her."

"Boys, calm down," said Dottie. "If you want, I can bake some cookies."

"Nobody wants your stupid cookies, Dottie," spat The Lawyer.

"I do," said The Prosecutor.

"I... could have some more too," admitted Gabe.

"Very well, why don't you all sit down and let me do my magic," said The Secretary as she put on an apron and picked the ingredients out of the cupboard while all the others reluctantly sat down.

An awkward silence took place as The Secretary started preparing the dough. Gabe had so many questions for his brother, but clearly it was not a good idea to poke someone so angry at him who was also twice his size. The silence was crushing him, though, so he decided to say something.

"Hmm... Dottie, right?" asked Gabe, tentatively.

"That's correct, sweetie," said The Secretary.

"So, who are... I mean... what's your story?"

"Well, I was the Secretary for a Don in Chicago in the 1950s. Turned out the Don thought I knew too much and gave me cement shoes. My bones would be in the bottom of Lake Michigan by now if it wasn't for The Manager who sent over your brother's predecessor to rescue me and work here."

"What's the point of telling him all that, we are just going to brainwash him anyway after the judge comes to a verdict," protested The Bailiff.

"Well, it's always interesting to have someone different to talk to, don't you think so?" considered The Secretary.

"Not when that person is a whiny punk ass little bitch," spat The Bailiff.

"Language, Miguel! There are ladies in the room," urged The Secretary.

"A true lady doesn't need to let people know that she's a lady," poked The Lawyer.

"Oh, *Madame*, quoting Thatcher again?" said The Secretary as her smile turned acerbic and more toothy. "We all know how you value your conservative values, no need to show off for your equally non-unionized colleagues."

"First, it's Baroness Thatcher for you, peasant. Second, conservatism is a very honest ideology for honest persons who never worked for criminals."

"And yet you are defending criminals from time justice."

"I defend the ones I believe to be innocent."

"Nobody is innocent in the Time Court," said The Prosecutor ominously.

"Cookies are ready!" chanted Dottie as she removed a batch of baked cookies from the oven.

"That was fast, weren't you just mixing the dough?" pointed out a perplexed Gabe.

"Time flows differently here, honey. Didn't your attorney explain that to you? That was supposed to be her job."

"Don't tell me how to do my job, *Mademoiselle* Salvatti, "said The Lawyer, hissing the first S of her surname. "I could do that if all of you weren't snooping around. And you know what? Let's go to a more secluded time, *Monsieur* Chagas."

And with that The Lawyer stood up and trotted into the darkness. Gabe looked sheepishly at the other remaining members of the Time Court, but only found compassion in The Secretary's eyes as she gave him a warm cookie.

"You should follow her, sugar," advised The Secretary. "She's a pain in the ass, but she's on your side."

"How can I be sure?" asked Gabe while eating the cookie.

"Because you wouldn't be given the opportunity of a trial if it wasn't for her intervention."

TERMINAL 3

Gabe nodded and began walking in the same direction as The Lawyer. This time his transit through the darkness at the End of Time wasn't as smooth as before. He felt like he was pushing himself first through water, then through jell-o, then through sand, then through gravel. And then he emerged somewhere totally different, somewhere he felt the blood flowing in his veins, air entering his lungs and making his cells age slowly but inexorably.

DAY
10,074,121,928,764

GABE COULDN'T SEE ANYTHING, AND soon he realized why: his eyes were closed. When he opened them he found himself in the middle of what seemed to be a nightclub. At first the place appeared to have an intimate vibe as it had only a dozen tables and chairs turned toward a small stage with a bar on one side. That is if the decor wasn't so garish, with carpet and wallpaper printed with a black-and-white zebra pattern, as well as a huge chandelier suspended from the ceiling that seemed to be made out of gold plated tusks and horns. Behind the stage, a huge logo featuring a rhinoceros with its body painted in zebra pattern displayed what seemed to be the name of that venue: "Zerhinbra". Gabe found The Lawyer at the bar, pouring rose wine to the brim of a very large glass.

"Anything for you, *mon chéri?*"

"I...I don't think I should drink when I'm about to have my trial."

"As you wish, in my case, don't worry, I'm French, I can hold my wine. I don't always have the opportunity to leave the End of Time, and, when I do, I like to indulge myself a little bit since alcohol needs time to kick in."

"So, are we going to the court from here?"

"This is the court."

"I've never been to a tribunal, always imagined them to be more somber."

"Well, The Judge has the privilege to pick the décor. She shaped the courtroom like the night club where she used to perform."

"I thought you needed a law degree to be a judge."

"Not a judge of drag queen contests in 25th Century Uganda, when the city of Kampala was Humanity's hub for those seeking sexual and moral indulgence, like Las Vegas and Macao in the second half of the 20th century and Vatican City during the 14th and 23rd centuries. I take that being a judge in those contests required a very sharp sense of discernment and fairness, otherwise the algorithm that The Manager runs wouldn't have selected her as The Judge."

"Glad to be back on Earth, I guess."

"Oh, this isn't Earth, *chéri*. We are billions of years after your time, the Sun already consumed our homeworld, and then consumed itself. It would have become a brown dwarf by now if all of that quadrant wasn't destroyed by the rampant expansion of the entropic anomalies that started in that Spaceport Terminal of yours. The Manager decided to place the court just a few million years before the End of Time, in order to minimize ripples that our frequent travels to this space might cause."

"So, if this isn't Earth—"

"The time court was carved inside a meteor that is headed to a black hole. Very discreet, even if there aren't many sentient creatures left in the Universe at this point that could have a chance to find us in here. Any other questions?"

"I have millions of questions."

The Lawyer sighed and took a long sip that emptied her glass. She then poured herself another glass of wine.

"Let's focus your curiosity on the trial, *chéri*. Knowing too much about the cogs that make the Time Court work won't help your case and, anyway, those memories are supposed to be erased."

"Okay, I guess…"

"So, during the trial, you can either demand to stay in the time from when The Bailiff extracted you, or go back to nineteen years after you were conceived by parents that irrefutably belonged to that stretch of time. We have a case at the Time Court because, technically, you belong to both, which has no precedent. The task at hand here is to decide what you want so we can make our arguments and try to persuade The Judge that this is the best outcome in order to preserve the normalcy of time."

"So my wishes don't matter?"

"Not to The Judge and certainly not to The Prosecutor. They do matter to me, though. I… was very touched by your situation. When I had to be my husband's attorney in the Directory's court, he was being sued for violating the terms of his exile to England. He wanted more than anything to go back home, to Brittany. That's why I picked your case, *Monsieur*. You deserve to be home, whenever home is for you."

"I… I'm not sure where… I belong, to be honest."

"Not where, when. If you would allow me an educated guess… during your whole life after your mother was extracted, you always wondered what happened to her. Wouldn't you want to go back to your mother?"

"I want her back in my time. To the life we had."

"That's not possible, *Monsieur*. The Time Court decided that she doesn't belong there. I am afraid we can't appeal this decision."

"I think I'm beginning to understand."

"So, what will be your plea to The Judge?" asked The Lawyer as she opened another bottle of rose wine and filled her glass a third time.

***

Gabe found it uncanny that, as soon as The Lawyer and he had decided on their course of action for the trial, the other members of the Time Court started showing up at the Zerhinbra. The Secretary was the first one, carrying a very large suitcase. She took a typewriter as well as some paper files from inside it, and placed her material on a table at the left side of the stage. After that she went straight to the bar and announced to no one in particular that she was preparing herself a Shirley Temple since it wouldn't be appropriate to be inebriated during the trial. The Lawyer showed her the bird and whispered to Gabe that The Secretary's Shirley Temples were the kind they served at the US Embassy in Ghana's secret orgies rather than the ones she had the time she was shooting Annie. Gabe nodded politely, pretending to understand the references. After that The Prosecutor arrived with an armful of parchments and sat at a table at the right side of the room. When his eyes met Gabe's, The Prosecutor said that he might be wondering why he used parchments, and his reason was that the old ways were the best. The Secretary put a cup of tea on The Prosecutor's table and, on her way back to her station she stopped by Gabe and whispered that The Prosecutor apparently invented paper during his life in Ancient China and was prouder of that accomplishment than any other of his achievements as an Imperial Prosecutor. Gabe was looking forward to hearing more random gossip that he lacked the context and knowledge to understand, however the lights began to dim leaving only the stage illuminated, where The Bailiff, clad in his armor but not his helmet, appeared and announced: "The Time Court is now in session, all rise for the Honorable Judge Goldina Blingoldz."

Gabe stood up as the stage went dark for a few seconds then lit again, this time with a frenetic flickering of red and purple stroboscopic lights accompanied by the beats of electronic music that sounded ethereal and very unfamiliar to Gabe's ears. The Bailiff was no longer on the stage, being replaced by a very large disco ball that was spinning midair, without any sort of visible support. The floating disco ball suddenly shattered in millions of shiny shards and Gabe yelped, thinking that he would be lacerated by them. It turned out that the shards were only extremely realistic holograms, and as soon they vanished a drag queen, dressed in a cascade of golden puffy fabric and featuring a very large golden crown on her head appeared on the stage. She was The Judge and she was ready to roll. The Judge started dancing in the rhythm of the music, as holograms of African Savannah animals paraded in the air. The spectacle was so overwhelming to the senses that Gabe instinctively took a step back, just to realize that his back bounced against something hard and big. When Gabe turned back he realized that The Bailiff towered behind him with a sullen, vigilant face.

After fifteen minutes of frenzied dance moves, the rumbling music stopped and The Judge, now completely drenched in sweat, ended her routine with a gracious bow to the audience. The stroboscopic lights and holograms were replaced by normal lighting while The Secretary put a standing microphone on the stage and gave The Judge a very large glass containing an indigo colored drink topped by an assortment of tropical fruits and cocktail umbrellas.

"Good whatever-the-time-is-now everybody! How are you doing?!" asked The Judge, still puffing with exhaustion from her performance. The Prosecutor was the only one who answered with the unexpected high-pitched shriek of a loyal fan girl.

"Oh, there we have Cao Lun, The Prosecutor or, as I prefer to call him, Lunny."

"I didn't sign for that," mock-protested The Prosecutor.

"Oh, you did, I have the *paperwork.*"

The Prosecutor laughed his ass off while The Secretary and The Bailiff rolled their eyes.

"We also have here our handsome, hunky Bailiff, Miguel Chagas, a man who always wears a frown. The stage is available in case you decide to strip off the frown, and maybe also the armor, m'kay?"

Again, The Prosecutor was the only one laughing. The Bailiff's armor creaked a little, hinting at the contorting muscles underneath it. Gabe was really confused by the terms of the joke, but before he could pursue his reasoning, The Judge already moved to her next target: "I'd like also to introduce my amazing assistant, Miss Dorothy Salvatti! Dottie, I love your shoes, gal! I told you that Chanel is way more your style than Cemex."

Gabe let out a chuckle as he got that one. Cemex was a brand of cement. He soon regretted his attitude, though, as The Secretary's constant smile turned a bit chilly for a few seconds.

"We have with us our dear *Madame* Vicky over there, whom is in some level of alcohol induced coma, as usual."

Gabe turned his attention to The Lawyer next to him just to realize that she had passed out with her head on the table.

"And last but not least, we have here our panicking defendant *du jour*, Mr. Gabriel Chagas! Any words you'd like to share with us before we start, cutie?"

"Ah… how can I defend myself without a lawyer?"

"Oh, I'm sure she is with you in *spirit*. Or, in her case, d'Anjou rose wine."

Again, The Prosecutor was the only one to laugh.

"But… I don't know how to proceed, like, I barely understand your jokes."

"Oh, someone doesn't like my jokes, huh?"

"No, I don't mean—"

"You can go to the ticket booth if you want a refund. Oh, wait, there isn't one!"

"It's more like I didn't get—"

"They are contextual jokes with comedy rules from a different time than yours," explained The Judge with a frown. There was nothing she hated more than to explain a joke. "Or maybe you are just humorless, so thanks for ruining the vibe! Let's start, then. Lunny, what is the Prosecution's take on the case?"

"The Prosecution supports the thesis that the Defendant should be kept in his current time."

"Wait, that's what I want too!" said Gabe.

"Excellent, where's my gavel, Dottie?"

"But with a caveat," added The Prosecutor. "It seems that the defendant was immune to the quantum induced oblivion after his mother was deported, probably due to his unusual double-status. Hence, he must be manually stripped of all memories of his mother and must believe that his upbringing took place completely within the Los Angeles Metropolitan Foster Care System."

"No biggie, right Gabbie?" asked The Judge, who after looking everywhere on the stage had just found her golden gavel under the folds of the red velvet curtains behind her.

"Yes, biggie! I don't want to forget my mother! Plus, what do you mean by manual stripping of my memories?"

"Oh, just a neat lobotomy," said The Judge. "But, don't worry, there's a robot in a clinic in Nairobi that does it. You can't believe how advanced neurology is in the 25th Century. I saw with my very own eyes that robot lobotomizing someone and after the guy was like, wow, practically the same, except he couldn't talk, hear or see."

"I... I don't want that!" said a shocked Gabe. "I want to actually ask you people to return my mom to my time!"

"Oh my sweet savannah baby Jeebus in a cradle of cheetah fur!" yelled The distraught Judge. "I was hoping we could all call it quits early and drink till we pass out before going back to the End of Time!"

"Sorry, but I'm not okay with what the Prosecutor wants," said Gabe firmly.

"Fine, you get the Super Deluxe Trial package with all the arguments, counterarguments and bling. Lunny, make your point!"

"Thank you, your honor. I studied carefully The Defendant's background. He was born in the stretch of time he was extracted from by The Bailiff, so in a quantum perspective I believe that sending him back to the time of his conception plus nineteen years would have more entropic dangers of creating time ripples. But the fact is that in his current time, those ripples are already present, more precisely at the area known as Terminal 2 of the Kornelia Kardashian-Bezos Spaceport—"

"Which were created by the impulsive behavior of this court's Bailiff!" said The Lawyer suddenly as she jolted her head up from the table.

"Hi Vicky, welcome back," greeted The Judge. "Lunny is making his opening statement, don't interrupt him."

"As I was saying, the entropic ripples couldn't be caused solely by the extraction of Maria Aparecida Silva Chagas from a time she didn't belong to. It was caused by the years she lived there. The Manager's choice of that time and place for the extraction operation was not casual. An illegal time travel quantum hole had been opened accidentally on those same premises in the early 21st century, when the Spaceport was known as an airport called LAX. The Manager decided to concentrate the crack in the fabric of time in that very location which was already damaged. We all trust his, her or their judgment. But we also know that it's the consensus among physicists that the Slow Ye Irreversible Great Collapse of the Universe started in that very locale during The Defendant's first day of work as a Terminal 3 security guard. They call it 'Day 1', and it's our duty to cram the most days possible between 'Day 1' and the day when time ends, as nothing is more valuable than time, not even life, as existence can transcend life through the monuments, relics and recordings of a fallen civilization or an individual who passed away, but no past can be registered without time. And, to achieve such a goal, we must tackle the direct cause of the anomaly, which, in my opinion, is not Gabriel Chagas, but his mother's incursion in a time where she didn't belong. She must be erased in every possible way from his time. And yet, she still remains in his memory, and that will only change with our intervention."

The Prosecutor sat down as the Court had recoiled in a grave mood. After a few long seconds of pondering The Prosecutor's argument, The Judge finally spoke: "The Defendant can have the floor now."

"Thank you, your honor," said The Lawyer, as she stood up in a shaky, tipsy movement. "I do respect The Prosecutor's concern, although they reflect his recurring bias toward the wellbeing of the system over individuals. We are talking here about a man who prosecuted innocent women in order to perpetuate the power of a cruel Empress only because he believed that this was the Mandate of Heaven!"

"Objection! The Lawyer is using *argumentum ad hominem*," interrupted the Prosecutor.

"Sustained," ruled the Judge. "Please, you're classier than that, Vicky. And we've been there before, you are Western, Lunny is Eastern, yadayada slightly racist!"

"Very well, my point is diametrically opposite to the one conveyed by The Prosecutor, but not because of his background... only. He also fails to point out in his reasoning that if the entropic ripples in space and time are, yes, associated to the presence of an individual that doesn't belong, that is not only just circumstantial evidence, but also a distraction from inquiring on the consequences of that individual's absence. Some physicists argue that the first signs of weakening of the fabric of time, back in 2020 caused by *Madame* Chagas' involuntary travel to the end of the 21st century had little to do with the portal itself, and more to do with her absence from her time of origin."

"And to which she was sent back," pointed out the Prosecutor.

"Indeed, but again, Cida Chagas is not the defendant here. And yet, sending her back to the early 21st century didn't solve the ripples. The Prosecution claims that the presence of Gabriel Chagas close to their place of extraction actually seemed to trigger an expansion of those entropic anomalies. We tend to forget that Gabriel Chagas also traveled to the future with his mother, or at least the blueprint of him, as an embryo in her womb. Can the Prosecution see all the subtleties he is ignoring for the sake of accepting an oversimplified understanding of time and space? It is the Defense's perspective that the anomalies were caused by this very Time Court's intervention and the best way to deal with them is to acknowledge that The Defendant is an individual who happens to belong to two timelines, not one. His dual chronologic status is not an aberration to be corrected or restrained. Instead, he is special, with a potential for unique achievements that have never been accessible to normal sentient lifeforms."

The Lawyer sat down, and again, the Judge and also the Prosecutor were mulling over her words for a moment.

"I...we didn't talk about any of that," whispered Gabriel to The Lawyer.

"Relax, I know what I'm doing," she reassured him, although the wafts of alcohol from her breath weren't very reassuring.

"Would The Prosecutor like to deliver his rebuttal?" asked The Judge.

"I'd like to interrogate the defendant first." said The Prosecutor.

"Very well, the floor is yours."

The Prosecutor approached the table where Gabe and The Lawyer were seated. He scanned Gabe attentively, his eyes no longer carrying any of the affability that Gabe had seen at the End of Time. This man was his enemy and his gaze was cold as a blizzard.

"Mr. Chagas, as I mentioned before, I analyzed your social background in depth. It seems that, since you were very little, you had a hard time socializing. Like when you were in kindergarten, and your fellow students covered you in glue and modeling clay, and your teacher had to call an amber alert when they couldn't find you after 12 hours of searching."

"I was a small kid, small kids tend to get bullied, right?"

"By every other kid?"

"I... I don't know."

"You don't know, because you never managed to build a bond with anyone else in your time, except your mother. And that only bond was gone when she was deported and you were sent to foster care, where you never managed to have any sort of healthy relationship with the other youngsters."

"That's not true, I kinda connected with the other foster kids."

"All your connections involved a bruising fist connecting with your body through a punch."

"I... I was a small teen."

"The Defendant consistently failed during his young life to connect meaningfully and positively with other individuals. We all know that this pattern of a bullied person happens when certain people don't fit within the social standards of a certain time and space, and in Chagas' case, that was quite literal. When emancipated he worked as a janitor, without any coworkers, only operating non-sentient robots. Would you say that in your new workplace at Terminal 3 things changed, Mr. Chagas?"

Gabe almost answered yes, that it did. However, he just remembered Chip saying that he didn't belong at Terminal 3. And oafish Mason bullying him and awakening a sense of aggression that he did not know that he had. And Sue's indifference to his incursion into Terminal 2 and its dangers. And Brenda... well... She had fired him. He tried to think that maybe Wendy liked him, but based on his last encounter with José he might not be a good influence on her mental health.

"Things stayed the same... in a different way," mumbled Gabe.

"As we know, your time as a security guard was short-lived as you were fired after five days when your boss discovered that you are the son of Mrs. Chagas."

"Wait, that's why Brenda fired me? I didn't—"

"And then you returned to your former job, where you are going to do a terrible thing."

"What terrible thing?" asked a puzzled Gabe.

"Don't worry about that, *chéri.*" said The Lawyer.

"No, I want to know! Like, you guys are going to erase my memory anyway, right?"

"Demand granted," said The Judge. "Dottie, can you please read the records for the expected end of The Defendant's life."

The Secretary picked a sheet of paper from her files and blushed. "Should I really?"

"Go for it! I can take it!" encouraged Gabe.

"Well, you will work for a few months in your former position as a janitor. Then one night you'll feel really bored and will find out that you can easily reprogram the scrubbing robots to perform other tasks and—"

"I will lead a robotic take over of the world because I will have too much rage and angst in my heart and a need to seek a violent outlet for a lingering lack of fulfillment? Like, I will target bullies with my mechanic army, but then realize that, by doing so, I'm becoming a bully, then, with that realization, I will tragically—"

"No, sugar. You'll fail to gauge the intensity of the repurposed robot, and you'll die of machinery-induced erotic asphyxiation."

Gabe looked very disappointed.

"I rest my case," said The Prosecutor, returning to his table.

"The Defense can now have the floor," announced The Judge.

"Let's follow up on that. Can you read us from your files what happens if Gabe is not fired, Dottie?" asked The Lawyer.

"Objection! We should not use data from alternative timelines that were changed due to our intervention!" said The Prosecutor.

"Sustained," ruled The Judge. "Firing Gabby was his boss' call, Vicky, we shouldn't intervene."

"We will need to intervene, as Brenda Roy now remembers *Madame* Chagas as well. Isn't that the whole point of The Prosecution?"

The Prosecutor was rendered speechless and started to nervously go through his parchments.

"Oh, looks like someone didn't think everything through," teased The Lawyer. "I rest my case."

"I can deal with Brenda," offered the Bailiff.

"Please stick to your station, Miguel," warned The Judge. "When the trial is going on, your job is only to be a formidable standing hunk and make sure that The Defendant abides by the rules of this court."

"I'd like to call a witness," said The Prosecutor suddenly.

"You didn't file for witnesses at the start of the process, Lunny," said the Judge. "We can't just stop now and make Miguel go all the way back or forward in time to fetch whoever you want for a witness."

"Oh, my witness is right here. His name is...Miguel Chagas."

"I...well, that's unusual, and I'm sure Vicky is gonna object."

"I'm fine with that," shrugged The Lawyer.

"Really?" asked the perplexed Judge. "Very well, Lunny, there isn't any kind of logistical obstacle to your demand. Granted. Miguel, could you please bring all that manbeefiness forward?"

Miguel approached the stage as The Prosecutor stood next to him.

"Mr. Chagas, please tell us more about your ideas related to the Brenda Roy problem."

"Objection, your honor!" said The Lawyer. "The defendant's name is Gabriel, not Brenda."

"Your honor, the mandate of this Tribunal is to minimize entropic ripples in the fabric of time," argued The Prosecutor. "We may not be talking directly about The Defendant but we are addressing the anomalies related to him."

"Overruled," determined The Judge. "Answer Lunny's question, Miguel."

"Usually when a time traveler tries to alter the course of time I, as Bailiff, can eliminate the traveler, as this action sends less ripples than whatever they had planned if they succeeded."

"I see," interrupted The Lawyer. "Why have a Time Court at all if The Bailiff can just go on a killing spree?"

"Vicky, now you are just being a bitch," said The Judge. "Let that big chunk of dream meat finish."

"I'm talking precisely about cases where elimination is the best but also the only solution," continued The Bailiff. "The fact is that Brenda Roy never developed any major bond after Cida Chagas' extraction. She has been living an existence of self-loathing, bitterness and xenophobic hate that filled the gap in the memory caused by mom's… I mean… Mrs. Chagas' deportation. She can only go downhill from there now that she has her memories back and a hate that is now out of place. Eliminating Brenda Roy would be the right call for a greater good and a merciful act towards her."

"What the hell is your problem!!!" interrupted Gabe. "I think mom and Brenda were in love, why do you hate us all so much?!"

"Again, Defense, come on. Speak during your time. This is getting old," said The frustrated Judge.

"Actually I'm done with my questions to the Witness," informed The Prosecutor.

"Very well, The Lawyer can have the floor."

The Lawyer studied The Bailiff's face for a moment, and then she spoke: "Mr. Chagas, why do you hate your brother so much?"

"I just hate him," nervously shrugged The Bailiff. "Look at him, he's a shrimp and his face is so punchable."

"I get that a lot," said Gabe.

"The Prosecution suggested earlier that Gabriel Chagas is a bully-magnet, which hints at the fact that he is an individual in the wrong space and/or wrong time," explained The Lawyer. "But The Bailiff himself, who was born only nine years before The Defendant was conceived, seems to display those instinctive bullying inclinations toward Gabriel Chagas. Such antipathy toward The Defendant was clearly nurtured during The Bailiff's stay at the End of Time, no less, where time can be neither wrong nor right for anything."

"I mean… it's not out of nowhere…" The Bailiff tried to clarify. "When Mom was trying to immigrate to the United States in 2020, the customs officer guessed that she was pregnant with that shrimp. She was sent to the X-Ray room where they'd scan mules carrying drugs because X-Rays are very dangerous for fetuses, so she'd need to either lie about her pregnancy or admit it and get deported. That country was going through a xenophobic, almost fascist time, and those officers would not allow her to deliver a baby in American territory because by their laws in those days would give American citizenship to Gabriel. If it was not for him, mom and I would never have landed in that lost and found room and… I would never have touched the time traveling device. I would never have been deported to fucked up Brazil and lived as a stray kid until you guys took me in."

"You seem to think about that a lot," pointed out The Lawyer.

"I think about that all the freaking time, Ma'am!"

"When we live in the End of Time for so long it feels like we have all the time in the world and, at the same time, none," said The Lawyer. "The result in our mind is hard to describe, but I'd say that we have lots of time to think through things, but also, because there's no time, those thoughts happen in what feels like a loop. That's true for me and the grudge I have towards my husband. And I'm sure it is also true for The Bailiff, to whom I'd like to ask a final question. If it was entirely up to you, what course of action would you want for Gabriel Chagas' case?"

"I wouldn't deport him. I would keep him at the End of Time as my mentee who will eventually be my replacement as The Bailiff of the Time Court when my body grows too old and frail for the job."

"You are way too young to be awarded a mentee. Remember, you only age during the time you spend on your missions or in this very Court."

"I'm aware of that. He could be a second bailiff then."

"There's no need for a second of anything in the Time Court, as we have all the time we need to go through every case, one by one."

"Yes, but—"

"And I'm sure you are aware that there is also a very good reason for that beyond the fact that we have all the time in the universe for our activities. The number one grants quantum uncertainty, as when and where cannot be determined by a particle alone, you'd need two or more for that. Such a thing would ruin the principle that boosts our operations of collection and deportation without causing entropic ripples in time."

"That's what I want, not what we need," clarified The Bailiff.

"Fair enough, but that entails another question. Do you want someone you just described as a shrimp with a punchable face as a permanent fixture by your side?"

"So he could have a taste of what I need to endure!"

"So you could suffer together."

"Exactly!"

"And stick together through thick and thin."

"Nothing is thick in this job."

"I'd like to ask The Defendant to stand up and hug The Bailiff."

"Objection!" said The Prosecutor. "Now The Lawyer is just resorting to gimmicks to detour us from what matters."

"Overruled," said The Judge. "I kinda wanna see where she's going with this. Better be good, Vicky!"

"I don't want to be hugged by that shrimp," protested The Bailiff with a surly tone.

"Very well, you are authorized to push him away, or even punch your brother," said the Lawyer.

"What the hell are you doing?" whispered Gabe to The Lawyer. "That guy is huge, one punch and I'm dead."

The Lawyer shushed Gabe discreetly and refocused her attention on The Bailiff: "But you need to assert your non-compliance physically. Those are very fair terms. I'm sure this court will accept my experiment."

"I have no qualms with that," said The Judge.

"Very well, so please, hug your brother, *Monsieur* Chagas," said The Lawyer to Gabe.

Gabe gulped as he slowly approached the sullen, towering figure of his brother. There was nothing particularly huggable in that cold-looking, armor-clad, enormous body, and he flinched for a moment when he saw the huge gauntlets that dangled from his thick arms coiling, readying themselves to punch. And yet, Gabe found the strength to overcome his fear when he suddenly remembered that this man could be a stranger, but that stranger was a brother he never knew existed. A brother who took his mother from him and resented him for doing the same. Gabe wasn't sure if he resented Miguel at all, but he realized that musing on his feelings toward him took away the fear his brother inspired and replaced it with something else: curiosity. About having a brother. About having a family again. About maybe being loved by someone else other than his mother for the first time in his whole life. That wasn't mere curiosity: it was thirst, and that thirst was so unyielding that the eventual punch of that huge metallic fist that would certainly shatter every bone in whatever part of his body it landed seemed like a small price to pay to discover what a hug would give.

"Are you going to hug him or not?" urged The Judge, impatiently.

Gabe just realized that he had been standing still for almost a minute just inches away of his brother, his arms open, just like he did in his first day of work when he tried to hug Chip. And then, suddenly, Gabe was jolted by the impact of two heavy, metallic gauntlets against his back. They dragged his scrawny body toward Miguel's much larger one. Miguel hugged Gabe in a somewhat brutish way, as he discovered that he, too, could be tender, or at least try to be. The Court remained in silence for about a minute, observing respectfully the two brothers bonding for the first time.

Only when Miguel opened his arms and faced Gabe in absolute confusion over his feelings toward his little brother, did The Lawyer dare to speak: "I could always smell a rat when it concerns the bullying theory that The Prosecutor shared with us, which is part of this Court's handbook. Yes, one who is bullied might be out of place or time. But, through this perspective, we give too much leeway to bullies, assuming they are those unchanging brutes that are just a social or cultural given in a determined locale at a certain historical moment. We tend to associate a historic age less to its struggle and more to that age's main bully, like Robespierre for the French Revolution, Adolf Hitler for World War 2 and Tiffany Trump for the One Day War. But the fact is that we don't think enough about how the bullies who are not magnified by history and society beyond redemption can change and what can make them change. A bull-inducing individual with a great deal of resilience and grit may change things as long as they are not totally powerless. We all know that the staff of Terminal 3 is a nest of bullies, and still The Defendant in a matter of five days did fit in there, against all odds, contradicting his life experience and his status as a bully-magnet. We should allow Gabriel Chagas to go back to his time with his memories and tell Brenda Roy the truth about his mother, who happens to be the woman she loves. In exchange, we'd ask both of them for their discretion in discussing our activities. I rest my case."

"Thank you, Vicky, that was brilliant, and very touching," said the Judge. "I shall—"

Suddenly a brown envelope materialized in the air and landed on The Secretary's desk. She opened it under the puzzled gaze of The Judge. After scanning the sheet of paper that was inside with somber eyes, she handed it to The Judge, who read it with similar sobriety.

"It's from The Manager," informed The Judge. "He, she or they are demanding the Trial of Brenda Roy and ordering The Bailiff to fetch her as soon as I deliver my verdict on Gabriel Chagas', which I am ready to do now."

"All stand!" said The Bailiff.

All those in the room stood up except The Secretary, who kept diligently typing.

"I was very touched by The Lawyer's perspective," said The Judge. "But with all due respect, those are very fringe theories and they don't answer the greatest issue at hand, which is the expansion of the ripples in time and the entropic anomalies in Los Angeles Spaceport and how the defendant's very first day of work in that place turned out to be what is seen by the consensus of most physicists as the first day of the Slow Yet Irreversible Great Collapse of the Universe, also known as SYIGCU. It is too much of a coincidence to not see a connection, which is supported by the bullying theory that Vicky decried. I'm afraid that we have no other choice but to stand on the side of caution. Gabriel Chagas, you are sentenced to the brainwashing of your memories of your mother and to be sent back to your current timeline. The sentence will begin after The Bailiff fetches the robotic neurosurgeon in 25th century Nairobi."

The Judge slammed her golden gavel on the table as both The Bailiff and Gabe stared at her wide-mouthed.

"Ah, another thing, Miguel," said The Judge. "After you are done with the brainwashing of your brother, can you please return the defendant and possibly use the same trip to extract Brenda Roy? I mean, not telling you how to do your job, of course. Which makes me think, don't return the neurosurgeon robot after it lobotomizes Gabriel, we might still need it for Brenda when—"

"Your honor, I'd like to request a temporary suspension of Mr. Chagas' brainwashing," demanded The Lawyer.

"On what terms, Vicky?"

"He will be The Defense's witness in Brenda Roy's trial."

"Whatever. Granted. That's less work for The Bailiff. Now, this Court is adjourned because my head is spinning and I desperately need another drink."

"On it!" said The Secretary, as she darted to the bar.

Gabe noticed that his brother was no longer in the room and all the other members of the court were now assembled around the bar, including The Lawyer. He was not sure what was going on, but if they thought that he would just stand still while they messed with his brain, they assumed wrong. Gabe ran to the golden front gates of the Zerhinbra, opened them, and sneaked out.

***

Gabe found himself in a dim corridor illuminated only by the lights coming from the now open gates of the Zerhinbra. All he could see were the rocky, irregular walls of the tunnel he found himself in that ended a few yards ahead, at another double-door. Gabe ran to those and opened them. As he stepped through, Gabe found himself in a room made entirely of glass, at the center of which stood six orange androgen humanoids that looked perfectly alike. Gabe recognized them as natives of Beta Torin, as there were a few of them living in Pomona. And by the frowns on their faces it seemed that he was interrupting something important.

"I'm so sorry, just passing by!" awkwardly apologized Gabe as he rushed toward another gate at the opposite side of the room from where he had entered.

He opened it and found himself in another rocky tunnel, like the first except for the fact that this one led to what looked like a perfectly circular, doorless blue hole. As soon as Gabe crossed that blue hole, though, he realized that he had dove into an aquatic environment. He swum through the transparent waters of a hall of sapphire and emerald columns in which six creatures that seemed to be tritons from a fairy-tale book looked at him in confusion. He couldn't remember seeing that species of alien before in real life, but he did notice that the largest triton propelled himself toward him with a trident in hand and gritted fangs. Gabe swum to another hole and landed in another corridor, gasping for air. This time there was another doorless hole at the opposite end of the tunnel that seemed more like a cave entrance, from which came a flickering, mellow orange light. Instead of just barreling in, he decided to skulk his way into the next chamber.

Gabe found himself in a dry room with rocky walls that wasn't much different from the corridor he had just crossed, except that it was a vast chamber instead of a narrow tunnel. The only fixture of that space was a bonfire (or bonefire, since the fuel was bones instead of wood), at which five large, lupine aliens seemed to be roasting a sixth. Gabe recognized these creatures, they were from Gamma Malvina 6, just like his landlord in Pomona. And like his landlord used to do on the day Gabe was due to pay his rent, they turned their muzzles full of sharp teeth to him after they caught his scent in the air. They all charged toward Gabe, their upper paws filled with sharp claws ready to shred him, although he was more worried about the inconspicuous rear claw that they were surely readying to deliver a death blow as soon as Gabe entered their range. He witnessed his landlord using his rear claw once. Not pretty. And then, suddenly, Miguel landed between Gabe and the lupine aliens.

"I apologize for the inconvenience," said The Bailiff. "But this is a key witness who ran away from the Human Division's Time Court. I'm afraid you guys can't eat this one."

"Then get him out of here!" growled one of the Gamma-Malvinese.

"I actually would like to ask you guys if... I could borrow the room."

"Can't you see we are busy?"

"I see that there is no trial going on right now, maybe you could take your... Defendant to the End of Time and... finish him there?"

The Gamma-Malvinese howled in anger but complied with Miguel's demand. They begrudgingly picked up the carcass that was being roasted in the pit and suddenly disappeared.

"Do they... eat their time travelers?" asked an astonished Gabe.

"Different species, different justice systems. Only a few rules are universal, like prioritizing an upcoming or ongoing trial over one that is completed, and that's why they had no choice but to yield their court room for the time being."

Gabe nodded and for a moment an awkward silence fell.

"So, are you going to take me to the Human Courtroom now?" asked Gabe.

"No need to rush, The Lawyer is talking to Brenda Roy, explaining to her what is at stake, like she did for you," informed The Bailiff, as he stared at the fire.

Again, an awkward silence. Gabe felt like he had to say something, but he was afraid of mentioning anything that could make his brother angry with him again. He wanted to know the brother he never knew he had, but he was also aware that this brother, until a few minutes ago, hated him with all the fire in his soul. He also pondered the point of trying to get to know his brother if he would soon be forced to forget him anyway.

It was The Bailiff who broke the silence, as he sat by the bonfire, still averting his eyes from Gabe. "Did you... ever go camping with mom?"

"That's... a question I was not expecting."

"You don't need to answer."

"No, never camped either with mom or without her. She used to say that nature had lots of itsy-bitsy critters that she was afraid of."

"After mom left and I was alone on the streets of São Paulo, sometimes I would land in a shelter for children called *Fundação CASA*. Food was gross, most of the employees there had either thrown in the towel and were there only for the paycheck or were some sort of crook. Given a chance, I would always run away from that fucked up place. But they had one thing I liked. A TV in the mess room, and sometimes they showed American movies... I really liked them, even before mom disappeared in LA. And sometimes those movies showed those families that were all cranky with each other, but also happy despite their problems and flaws. In some of those movies the family would go camping, usually in places full of pine trees that are not very common in Brazil. I... I always wondered how it'd be to go camping with... mom."

"I can relate... I mean, with the shelter thing, not the camping."

"You had three meals a day, education and nobody trying to stab you unless you stabbed them first."

"Well, it could be rough sometimes. I was the smallest kid in foster care. I would look up at the big guys... like you. And hope they didn't kick my ass."

The Bailiff stood in pensive silence for a moment. "I did... protect some of the small kids. But you can only go so far as the big kid when you... don't belong."

"I tried to belong... I mean... The girls were more receptive."

"My shelter was only for boys. You are lucky."

"Girls are the meanest, especially when they are bigger than you."

"Come on!" chuckled The Bailiff in disbelief.

"Bich Nguyen."

"What?"

"She was… a girl… that I tried to bond with… you know, as you said, to belong. I… I lost my virginity to her."

"Tell me more."

"It's embarrassing."

The Bailiff shrugged. He picked a long bone from the ground and started poking the bonfire, stirring the flames. Gabe sighed and sat down next to his brother. The fact is that he had never shared what he was going to share with anyone, and he ached to talk about it with someone for so long, someone he could trust or would at least listen: "I was Bich Nguyen's eighth… you know."

"How do you know that?"

Gabe pulled up his left sleeve and showed a series of small, aligned scars on his forearm that looked like polka dots. There were nineteen in all. Gabe pointed at one of them that was particularly faint: "See, that's me. Bich pushed the cigarette less forcefully when she recorded me because she said that it was a pity fuck."

"Why would she do that to you?"

"To keep track of how many—"

"Why would you let her do that?!"

"She was bigger than me and… I wanted to bond with someone. I wonder how she managed to keep track of her fucks after she was transferred to another foster home."

"Then things improved, right?"

"Well, there was this girl, Trix. She was different, but not by much. I mean… Let me show you my right arm and you are gonna understand—"

"No need," said a shocked Miguel.

"I thought you were aware of all that. Don't you guys in the Time Court know everything about everyone?"

"No, just what The Manager wants us to know for the cases and operations."

"Who's The Manager?"

"I don't know, nobody knows. He, She or They send envelopes through Dottie with information and commands."

"Is The Manager a god or something?"

"I don't think so. God is supposed to listen to your prayers and shit. There is no such thing in this universe."

"I don't really believe in gods or anything like that... but mom did. She used to pray to angels and to Our Lady of Aparecida, her patron."

"Yes, she does."

"What do you mean by she does?"

"Forget that."

"Do you... still see her?"

"Not the way you think."

"Can I see her?"

"Trust me, it's not worth it."

"You are hiding something."

"Come on, we are having a good time here. Don't fuck this up."

"I'm ready to go back to the Court, Miguel."

"Please, Gabriel..."

"Then tell me everything."

"When I said that The Manager doesn't listen to prayers... this isn't a prayer... do you know what I mean?"

"So fuck The Manager, whoever that person is, for snooping on our conversation. Tell me—"

For Gabe it was just a blink. In one moment he was by a bonfire in a cave with his brother. In the next, he was back at the Zerhinbra, with the exact same people as before plus Brenda. The Bailiff, standing by the stage, sullenly asked for all to stand, as the court was back in session.

***

Brenda and Gabe looked at each other in surprise. Even though Gabe knew that Brenda was coming, and Brenda was briefed by The Lawyer about Gabe's presence, seeing each other in these odd surroundings and even odder circumstances was still hard to process. Now there was a mutual awareness of the bond between them.

Their steady eye contact was only interrupted by The Judge's voice: "Excuse me, the awesomeness is in this direction!"

Brenda and Gabe turned their attention to The Judge, who interrupted her dance routine as neither Brenda nor Gabe were paying attention to it.

"Sorry, Ma'am, would you mind…starting over?" suggested Gabe.

"I do mind and it's your loss. I never perform the same choreography twice. Anywho, let's get this going, I'm grumpy now. Lunny?"

The Prosecutor opened one of his parchments: "Brenda Roy was extracted from July 9th, 2119 under the assumption that she acquired knowledge of the existence of this court, through the activation of the double-take principle as she met the Bailiff for a second time. Such awareness might be a risk to the fabric of time. The Prosecution's plea is for the erasure of every one of Brenda Roy's recollections, starting at the encounter with the Bailiff on July 7th, 2119. The consequences of such intervention would be supported logically in her home time as clinical amnesia, as the Defendant was struck in the head by a flying baton just after meeting The Bailiff a second time, which leads us to believe that we will foresee minimal rippling effects."

"If you erase my memories I'm gonna erase your balls," hissed Brenda.

"Ha! Lunny doesn't have balls!" teased The Judge.

"It was… a common procedure during the Han Dynasty for men to ascend socially without representing a threat to the throne," clarified The Prosecutor defensively.

"Didn't you have to drink poison because you became a threat to the throne at the end?" asked The Lawyer.

"Can we just focus on the case at hand?" begged The now unnerved Prosecutor.

"Very well, what does The Defense have to plead, besides threatening The Prosecutor's non-existent balls?" asked The Judge.

"The Defense disagrees with The Prosecution. *Madame* Roy has suffered enough at the hands of this court by having now access to the painful recollections of the extraction of *Madame* Chagas, but also of the love she had toward her. Submitting her to the same procedure all over again would not only lack humanity, but would likely fail as the whole process is based on the uniqueness of a certain experience that is quantically erased from someone's memory through the principle of uncertainty."

"We could just use the same lobotomy robot we are going to employ for Gabriel Chagas," argued The Prosecutor.

"I thought this Court was averse to trial and error," counter-argued The Lawyer with a sassy smirk. "It was that very aversion that lead The Judge to side with The Prosecution in Gabriel Chagas' case."

"First, there's no trial-and-error with the lobotomy robot. I have seen it doing its magic, it's a sure shot," asserted The Judge. "But also, you are right that, indeed, there are no precedents for Brenda Roy's situation."

"Not in the Human Time Court," pointed out The Prosecutor. "But I heard that in the Gamma-Malvinese Time Court they roast and eat a Defendant that is deemed too dangerous for the time fabric's cohesion."

"What the fuck, Lunny!" reacted The Judge.

"She threatened to cut off my balls!"

"And you have no balls to cut off, just like The Defendant's memories are now beyond the Event Horizon of Oblivion," said The Judge. "I'm willing to listen to Vicky's proposal."

"My proposal is still the same. Let *Madame* Roy and *Monsieur* Chagas return to their times, with their memories intact, as long as they solemnly swear to keep secrecy about the existence of this Court and to, eventually, collaborate with our operations. We could use allies and informants posted right by the original point of the Slow Yet Irreversible Collapse of the Universe."

"You mean the SYICU?" asked The Judge.

"Nobody uses that acronym but you, your honor," said The Lawyer.

"And wouldn't you like to start using it?"

"No, your honor."

TERMINAL 3

"Why not? Don't you like the ring of it?"

"Your honor—"

"I must object to the defense's preposterous suggestion," interrupted The Prosecutor. "Both Brenda Roy and Gabriel Chagas still nurture feelings towards someone situated in their past. Those feelings will just send entropic ripples through time, worsening the anomalies at Terminal 2. Since you don't agree to follow the totally reasonable procedure adopted by the Gamma-Malvinese Time Court, let's keep both Defendants at the End of Time with us, as guests, and replace them at their original times by emotionless robots that will pretend to have a premature death."

"I... I must say that Lunny's solution is a bit harsh, but, as usual, minimizes entropic risks," said The Judge.

"What if we can give both the Defendants a sense of closure on their feelings about *Madame* Chagas?" suggested The Lawyer. "We could let them see Cida in her normal life, back in the time we sent her."

"I'd give anything to see her again, even if it's just once more," mumbled Brenda, touched by this prospect.

"How can we know if that won't make things worse?" questioned The Prosecutor.

"Our Bailiff will supervise the experience and measure the quantum impact *in loco*."

"Can you extract them if things turn dangerous or Cida Chagas starts remembering what she had forgotten?" asked The Judge to The Bailiff.

"Yes, Ma'am. I can with only a few adjustments to my equipment."

"Very well, you have my leave to follow the Defense's suggestion then," announced The Judge while slamming her gavel on the table.

Gabe was ready to ask a question, but then the sight of the Zerhinbra crumbled in front of his eyes, as he felt what was now to him the familiar pull of time travel.

DAY -32,752

GABE FOUND HIMSELF IN A DIM, DUSTY room in which different kinds of objects were hoarded on rows after rows of shelves. He noticed a confused Brenda and The stoic Bailiff standing next to him.

"Where are we?" asked Brenda.

"June 12th, 2029," answered The Bailiff.

"Where and when are not different for the Time Court folks because time and space are kinda the same," clarified Gabe with a smartassy smile, as if he didn't learn that only a few hours ago.

"Cool, what's this fucking place?" asked Brenda.

"This is Los Angeles Airport's lost and found room," answered the Bailiff as he scanned the shelves. "There's an incipient entropic anomaly here that will evolve to be a time-gravity hazard on these same grounds, when it becomes, in a few decades, the complex of buildings you know as Terminal 2."

"Is… Cida in here?" Brenda asked with a gulp.

"No," answered The Bailiff as he passed to Brenda a few pieces of clothing he found on the shelves. "It's just safer to timetravel to this spot since the time fabric here is already weakened. After you have dressed in these outfits of the current time, I will teleport us to mom... I mean, Cida Chagas' current location."

"I'm not wearing this colorful shit," protested Brenda, as she examined the pink polo shirt, khaki shorts and purple rubbery shoes of a brand named Crocs which The Bailiff had given her.

"This is what... women like... you wear in this historic time wear. You want to blend," said The Bailiff.

Miguel pressed a button on his gauntlet and suddenly his armor crumbled, becoming a small cube on the ground. He then picked some battle fatigues and boots from the shelf and began to dress.

"What about me?" asked Gabe.

He soon got his answer, as the small cube on the ground suddenly leaped toward him and glued against his chest. The cube then started unraveling itself, expanding while covering Gabe's body in his brother's armor duly adjusted to his smaller size.

"You are going to be me," instructed The Bailiff, eliciting a frown from Gabe that lead him to clarify his statement. "Mom... I mean, Ms. Chagas had one child before she traveled to the future, when she delivered a second one. He was raised in that future and happens to be you, Gabriel. Even with her recollections of her... offspring erased, there was a gap in her life with the potential to send entropic ripples in this time. To minimize it, after she was deported she was given manufactured memories of raising her only child after immigrating to the United States. That child happens to be the one who traveled with her from Brazil: me. My cover identity in this time is of a sergeant serving in the US army who comes by every two years or so to visit his mother."

"That's not very often."

"She... asks way too many questions when I'm around and that makes my EHS go nuts."

"EHS?"

The Bailiff points at a device that looks like a wristwatch attached to Gabe's gauntlet and then removes it, attaching it to his own wrist.

"An Event Horizon Scanner. It's going to tell you if you are affecting the fabric of time in a negative way. To keep it short, if it remains green, it's fine. If it turns yellow, be cautious. If it turns orange, get the hell out. If it turns red, you screwed up."

"Mom will find weird that her son is suddenly one foot shorter."

"Oh, almost forgot," said The Bailiff, touching a button at the shoulder pad of Gabe's armor.

Gabe suddenly felt a jolt followed by an extreme feeling of dizziness. One moment he was looking up at his towering brother, and the next... he was looking down at... himself?

"Am I... tall?" said Gabe, but with his brother's mouth and in his baritone voice.

"You are me," explained Miguel in Gabe's body. "For now."

Gabe looked at his brother's hands, now under his control, with fascination.

"Man, look at the size of these fists! I bet I could crush a skull with them."

"Don't get used to them."

***

As soon as Gabe was done with the power trip triggered by borrowing his brother's body, the threesome teleported to a different location. They were now in a parking lot by the intersection of two large avenues that, according to signs, were named Slauson and Normandie, in what looked like the commercial hub of a somewhat decayed neighborhood. It was composed mostly of auto parts stores, Hispanic evangelical churches, Caribbean and Central-American diners and S&M themed sex shops. Both Gabe and Brenda started coughing as the air was saturated with smoke, despite the fact that the sun was shining in a blue sky.

"What the hell is wrong with the air here?" asked Brenda, as she started coughing.

"Welcome to LA during the last years before combustion-based automobiles were outlawed," shrugged The Bailiff. "Anyway, mom is over there."

Miguel pointed at a small shop with cracked purple walls on which a sign read:

XOXOTÔMICA
Lesbian Haircuts and Subaru Licensed Mechanic

"Stay in character, Gabriel. Your name is Miguel, you just came back from the frontlines of war in India."

"What about me?" asked Brenda.

"You are just a client, I guess. Just don't act too weird. If you need me I'll be at that *Pupuseria* next door," said The Bailiff as he walked to a small Central-American restaurant, leaving Brenda and Gabe behind.

"I can't believe that… she is there. Just there," said Gabe.

"I know," said Brenda.

"I mean… we are so close now, and—"

Brenda didn't listen to what Gabe had to say, she just darted into the shop.

The Xoxotômica was as Spartan inside as it was outside. A repurposed warehouse where half of it was a hair salon, with a single barber chair facing a mirror and a couch on the side, and the other half a mechanic workshop. The only two ornamental objects in the establishment were a rainbow flag dangling from the ceiling and a small shrine in a discreet corner that displayed an Our Lady Aparecida statue. A sturdy dark-skinned woman wearing grease-stained dungarees was hammering a car engine in the auto shop side of the Xoxotômica. She turned her attention to Brenda and nodded curtly to her: "Car fix or hair fix?"

"I… I don't have a car."

"Cida! You got a costumer!"

Cida walked from the back of the warehouse. She was older than Brenda remembered, having aged seemingly at the same rate she had. Cida was still the tiny, slender doe of her memories, but was now clad in baggy cargo pants and a loose polo shirt instead of the tight spandex she preferred when jogging along the Santa Monica boardwalk. Her hair wasn't as long as Brenda remembered, but short with puffy waves on the top of her head.

"Hey, you're a first timer, right?" asked Cida.

"I… Well… I—"

"I mean, never saw you before. Did anyone refer you to us?"

"No, I was just passing by and… I saw the sign."

"Cool. I have a customer coming in thirty minutes. I hate to rush things, but if you want a cut it needs to happen now."

Brenda started cackling. It was hilarious to hear Cida rushing things for a change. When Brenda stopped laughing she noticed Cida staring at her with a frown.

"Oh, sorry, I was just… finding it funny that this is both a hairdresser and a car mechanic place."

"Yeah, Zenika and I couldn't agree on what we wanted, so we decided to go for both, and it kinda paid off. Lots of lesbians drive Subarus. I mean, you must drive one too, right?"

"Yeah, of course," bluffed Brenda.

"The name was a bit of an issue though. Zenika had an idea and I wanted something in my mother language, so… we went with Zenika's idea, but in Portuguese."

"This is married life for you, in case you are wondering," stated Zenika from her corner and without taking her eyes from the task at hand but clearly paying attention to the conversation.

"What does the word *Xoxotômica* mean?" asked Brenda.

Cida blushed, embarrassed, and Brenda almost cried. Now, that's the somewhat insecure Cida she used to know.

"Probably something dirty," said Brenda, as Cida nodded in confirmation.

"Oh my god! *Anjinho*!" suddenly screamed Cida, as she noticed Gabe standing at the doorway. She rushed toward him, hugging him and giving it her best to shower him with little pecks on his cheeks as she stood on the tip of her toes.

"I thought you were in India? What happened? Oh my god, are you injured? They discharged you because you are injured? Are you—"

"I'm fine, mom. Just... visiting," said Gabe, his face flooding with tears.

"Why are you crying then?"

"I'm happy to see you, dammit."

"You never cry."

"Those are tears of joy, mom."

"Seriously, you *never* cry, Miguel. What's wrong?"

Brenda cleared her throat loudly as she glanced at the EHS on Gabe's wrist. When he looked down, he realized that the display transitioned from green to yellow. "I think... it's an allergy."

Cida seemed to accept that explanation as the display returned to green.

"I... I can see that you have a client now. I will just sit down while you take care of her."

"Thanks, *Meu Anjinho*," said Cida, as she turned the barber chair toward Brenda, who flinched for a moment, but decided to sit down. "Why don't you go give a hand to Zenika?"

"I don't think I know how to fix cars, mom."

For a moment Gabe was afraid that the display would turn yellow again, but it remained green. Cida started combing Brenda's hair and massaging her scalp. Brenda was in absolute bliss.

"Well, it's an opportunity to learn. You could make a living at that instead of going out there fighting those damn wars," said Cida, as she grabbed a pair of scissors and got to work on Brenda's hair.

"That's what he chose for himself, Cida," said Zenika.

"I mean... not only because it's dangerous," pondered Cida. "I bet it's lonely too."

"I have... companions on... the frontlines, mom."

"I bet they are a bunch of bullies," said Cida.

"They can be difficult, but they have lots of potential. They kinda accepted me. And they don't seem to be the kind that accepts anyone easily, so, for the first time in my whole life I think I'm finally doing something right, mom. And I'm following your footsteps!"

"Are you a hairdresser?" asked a puzzled Cida.

"I... yeah... kinda... I... shave... them. Yeah, I shave the soldier's heads."

"Well, I'm flattered," said Cida.

"He's a good kid, Cida," mumbled Brenda.

"Sorry?"

"I mean, he looks like a good kid, Ma'am."

"Oh, I'm proud of him, all right."

"Your family is lovely," said Brenda, teary.

"I just wish my son would visit more often and my wife would learn how to use the carpet mat instead of staining the kitchen floor with grease every time she waltzes in there for a snack."

"I told you that I'm gonna clean that shit. Relax," said Zenika in her usual phlegmatic tone from her side of the shop.

"I'm a little jealous," admitted Brenda.

"I'm sure you will find someone soon. I mean, you are quite handsome, I must say."

"Thank you."

"And... I'm done with you," announced Cida, as she picked up a small mirror to show Brenda the back of her head. They had very similar haircuts now, very short on the side and puffy on the top.

"I like this... lesbian haircut," said Brenda.

"Well, the old cut you had was quite lesbian too."

"Yours is lesbianer."

"Glad you liked. That will be sixty dollars."

"I... Sure, let me find my holotablet... I mean..."

"That'd be on the house," interfered Gabe, attracting a confused expression from Cida. "You know, because... that woman is actually my friend!" The EHS turned yellow, which didn't go unnoticed by Gabe. "I mean... actually... mom, she's my fiancée!"

Cida dropped the scissors in absolute shock, and the EHS turned orange. Brenda noticed that and immediately stood up. "That's a lot for your mom to take in, *honey*! Why don't we both go next door to fetch some pupusas and let her digest the news!"

Gabe tried to say something but Brenda quickly dragged him to the door while a widemouthed Cida stared at them.

Brenda punched Gabe hard in the face as soon as they stepped on the sidewalk. "What the hell is wrong with you?"

"I'm not a smart person and I panicked! I'm sorry, Brenda!" said Gabe, as he rubbed his now bruised face. He deserved that one, and, for some reason, he felt it was overdue. "If you want to go back there, I'm sure we can work out something—"

"Nevermind," said a suddenly morose Brenda. "Honestly, I've seen enough. I'm... just glad that she's happy."

"I... I don't know what to say, Brenda. When I was a kid my mom told me that she was seeing someone, but never whom. What I can say is that, when she started working at Terminal 2 as a security guard, she was happier than usual."

"Happier than we saw in there?"

"As happy, I guess. The point is, I... I'm sure that you could have made her happy."

"That's quite neat of you to say that, rookie, but you know that's not true. I would not have forgotten her if it was meant to be."

"It was not your choice, remember? They talked at the trial about the quantum thingy and—"

"You never forgot her."

Gabe realized there was nothing he could say to cheer his boss up, but at least she seemed resigned to her situation. For the first time since Gabe met Brenda, her tense stance was mostly gone. She was still an intimidating woman that would make anyone step lightly around her. But the aggressiveness for the sake of aggression seemed to be gone.

"It must be harder for you, rookie," Brenda said, while fighting back tears.

"Well, I had a last chance to see my mother, the one I thought was dead. I should be grateful."

"You know, if you ever need to… talk about stuff… that you would only say to Cida… you can always swing by my office after your shift is over."

"Does… that mean that I'm not fired?"

"That's right. But don't screw up, no special privileges just because you are the son of the first and only woman I truly loved."

"Talking to you after my work shift will be a special privilege, and I'm grateful for that."

"Don't make me revoke it."

***

Gabe and Brenda entered the pupuseria. It was a small, quaint restaurant with walls that featured both Meso-American indigenous artworks and posters of masked, muscular wrestlers. The only patrons seemed to be Miguel and… to their surprise, The Judge, in her same golden outfit from the court.

"What happened to my face?" asked The Bailiff with a frown when he noticed the red mark where Brenda had punched Gabe.

"Oh, I… tripped, no biggie. What are you doing here, ah… your honor?" asked Gabe.

"I do love some pupusas," said The Judge, as a plump woman who appeared to be of native Central-American ancestry, clad in a floral dress and apron, approached the table and put down a tray filled with an array of the steamy, stuffed flatbread snacks.

"*Gracias, Tía Yéssica!*" said The Judge, to whom the woman gave a curt nod before walking away.

"So you guys can just travel through time to eat whatever you want?" wondered Gabe.

"Sure, as long as the EHS doesn't turn yellow," shrugged The Judge. "The owner of this place thinks that we are hipsters or a film crew from WeHo or whatever makes sense in her head, hence no ripples. And… talking about ripples, how do you feel after having met Cida?"

"I feel better," admitted Brenda frankly. "I... I'm glad that she is happy."

"Very well, what about you, Gabe?"

Gabe gulped.

"Not so good, huh?" assumed The Judge.

"I... I'm not sure."

"There is an alternative for you that we haven't mentioned. For the sake of time fabric, Cida Chagas can only have one child and... you can take Miguel's place in here, as long as you are satisfied with seeing her every two years or so, until she passes away."

Gabe thought for a moment while studying his brother's face: "Do I get to keep this body?"

"Yes, but—"

"I'm joking. Mom has only one son now, and his name is Miguel. It's his turn with her."

"You don't need to do that for me, Gabriel," said The Bailiff. "Really... It's okay."

"I'm doing it because it's the right thing to do. I don't want to shred the universe or something crazy like that. But when Mom is gone, and you still feel like being part of a family, you know *when* to find me, Miguel."

EPILOGUE

Personal Diary of The Bailiff of the Time Court, Human Division (excerpts).

June 12th 2029, 36,127 days before the beginning of the Slow yet Irreversible Great Collapse of the Universe.

After Gabriel and Brenda left, I had to stay away for a few months until I could go back to LA in order to clarify to mom that, no, I wasn't engaged to a butch lesbian. It was just a joke. And then I had to explain why I was joking, since, according to mom, I am humorless. That normalized the entropic rippling that Gabriel started, but made mom start acting a bit obsessed about my status as a single man. I'm not great at storytelling. I can only dodge her pestering questions on why I don't meet anyone with silence, and it doesn't take long for the EHS to turn yellow and me having to say that the colonel had called and wanted me somewhere different. With the siege of Hyderabad having ended the Indian War, that excuse is not very solid, I will need to stay away from home longer than I wish for the sake of the time fabric stability.

May 5ᵗʰ 2032, 35,069 days before the beginning of the Slow yet Irreversible Great Collapse of the Universe

I decided to make a surprise appearance for mom's birthday after not seeing her in the last three years (for her, for me it was just a few minutes). It always makes me a little uncomfortable to see that she has new white strands of hair and wrinkles on her face that weren't there just a moment ago. I wish she would do like 50% of the women and 90% of the men of her time in LA and get some plastic surgery done. But she's not the vain kind, nor does she need that to be happy. I guess I'm just being selfish and need to remember that I'm here for her, not the opposite.

Mom has a happy life without me, but it feels good to see that my presence on her birthday makes her even happier, at least for a moment. There were a great number of her clients at the party. Zenika apparently had just launched her own Subaru dealership and mom had the opportunity to expand, by opening other lesbian hairstyling salons. Based on the party's attendance, it was quite clear that Xoxotômica was becoming a staple in Los Angeles' edgier lesbian scene.

The EHS only turned yellow when she started asking me if I was seeing someone. When I answered no, she called for one of the few guys at the party, a big burly bear of a man named Hamish. Mom whispered that he was single and pointed out that my face had just turned red like a beet. The EHS turned orange and I said that I had to take a call from the colonel. I sneaked away from her place, and programmed an email to be sent to her tomorrow, telling her that the colonel had called, as things were getting worse in Burundi.

TERMINAL 3

December 25th 2038, 32,646 days before the beginning of the Slow yet Irreversible Great Collapse of the Universe.

I showed up for Christmas many years later with an apology as a gift for mom. She said that I was an adult and she was happy that I had things going on in my life, *"whatever these things may be"*. This time, however, I tried to anticipate the cause of the upcoming ripples that forced me to leave in a rush on the last two visits, and brought Cao Lun with me, claiming that he was my husband. At first mom and Zenika were exhilarated, but it turned out that Cao is a petty bastard who refused to eat any of the Christmas food except for the cookies. Zenika had to call a Jewish friend of hers to ask about which Chinese restaurants would deliver on Christmas.

But the fact is that mom is smart and sensitive – I took the first quality and Gabe took the second. She could see the total lack of chemistry between Cao and I. When the EHS turned orange I knocked out Cao with a punch while nobody was looking and told them that he was having an allergic reaction and had to take him to the closest hospital. After I left I sent her a text message saying that the colonel had summoned me for the raging war in New Zealand.

February 21st 2044, 30,529 days before the beginning of the Slow yet Irreversible Great Collapse of the Universe.

I showed up to mom's place and, for the first time, it felt somber. The happiness had left her. She had stopped working since Zenika passed away a few months before my arrival. I apologized for not making it to the funeral and she said that she wasn't expecting me anyway. I wanted to tell her that she should try to meet somebody. But there was no point in doing so. She was about to rest, after all. The EHS stayed eerily stable and green for the whole day, maybe because we didn't talk much, just watched some movies together, or maybe due to the fact that there wasn't much to affect in the fabric of time, considering the event that was about to happen in just a few hours. All of the movies we watched were old action popcorn flicks from the early 21st century featuring an actor named Chris Pratt. She claimed that he was my favorite actor, which is ridiculous and I have no idea why she'd think that. I'm an action movie buff, but my favorite action movie star is, by far, Gaten Matarazzo.

With the EHS stable I dared to tell her that I was going to spend the night at her place instead of inventing another war mission I had to attend at the last minute. I thought she would be comforted by that, but instead she seemed puzzled yet also determined. These are two stances that usually don't go together, and I had to double-check my EHS to be sure that such emotional paradox was not affecting the fabric of time.

"I guess I will finally be able to ask questions that you've been dodging for years," she said while standing up.

"Mom—"

"It's lots of questions. Need some coffee," mom said, heading to the kitchen. I rushed in front of her, blocking her way.

"Let me guess, Miguel. Do you need to go to Whateverland all of sudden?" she asked with a frown, "Because you always need to leave when that watch of yours turns yellow or orange, don't think I haven't noticed. But, right now, it's still green."

"I… I will answer all your questions, mom. Please, go back to the living room and let me make your coffee."

She flinched for a moment, but soon sighed and sat back on the couch, yielding to my small attempt at kindness. I wish I could have been more present. I wish I could have been there for her in person, as a real son would be. This is my last chance to make up for all the lost time and be a son to my mother. I was determined to make her coffee and answer whatever the questions she might have, even if the stupid EHS turned red.

After a few minutes I brought her a mug of strong coffee. I wasn't sure if that's how she liked it and was relieved when she nodded in approval after the first sip.

"I started remembering that day when you came back from India," she said, pensive. "You showed up with that woman who you claimed was your fiancée."

"Yeah, I told you—"

"—I know. Her name is Brenda Roy. She was the first woman I dated. And loved. Before you deported me."

"You shouldn't know any of that. How can you remember?"

"Little by little. The first thing I remember was when I landed in the future. How the simple fact that I was human was sufficient to get the documents I needed and a place to live, no questions asked. Such a difference from these times of hate we are going through right now in our world, huh? Then I had my baby... his name is Gabriel. He's your baby brother, Miguel. But you probably know all that."

"Mom—"

"I never said anything. I didn't want to forget again, whatever spell or trick you played on me was wearing off and I was afraid that you would force those memories out of me again."

"Why are you telling me all this now?"

"Your watch is green. You are not nervous, nor ready to run away. You are just sad. Who are you, Miguel? Really?"

"I'm the Bailiff of the Time Court, Human Division. They are the ones who ordered you to be deported back to early 21st century. This is when you belong, mom."

"Some people say that I don't belong in LA or the USA. That I should go back to Brazil."

"That's not the same. Time and space are different. I mean... actually they are the same, but—"

"You and your brother are so different...he got my size... and his father's...brain. You got your father's size...and heart."

That stung like hell. But I sucked it up. I deserved that. I deserved worse than that.

"There's nothing I can do to change that, right?" she asked. "To get him back?"

"Gabriel is fine, he's just...in the future."

Tears were cascading down her face.

"Do you want me to bring you a tissue, mom?"

"I just want my sons. My two sons."

I thought about telling her the truth about that strange day when she met Brenda and Gabriel disguised as me, but that would probably just make it worse, as it would lead to another truth that she should not be aware of: fetching Gabriel would be as easy as fetching a tissue. I could only resort to a lie: "I can't."

"I see. That Time Court of yours decided that I can't be a mother to both of my sons, but do they also say that you can't be a brother to Gabriel?"

"It's not like that, mom."

"Did they?"

"No, but—"

"Promise me that you are gonna love Gabriel, Miguel. Promise me that you are gonna protect him. He's not… as strong or… as smart as you. He… he needs to be protected."

"Mom—"

"Promise…me…" she said with her now slurred speech.

Mom was trying to speak, but the words would not come. The cup of coffee slipped from her hands and crashed to the ground. Her head leaned back and she soon fell asleep, succumbing to the tranquilizers I slipped into her coffee. She was too good to be awake and aware of what was coming next.

I carried her to her bed and I kissed her good night. After that, I looked for her wallet and snatched her driver's license. I was going to need that in a bit.

February 22nd 2044, 30,528 days before the beginning of the Slow yet Irreversible Great Collapse of the Universe.

When I arrived in LA at the intersection of Normandie and Slauson the area was quite foggy. This was unusual, since most automobiles were, in this time, electric, although that made no difference since there was no traffic. Only dust, fumes and flames. Eight hours had passed since I had dropped mom in bed and three since the nuke was dropped in LA, starting and also ending the last recorded war between human factions. I could see through the smoke that the downtown skyscrapers were relatively intact, having withstood the blast. The old, small concrete buildings from South LA…not so much. Mom's house didn't stand a chance, it was all debris.

TERMINAL 3

Except by the dancing flames, the city stood still as I went through the rubble and started digging until I found her. Or what remained of her. At first I tried not to stare at the body for too long. This is not how I wanted to remember her. But I couldn't avoid the sight of her, my eyes locked on her corpse and lingered there, despite my efforts to look away. I need to forget the sight of her like this. I need to lose the memory of this exact instant. How can a son forget his mother? I can't. I must only remember the beauty and love of my mother. No. Our mother.

"I promise," I muttered, not to the corpse, but to the woman who was alive just a few hours ago. The one I can't and won't forget.

And then I put her driver's license inside her charred fist.

July, 11ᵗʰ 2119, 7 days after the beginning of the Slow yet Irreversible Great Collapse of the Universe.

Crossing back from the End of Time to Terminal 2 was easier by now. Teleporting from Terminal 2 to Sierra Madre Memorial Cemetery not so much. Not because of any sort of entropic hazard, as teleportation, unlike time travel, was a relatively simple process. What made this particular teleportation hard was that I knew what I was going to find at my destination.

The first thing I noticed after completing the teleportation process was the imposing wall of mountains across the Northern horizon. With the exception of those mountains, the area around me was relatively flat, filled with hundreds of thousands of granite, knee-high poles aligned endlessly on the grounds of what used to be one of the smallest suburbs of Los Angeles. The former city of Sierra Madre was named after the avenue that crossed it, not the mountains that overlooked the area. Those mountains were called San Gabriel. They were beautiful, but they were also the doom of this suburb and all the others that sprouted up within the shadows of those mountains, Altadena, Hastings Ranch and Monrovia, to name a few. The edges of the basin were the areas most heavily affected by the nuclear attack, since the blast had nowhere to expand and just bounced against the mountains, steamrolling the adjacent suburbs with fire. Those grounds made bare turned out to be the perfect place for a Memorial Cemetery for the One Day War victims.

I walked through the rows of poles, scanning the small metallic plates that were affixed to each one of them. They were all identical in shape and in the spray of rust that covered them. Each had the same inscribed message:

Unknown
† Los Angeles, February 22, 2044

She was somewhere. She was not unknown. I knew her. I was going to find her. And I did. Her pole looked like the other poles, her plate was a small rectangle like all the other ones, but hers read:

Maria Aparecida Silva Chagas
☆ Goiânia, May 5, 1993
† Los Angeles, February 22, 2044

I'd seen enough. I started getting ready to teleport myself back to Terminal 2 and, from there, to the End of Time, when I heard a puffing sound behind me. As I turned back I noticed Gabriel carrying a huge backpack and dragging a second one.

"There you are, Miguel!" he said while panting out of exhaustion.

"How did you know I'd be—"

"I was thinking… During my Trial, Madame de la Villirouët said that the way to eliminate uncertainty is by dealing with two variables. For us to meet again, two things must happen. You would need to come to whenever I am and I would need to go wherever you are. Today is my first break from my work at the spaceport, and my first chance to find you somewhere that matters for both of us—"

"Gabriel—"

"I just assumed that you'd be wherever mom is, as you always have been when circumstances allow. There is a small memorial in Marina Del Rey for the victims of the spacetime anomaly that shut down Terminal 2... I mean... entropic anomaly, that's what you guys call it, right?"

"Yes, we—"

"Anyway, I usually go there every month and bring some flowers and was gonna go there today. But then... I had a second thought when I realized that mom didn't die there, she was just deported to the past. I wondered if she could have passed away on the One Day War, assuming she had not moved out of LA. I checked online for her name on the Sierra Madre Memorial Cemetery database and... she was listed."

It took me a few seconds to realize that Gabriel was done with his yapping: "And I thought you were dumb."

"A broken clock is right twice a day," said Gabriel proudly.

Gabriel dropped the backpack he was carrying next to the one he was pulling and sat down in front of mom's grave, staring at it for a moment. "I should have brought some silver polish," he pondered, "this plate is a bit tarnished, don't you think so?"

"Don't do anything. The less you influence a certain turnout of events, the less risk there is for the fabric of time."

"Well, I'm still giving her a gift," said Gabe, as he picked a white rose from his backpack and laid it in front of the granite pole.

"Were you carrying this backpack just to hold a rose?"

"Nope, we are gonna go camping."

I frowned in confusion. Was he crazy?

"The other backpack there is for you," explained Gabe. "I have this friend... I mean, I think he's my friend. His name is Chip and you guys are about the same size. So I asked him if he could lend me some clothes. That armor of yours can't be comfortable."

"Did you tell anyone about me or—"

"No! Don't worry, just told him that I know someone his size who was mugged and had no clothes—"

"Gabriel—"

"—Chip thinks that you are a lover or something like that, which makes no sense because I... I have this weird thing going where I'm only into women. And—"

"Gabriel, I—"

"—that's not Chip's case, just so you know. I wish you could meet him, he's a meathead, but—"

"Gabe!"

He finally stopped talking, and stared at me with those big eyes of his.

"Please don't take it the wrong way, but you are delusional. I'm not here to bond with you or anyone else. I... I just wanted to say goodbye to mom. I don't even think we are gonna see each other again."

"Why not?"

"Because the fabric of time can—"

"Your watch says it's fine."

I looked down at my wrist, and, indeed the EHS was green, reading a mere 0.01% of risk of entropic rippling. "I don't understand... The mere fact we are talking should be dangerous."

"I guess we are doing something right here?"

"Something not wrong, actually."

"So, camping?"

"In a cemetery?"

"There's a trail over there, beyond the trees. They go all the way up the mountain and lead to a campground, unless Sue was trolling me about that. Why don't you go to the public restroom and change?"

"I'm not changing. I can't risk anyone noticing me in a time I don't exist."

"So, do you mean that all those people looking at us right now think I'm just a crazy dude talking to himself?"

"You are not the only one. See, that homeless woman over there is also talking to herself."

"So, what do you say, Miguel?" said Gabe as he stood up and faced me.

I looked up at the mountain. I wouldn't mind seeing what was up there. It would be nice to be somewhere stable for a while to think. At the End of Time I would muse about certain goals to no avail, as thoughts that take place there are often inconclusive. Here I could think, and decide what to do. And I could talk. I could tell Gabriel how I feel about the injustice of mom dying in that nuclear blast, of her not being here with us. I could tell him about everything except the promise I made to her. And you know what, screw it if my EHS turns red. Maybe it's not reasonable to expect the fabric of the universe to keep its cohesion if my family can't stick together as well. Maybe it was time for me and Gabriel to save our mother. "Let's climb up that rock, brother."

TERMINAL 3

ACKNOWLEDGEMENTS

This project would not have been possible without the financial and emotional investment made by Shane Lindemoen, this novel's editor and publisher, who first believed in a manuscript that no one else wanted to touch with a ten foot pole, then barreled through the year of the plague and many personal struggles in order to publish Terminal 3.

Before him, the journey to write Terminal 3 was only possible with the crucial support from my mother Marlene, who welcomed me back to her house for a while after I survived a psychological collapse triggered by a major professional setback; and later from my awesome, perfect, handsome husband Jim, who patiently supported my creative needs in many ways.

I am also thankful for other friends who gave me so much, like Billie, who has a generous heart and helped to proofread an earlier draft of this novel; Pedro and Priscila, who always send good vibes my way; my dearest sister Iona and my nephews Tomás and Ravi; and those who are now gone but will always live in my memory such as my father Moura and my friend J.D.

Finally, I would like to thank so many members of the SFF community that supported me, like Jonathan E. Hernandez who agreed to write an awesome review for Tor.com based on an early draft of this novel, Roman Godzich, Valerie Valdes, Alex Shvartsman, Jordan Chase-Young and so many others.

ABOUT THE AUTHOR

Illimani Ferreira is a Science Fiction writer currently living in the United States, more precisely in Southern Delaware, where he is trying to figure out if, as a person who grew up in Brazil's central savannas, he is a beach person or not. Illimani shares a life with his spouse Jim and their yellow lab Maurice.

Illimani's website is: www.ifscifi.com